"A haun...

"Fast-paced and full of fear and intrigue ... Creates a sense of unease in the reader that persists right through to the book's satisfying conclusion." UNDISCOVERED SCOTLAND

Praise for Sue Lawrence's writing:

"Sue Lawrence is a rock star." GUARDIAN

"I found this book enthralling. It's a cracking story beautifully told." LORRAINE KELLY

"Lawrence's parallel plotlines advance in lock-step with each other over alternate chapters, with spooky similarities but also crucial differences, until they're entwined to great effect towards the end." SUNDAY HERALD

"A gripping tale." DAILY RECORD

"A deft mix of vivid storytelling, intriguing mystery and building momentum, skilfully interwoven with the history of the Tay Bridge disaster." SCOTTISH FIELD

"A satisfying tale of revenge served both hot and cold." SCOTLAND ON SUNDAY

"The intertwined stories ... will keep you in suspense until the very end ... An enthralling read and beautifully written." BRISBANISTA

"Lawrence's parallel plotlines advance in lock-step with each other over alternate chapters, with spooky similarities but also crucial differences, until they're entwined to great effect towards the end." SUNDAY HERALD

"A gripping tale." DAILY RECORD

Also by Sue Lawrence:

Fields of Blue Flax
The Last Train

DOWN
TO
THE
SEA

SUE LAWRENCE

CONTRABAND

Contraband is an imprint of Saraband
Published by Saraband,
Suite 202, 98 Woodlands Road,
Glasgow, G3 6HB
and
Published by Saraband,
Digital World Centre,
1 Lowry Plaza,
The Quays, Salford, M50 3UB,
United Kingdom

www.saraband.net

ISBN: 9781912235339
ebook: 9781912235346

Printed and bound in Great Britain by Clays Ltd, Elcograf S.p.A.

MIX
Paper from
responsible sources
FSC® C018072

10 9 8 7 6 5 4 3 2 1

To everyone at Lennox House, Edinburgh

Prologue

A dark shadow slid along the gloomy corridor, keeping close to the wall. A hand reached out and patted the handrail, following it along to the end where it stopped and the stairs emerged. Slowly, silently, the ascent began, one arm pulling up on the banister in the dim light. The figure turned right at the top then bent down, peering at the numbers on the doors along the passageway. Nine, ten, eleven ...

The correct number appeared and fingers clasped the wooden handle, turning it clockwise. The door was locked but a quick glance up towards the hook revealed the key dangling there. Without a sound, it was inserted into the lock, the handle turned and the door pushed open slowly, warily.

A low whistling snore could be heard and as the figure approached the bed, hand raised high, the occupant shuffled over under the bedclothes. The shape beneath the blankets was slight yet long, loosely coiled, head facing the wall.

Moonlight cut through a crack in the curtains and revealed a glint of metal. A blade.

And then there was a soft knock at the door, a faint rap. Once, twice, three times.

Part I

Chapter 1

1981

'What d'you mean, you can't get the key in? Here, let me try.'

Rona and Craig stood outside a large sandstone Victorian house, trying to unlock the door. Rona grabbed the set of keys from her husband's hand, selected the long brass skeleton key and bent down to insert it into the lock. She turned it to the right, then the left, but the latch wouldn't budge. 'Why would the estate agents give us a key that doesn't work?' Craig grumbled.

'It must work; they were always inside the house, waiting for us at the viewings. How else could they have got in?'

'Let me try again.' Craig pulled both the handle and the heavy wooden door towards him. He inserted the key, turned the handle and pushed the door open. 'It just needs to be pulled in tight before you can turn the lock round.'

'We'll need to get new locks anyway, this key's ancient.' Rona picked up the bags at her feet, stepped over the threshold and into the gloomy hall.

Craig flicked a light switch on the wall beside him but nothing happened. 'I'll have to put on the electricity. The box is down in the cellar.' He jingled the house keys in his pocket. 'Give me a hand, Rona? It'll be pitch black down there. Don't want to fall headlong down the stairs.'

Craig opened the cellar door. He peered down beyond the dark, steep steps. 'Hold the door wide open, would you? I can't see a thing.' He fumbled for the handrail to his left and stepped slowly down each broad stone step. At the bottom, he opened the mains box, flicked the switch and then felt along the wall to find the light.

Rona followed him down, tracing her hand along the cold, rough wall. Craig switched on the light and they looked around the spacious cellar. 'Have you been down here before?' Rona asked.

'The agent showed me where the mains box was that day your flight was late. Look at this place, it's huge.'

They stood on the chilly stone floor, taking in the large vacant room with bare whitewashed walls. There were a couple of wooden wardrobes at the far end. Rona went over to them and tugged at the door handles till they creaked open. She peered in at old cardboard boxes and piles of books. There was a strong smell of mildew. The whole cellar was dank and fetid. Craig pointed at a little red door, the top of which reached his chest. He tried the handle. 'This is locked too. I wonder what's behind it. Maybe it's some sort of cupboard? It's pretty low for an adult to get through.'

Rona shivered. 'This place gives me the creeps, Craig. It smells fusty and even with that light on, it's so dingy. We'll need stronger lighting.' She pointed up at the one bare light bulb above their heads. 'And there's a horrible echo.'

'Don't worry. We'll clean it all up, sort through those wardrobes and make it a nice storage space down here.' He grinned. 'Or a wine cellar.'

'Like that's going to be any use for what we're planning.' Rona rolled her eyes. 'And what about the attic? You went up there, didn't you?'

'Yeah, course I did. Nothing there apart from a huge ancient-looking pram.'

'A pram? I presume you asked the agents to take it away?'

Craig shook his head. 'But don't worry, I'll take it and all the stuff from down here to the dump this week.'

'Thanks, darling.' What an old nag she was becoming. 'Sorry to be so grumpy, I just want it all to be perfect. Let's get our suitcases unpacked in our rooms. Get the chest of drawers out of the car. We've loads to do before the furniture van arrives tomorrow.'

Craig switched off the light and followed Rona up the steps. 'Let's go round the rooms, check they're all clean.'

'They certainly should be, the amount the cleaning company charged us.' Rona and Craig headed towards the front door which was wide open, their suitcases still sitting on the doorstep. They lifted the suitcases inside. As Rona heaved the heavy wooden front door closed, the cellar door banged shut. Rona swivelled round to see it slowly swing open again. 'Can you lock that door please, darling? I'm not sure I like it down there much.'

Craig shrugged and headed for the door.

✕

Rona went out into the hall. She could hear Craig yelling from upstairs. 'Everything's okay up here, Rona. All the rooms seem spotless. How are you doing down there?'

'Good, the place is spick and span. Ready for the removal men tomorrow.'

'I'm on my way down, love. Let's have that celebratory drink.'

Rona looked at her watch. 'Bit early, isn't it?'

'Never too early.' Craig ran down the stairs and through a modern wood-panelled door into their annexe, which comprised a kitchen, sitting room, en-suite bedroom and a small box room which was to be a spare bedroom. Rona pulled out a bottle of champagne from a chill box and handed it to Craig. 'Here, you open that, I'll get the glasses.' She delved into a canvas bag. 'I've got some crisps somewhere too. I'm starving.'

Craig poured the champagne. They both stood in the middle of their empty sitting room, grinning. Rona looked all around, shaking her head. 'I can't believe it. It's going to be amazing, isn't it? Our very first house and what a size it is!' She sat down underneath the window, back flat against the wall, legs stretched across the floor.

'We lived in your flat in the Hawkhill for a year, so it's not really our first place.' Craig sat down beside her. 'I was just thinking, I'll miss not being able to pop into Cuthbert's for a mince roll on the walk home from Mennies.'

The stagger home from Mennies, to be precise, thought Rona. But at least the all-night bakery next door meant Craig ate something after those many nights lost down the pub. Rona was relieved that he seemed more focused now. Things were going to be fine. Those dark Dundee days were behind them.

Rona smiled at her husband. 'Look at this place! We own all this.' She flung her arms wide. 'A twelve-bedroomed Victorian house in Edinburgh with a garden and great view down to the sea and over to Fife.'

'Wasn't there a poem, or a saying, or something, about The King of Fife?' Craig mused.

'"The thane of Fife had a wife, where is she now?"'

'That's it. What's that from?'

'Was it Shakespeare?' Rona screwed up her eyes, trying to remember. 'Yes, Macbeth, of course, it was about Lady Macbeth.'

'That's right. She was a nasty piece of work, wasn't she? Anyway, back to our mansion.' Craig grinned. 'It's pretty amazing, but there's still loads of work to be done.'

'I know, but we've got our work schedule. Next week they start putting in the en suites, then it'll be the lifts. Should all be finished in three months' time. Then we'll be ready for our first residents.'

'Yeah, but only when we've got more staff in place.'

'Won't be difficult, we'll make everyone want to work here.' Rona sipped from her glass. 'Oh, that bubbly tastes weird. Metallic. Sorry, I thought it was a good one.'

'It's alcohol, Rona, who cares?' said Craig, taking a long gulp.

'I'm so pleased everything's clean. That makes the move much easier.' She smiled. 'I love the fact we'll be living in a house with so much history. Tell me again who built it?'

'Some sea captain, but he never actually lived here. It became the home of a family who owned a jeweller's in George Street, 1860-something.'

'Such a different feel when you walk from the old part into our 1960s annexe, isn't it?'

Craig nodded, then rubbed his fingernail over a small stain on the floor. 'How long is it we've got, legally, if we have a complaint or something? To go back to the estate agents?'

'Five days.'

'Tomorrow morning I'll have a really good look at everything in the main part of the house while we wait for the removal men.'

'Still can't believe how cheaply we got this place. Even the agents kept saying what a bargain it was.'

'You've looked at everything in detail, haven't you? There definitely aren't any snags?'

'Nope. Handy being married to a lawyer, is it?'

'Are you technically still a lawyer even though you've given it all up to run a care home?' Craig downed his second glass and poured himself another.

'It's going to be handy when it comes to staff contracts.'

Craig scratched his head and looked down at the bare wooden floor. 'Just like it would've been handy if I'd done my finals, and we had a qualified doctor on the premises.'

Why did he always feel the need to bring that up? 'It wasn't your fault, darling.' Rona raised her glass. 'Anyway, here's to Wardie House. Cheers!'

Chapter 2

1898

The girl walked up the cobbles of Laverockbank Road, then stopped to look back down the street and out to sea. The low, grey clouds reflected on the water, which was swirling up into frothy, foam-crested waves. 'A guid day for the fishin',' her mother had said before handing her a ragged bag of belongings and pushing her out the door. Her home, in the long row of tiny fishermen's cottages on the shore, was only a ten-minute walk, yet she felt she was miles away, so alien did it seem coming up the hill towards these big stone houses where the rich folk lived.

She had never been up this way. She'd never even been to Leith and certainly not to Edinburgh. But she had been to Granton one day in the summer for the gala day when she was allowed to sing in the choir. The Newhaven Fisherlassies, they were called. Aged thirteen, she had sat in the front row, cross-legged, wearing the uniform of all the Newhaven girls and women: a red-and-white-striped petticoat and yellow-and-white-striped apron with its deep pouch. And around her head, she wore a paisley shawl. Her mother had scraped all her thick, dark hair back off her face before tying the shawl round the back of her neck. She could still feel the skelp her mother had given her when she complained she was tying the shawl too tight.

Her big sister Dorrie, one of the older girls, had stood at the back of the choir of twenty or so and she and Ruby Gray had started off the singing. 'Caller Herrin'', 'Caller Ou'' and 'The Boatie

Rows' were the only songs she could remember off by heart. What a day that was! People clapped and told them what good voices they had, what a fine choir they were. Granton didn't have one and they wanted to hear Newhaven's girls' choir to see if it was worth starting one. Newhaven had a school and Granton was having one built; the nearby village wanted to copy everything. Only one mile along the shore, Granton seemed like a foreign land. Only once in all her fourteen years had she ventured out of Newhaven.

The girl gazed out at the water, looking beyond the harbour where a flock of herring gulls soared and dived. Though it was an estuary, the locals always called it the sea, it was so vast. She looked over the broad span of the Firth of Forth where she could just make out the hills of Fife.

Her father had said there was a king who lived in Fife, but Pa was always joking, so she didn't know if that was true. Her father used to smile all the time and was always cheery, even, according to her brother, when he was out in gale-force winds on the sea. When she thought of him she felt tears prick her eyes but then she bit her lip hard, to stop them. She just had to accept that Pa and her big brother Johnnie were gone now. All ten of the men and boys who'd gone to sea that day were dead, drowned. The fishwives said it was all the girl's fault. That she was cursed. The girl was devastated when even her own mother, in her grief, agreed.

The girl turned back round and looked up at the trees with their orange leaves rustling in the autumn breeze. She headed left and walked along the pathway towards the big house. Her stomach tightened at the sight of the imposing building ahead.

The girl stepped onto the doorstep and put down her bag. She bit her lower lip, distracted, as she tried to remember who she was meant to ask for. She gazed up at the great stone house then reached up to the door and pulled the bell. She looked down at her tatty dress and pulled at the hem. It was her older sister's and was far too baggy on her. Well, she had nothing else to wear. At least she had shoes on, black shoes that she'd only ever worn on Sundays and gala days, shoes that were now too small but her sister's shoes were still too large. She was more comfortable in bare feet but Ma had insisted she squeeze into these for the walk up the hill.

There was a grating noise as a key turned in the lock and then the huge wooden door creaked open. In the gloom, the girl could make out a plump figure with an angry scowl on her face. She was about to say her piece when the woman hissed, 'What's an urchin like you doing at this door?'

'I'm Jessie Mack, Ma said I'd to come and …'

'Aye, to come round the back door. The front door isn't for the likes of you.' The woman jangled the keys on a large metal ring in her hands, picking out a smaller one. 'I'll unlock it just now.' She pointed round the corner of the house and slammed the door in Jessie's face.

Jessie picked up her bag and trudged round the back, her shoes pinching her toes. She bit her lip once more. Hard.

Chapter 3

1981

Craig watched the removal van drive away, heading along the road to Leith, before he turned back into the wood-panelled hall where Rona was standing by the cellar door. 'Thought you locked this yesterday?'

'I did. Why? Is it open?'

Rona turned the handle and pushed the door wide. Craig frowned and patted his pockets. 'I've left my keys somewhere. Maybe the removers put some boxes down there. I'll nip down and check.'

'Just leave it for now,' said Rona, unable to repress a shudder.

'Don't be daft, it's just a bit gloomy. I'll put in a stronger light bulb soon.'

'We need to get on with unpacking all our stuff, that's all.' Rona wandered through to the annexe which was full of cardboard boxes. In the bedroom, the bed was piled with clothes from the hanging wardrobes. She walked through to the kitchen and plugged in the fridge.

'Cooker's arriving this afternoon. We can cook our first dinner in our new home tonight.'

'And sleep in our own bed,' Craig said, opening a box of kitchen utensils.

The doorbell rang and they both looked at each other. 'Who could that be?'

'The removers have maybe forgotten something,' said Craig, heading for the main hall to open the door.

'Hello there, just wanted to introduce myself. Saw you'd moved in.' It was the postman, holding out a letter.

'Thanks,' said Rona. 'Who on earth's writing to us here?' She turned the letter over. 'Oh, it's Mum's handwriting, it'll be a welcome-to-your-new-home card.'

The postman, a short man with thick-lensed glasses, put down his bag and beamed at them both. 'What are your plans for such a big house then?' He peered past them. 'My oh my, that's a good-sized hall you've got.'

'We're converting the house into a care home,' said Craig.

'Yes, once we've put in bathrooms, it'll be for twelve residents.'

The postman's eyes widened. 'Goodness me, that'll be a lot of work. So it's got twelve bedrooms, has it?'

'Not including our annexe, that's the new part,' said Rona, pointing off to the left.

'My oh my, won't this be something else? Like an old folks' home then?'

'Kind of. But it'll be more, well, luxurious – more like a five-star hotel but with medical provision.'

'My word! Good to see it occupied at last. Everyone up the road in Trinity was wondering how many more months it would take. Been on the market a long time, I was told.'

'That's right.' Rona smiled. 'Anyway, nice to meet you.'

The postman picked up the bag at his feet and slung it over his shoulder. 'Right-oh then. See you tomorrow.' He took a step, then turned back. 'And don't forget, I've always got time for a chat. Not like the young lads who go so fast on their rounds they don't even know their customers' names.'

'Thanks very much,' said Rona, waving him off.

Craig burst out laughing. 'Don't think we're going to get away with much, having a nosey postie like him.'

'Bless him, he obviously loves a good chat. He's maybe lonely.

We had a postie like that in Stornoway, really sweet. Mum used to bake a batch of scones especially for him calling. She'd start slathering on the butter and jam when she heard the gate click open.'

Craig smiled. 'Remind me, how long was the house on the market for?'

'I think just over a year. Maybe longer. They put it to fixed price then still had no offers till ours. I only saw it that one time, you were doing most of the viewings.'

Craig nodded. 'I just don't get it. I mean, a brilliant, solid house like this, just made for conversion.'

'Not everyone's got a spare twenty grand to spend on bathrooms and bedrooms for a whole load of old folk.'

'True,' said Craig, heading for the annexe. 'I'll start in the kitchen.'

'I'll make up our bed and sort things out in there.'

✕

Several hours later, Rona emerged from the shower room wearing sloppy tracksuit bottoms and a t-shirt, her hair wrapped up in a towel. She went into the kitchen where Craig was chopping onions. She went over to put her arms round her husband. 'It's chilly in here. You wouldn't think it was September.'

'Much bigger house to heat, love.' Craig turned to look at her freckled face and planted a kiss on her nose. 'Is the shower okay?'

Rona removed the towel from her head and shook out her curly red hair. 'Yup, much better than our old one actually.'

Craig turned back to the pan, tipped in the onions then shook in some cumin. 'Thank God for your dad's inheritance money. You still got some in that account?'

It irritated Rona that Craig was so vague about money – and he knew it. Was he deliberately trying to get a rise from her? 'Not much, most of it went towards the house. But you know that, Craig.' The nagging worry about money returned – had they overstretched themselves?

The doorbell rang.

'God, there it goes again. Our bell never rang once in Dundee but now we're in Newhaven that's twice in one day.'

'You get it. I'm not decent,' said Rona.

Craig turned the gas to low and headed for the door. Rona slipped through to the bedroom at the front and peered between the slats in the blinds at the open window.

Craig opened the front door to an elegant, slim woman with cropped dark hair, dressed in black with a bright-pink silk scarf. There was a wicker basket at her feet and she extended her hand, which Craig shook.

'Hi, I'm Martha from next door. Well, not really next door, your house is so big you've no close neighbours. I live in the small lodge house over the wall at the back.' She pointed to the left and continued in a drawling voice. 'Just wanted to welcome you guys. I've made you a stew.'

It was when she pronounced stew as 'stoo', that Rona realised their neighbour was American.

'Thanks. D'you want to come in? Meet my wife?'

'Sure,' she said, picking up her basket and offering Craig a dazzling smile.

'Come on through.'

Rona raced over to the dressing table and plugged in the hairdryer. She tipped her head upside down and blasted her hair dry. The door opened and Craig shouted over the noise, 'We've got a visitor!' Rona switched off the dryer and ran her fingers through her tousled locks.

The American was standing by the stove, looking out the window. She turned round when Craig returned with Rona. 'Nice view. And you must be able to see the sea from up on the top floor of the main house. You're lucky, my house has those huge trees in the way.' She held out her hand to Rona and introduced herself again.

'So where are you from?'

'California.'

'Where about?'

'Not far from San Francisco. Small town you'll never have heard of.' She smiled and looked at Rona's curly red hair and green eyes. 'How about you? You've got real Celtic colouring.'

Rona smiled. 'No getting away from it, is there? Stornoway, Isle of Lewis.'

'And you, Craig? You don't sound Scottish.'

'Essex, born and bred.'

'So how did you guys meet?'

'Both students at Dundee; I did law, Craig was a medic.'

'Couple of high-flyers …'

'Would you like a drink?' Craig pointed to the table. 'Take a seat.'

'Yes, you can fill us in on everyone who lives around here,' said Rona, fetching a bottle of wine from the fridge.

'Like I said, I'm your only close neighbour. There's no one else in our road. You have to carry on up the hill towards Trinity and those big houses there.' Martha sat down. 'But near us, there's no one. Well, there's the house opposite, I suppose, but you never see them. Youngish professional couple, both lawyers and both out all day till really late then always away at weekends. Used to be owned by the Bells, but they left about five years ago, when they couldn't manage the house. They were getting on, pretty old. Don't know where they went. They weren't short of a dollar or two so maybe they went into some fancy retirement home. They didn't have any kids to take them in.'

'Have you any family?'

Martha shook her head and took a sip of wine. 'Mmm, nice wine.' She turned to Craig. 'Riesling?'

Craig shrugged his shoulders. 'Dunno. It's just white wine to me. Sorry it's not colder.'

'I usually buy it.' Rona swirled her glass around. Why did this woman presume the man of the house bought the wine?

Martha shrugged. 'So what are your plans here? It's a bit of a relief you bought it, it was empty for a long time.'

'Did you know the previous owners?' Rona asked. 'The estate agents said they only stayed a few months, had to go back to somewhere abroad. Was it Hong Kong?'

Martha raised one eyebrow. 'That what they told you? They never really settled in. Said the house wasn't what they'd thought it would be and just upped and left. Then it lay empty for, what, two, three years?'

Craig pulled the tab on a can of lager. 'No idea why. It's perfect. A bit rambling, but good for our plans.'

Martha got up and walked towards the door into the hall. She peeked round the corner into the old part and nodded. 'Thought so. They didn't leave any furniture or curtains or anything, did they?'

'Just a few curtains, but that suits us fine.'

'Donnie was telling me you're going to make it into a care home.' Martha sat down again.

'Who's Donnie?'

'Our garrulous postman,' Martha said, smiling. 'He's new on this round but already it seems no secret's safe in Newhaven.'

Craig told Martha about the conversion plans while Rona sat back, studying the woman, trying to assess how old she was. She was well groomed and wore lots of make up. Her hair was definitely dyed, it was jet black. Perhaps ten years older than them – mid forties?

'Well, it's an amazing project. What put it into your heads to run a care home?'

'My gran lived with us at home on Lewis and my mum ended up looking after her full-time,' Rona replied. 'And I got to thinking, what if Mum hadn't been able to do that? Gran would have ended up in one of those awful old folks' homes which were like Victorian institutions, all cabbagey smells and no dignity. So we decided to give up our jobs and start one ourselves, more like a luxury home.'

Martha nodded. 'Yeah. The money you make should be good too.'

Rona bristled. 'Yes, eventually, maybe, but that's not the purpose.'

'I reckon you guys are pretty brave, setting up a care home. But, hey, life always comes round full circle, doesn't it?'

'What d'you mean?'

'Well, you know what this house was in the nineteenth century?'

'Yes,' said Rona, sniffing the wine in her glass. She wasn't enjoying the taste at all. Was it corked? Maybe it just wasn't cold enough. 'We heard it was built in the 1860s by some naval captain who wanted to be able to see the sea from his house. That was one of the things that attracted me. My dad ran a shipbuilding business and he just loved the sea.'

'Yeah, but then it became a poorhouse, you know, a place for folk with no money to support themselves.'

'What?' Rona and Craig both stared at her.

'Maybe that's why it was on the market so long and was so cheap.'

'It wasn't *that* cheap!'

'Calm down, Rona. Look at the size of the place! We did get it for a bargain.' Craig turned to Martha. 'But why did it become a poorhouse?'

'The sea captain sold it on to someone else, who then became bankrupt or something, and so in the mid 1870s, Wardie House became a poorhouse. It was used by poor people from Leith and north Edinburgh.'

'But hang on. If it was a poorhouse, would it not have had big dormitories instead of individual bedrooms?'

'I'm just telling you what a local historian told me.'

'Rona, remember I said some of those walls between the rooms are plywood? I think they would've been bigger rooms originally,' said Craig.

'I seem to remember him telling me that the previous owners had the idea in the 1960s to make it into a hotel, but they ran out of money. Maybe that's why you have twelve separate rooms.' Martha took another sip then looked at her flashy gold watch.

'How long have you lived here, Martha?' Rona asked.

'Oh, a few years, difficult to remember exactly how many.'

'And before that, were you—'

Martha stood up. 'Now, I really must be going, I'll leave you to your stew. Give it ten minutes or so in the microwave or an hour in the oven.'

'Thanks. See you around, then,' Rona said, as the American swept past them and out the front door, wafting a strong musky scent behind her.

Chapter 4

1898

Jessie tapped on the back door and waited. Soon she heard the noise of the key in the lock and the door opened. The stout woman stood there, glowering. 'Come away in, then, and don't you ever use that main door again.' She locked the door behind Jessie. 'This is the door you'll use. It leads only into the garden and that's all enclosed by walls.' She pointed at a small door in the corner. 'There's no way out, just in case you're thinking of heading back down the road.'

'No, 'course not,' stammered Jessie, looking all around the kitchen. The huge blackened range had several large pans on it and hanging on the rail at the front were a row of tatty, grey kitchen rags.

'Right. Clothes off,' barked the woman, walking towards the table where a pile of garments lay.

Jessie hesitated.

'You need to put on the same as everyone else. Here's your petticoat, shift, cap and stockings. Washing day's Monday so be sure you keep it all clean till then. Your bath day'll be a Friday. You're lucky, at most other poorhouses it's a bath once a fortnight but Matron's keen on everyone being clean.'

The woman leant over Jessie and sniffed. 'You stink of fish. It's a good job it's Thursday today.' She peered at Jessie's face. 'You've got a smudge. Wipe it off with one of those rags.'

Jessie hung her head. 'It's not dirt, it's my birthmark.'

The woman stared again at the broad, dark brown mole that extended from Jessie's upper lip to one nostril, then she sat down on a chair, her fat thighs wide apart under her grubby apron.

Jessie began to pull off her tight shoes, trying hard to stand on one leg without wobbling. 'I've never had a bath before, only a scrub-down in the basin in the kitchen.'

'Don't be getting too keen. You'll be in a queue, at least twenty of you in the same water. By the time the last person's been in, it looks like thin, greasy mutton broth – and cold at that.'

The woman helped Jessie pull her dress over her head.

'I'm Molly, by the way. I'm the cook here. You know you're to help me in the kitchen, don't you? The last lassie, Lizzie Smith, was sent off to Leith last night so I need you to start in the scullery as soon as Matron's seen you. There's still all today's porridge plates to be washed.' Molly pointed to a deep sink piled high with bowls. 'How old are you?'

'Fourteen, I just turned fourteen.'

'Just a year younger than Lizzie. Poor wee mite, she'll not fare well down at the docks. But that's how Matron punishes them.'

'My Uncle Jack says Leith's a fine place.'

'Aye, fine for a man maybe, not for a penniless lassie who'll soon have a bairn to mind. She's no choice of how to earn a bob or two down the docks.' Molly shook her head. 'Anyway, since you're four-teen, you can still sleep in the girls' dormitory. You might need to share a mattress, probably with Big Bertha. She's a bit simple – you won't be bothered by her.'

Jessie was used to sleeping with her sister and often their mother too. To sleep alone would have been a novelty. 'How many girls are there?'

'About twenty. Only twelve boys though, and there's twenty-one men and twenty-five women … well, if you count Effie.' Molly wiped her nose on her forearm and pulled some straggly hair back into her bun. 'The boys' and men's dormitories are at the other end of the house so you won't have much to do with them apart from mealtimes.'

Jessie shivered as she pulled on the full-length petticoat – the dun material was cold and slightly damp. Molly folded her clothes and stood up. 'Right. Come along with me. You've to see Matron now.'

✗

Jessie followed Molly out the kitchen door and into the dark corridor. She looked up at the gas lamps high on the walls, but none appeared to be lit. She turned her head up towards the windows and saw they were fitted with bars, like a prison. She had heard about prison cells from one of her brother's friends who had ended up there after attacking a Dutch sailor down at Leith. Jimmy said it was always dark because of the bars on the windows. She looked up through the gloom and could make out some paintings hanging along the walls. They were all of important-looking men wearing black suits with a white collar. Some had neat moustaches, some had long, bushy whiskers.

Molly stopped at a door and knocked.

'Enter!'

Jessie followed the cook inside a dim room, lit by the flickering flames of a fire in the grate. A lady sat at a desk, her pen poised over an inkwell.

'Jessie Mack, Matron.' Molly pushed Jessie forward.

'Come forward, child. I see you have changed already. But what is that strong odour?' Matron beckoned with a thin finger. She wrinkled her nose. 'Fish. Did Cook say when your wash day is?'

'Tomorrow, Matron.'

'Good,' she said, opening a drawer.

Jessie stood, too frightened to move, gazing at the woman raking around in the drawer. Matron was dressed all in black, with a high white collar at her neck, just like the men in the portraits.

Below the ruff of her collar sat a pearl choker, two strands, tight together. Her hair was drawn back into a bun so tight the skin was taut at the sides of her face. She removed a sheet of paper then nodded at Molly, pointing to the door.

Molly shut the door behind her and Matron gave a couple of dainty coughs. 'Yes, I recall now. Your people say that you're a hard worker, that you are used to cleaning and mending, though mending fishing nets is less precise than the mending required at Wardie House. Here, you will undertake all manner of work, whatever Molly or I need you for. Mainly kitchen duties at present.'

She sat up tall and peered straight ahead at Jessie, her dark eyes narrowing. 'This is a poorhouse, not a hospital. Neither is it an asylum and yet we do have some patients who are perhaps not as well as they ought to be in both mind and body. If you have any problems with them, man or woman, come straight to me, do you understand?'

'Yes, Matron.'

'And do not attempt to become friendly with any of the girls in your dormitory. They come from desperate circumstances, worse than yours. You will remain separate at all times, except for sleeping.' Matron ran her finger down a list of names on her desk. 'You shall share a palliasse with Bertha. It is up to you both to ensure the mattress is turned and the blanket aired.'

Jessie nodded. She had no idea what a palliasse was.

'The other girls sometimes need reminding to wash. In here, cleanliness is next to godliness. Once you have had your bath, you will assist at bath times with the younger girls and infants. I will have no unpleasant odours in this house. The Governor and I have sensitive noses.'

Matron tucked the sheet of paper back in the drawer. 'I shall have reports from Molly of how you are doing and we shall see how you fit in.'

'Thank you, Matron.'

'One more thing, Jessie Mack.'

'Yes?'

'No one else in here knows about the curse you are said to bring with you. The residents will, however, notice you are marked.' She pointed at Jessie's birthmark. 'You will ignore any talk of it. Also, if at any time I hear mention of witchcraft or ungodliness, you will be dismissed. At once.'

Jessie nodded.

'Now go and get on with your work. And tie up that hair. I will not have loose hair. Loose hair goes with loose morals.' Matron raised her chin. 'Be on your way.'

Chapter 5

1981

Rona pulled open a wooden shutter in the bedroom. There was a row of six round holes along the window ledge. She looked up and noticed another six indentations along the top. After a moment, Rona realised what these were: holes for bars. There must have been bars on the windows. She'd noticed them in all the other rooms. Why would they have needed those? That American woman said it was a poorhouse; bars seemed more in keeping with a prison.

Rona looked around the bedroom. This was a good-sized room, unlike the one she'd just been in which was so small it must have been a converted linen closet. They were going to be hard-pushed to get a toilet and shower in that one, but if it had been fitted out at some time in the past to function as a hotel, there must have been room for at least a bed and sink. She and Craig were taking a bedroom each, opening windows and shutters and taking measurements for curtains and carpets, before the workmen started.

This room was large and had two windows, both overlooking the back garden. Rona peered out and saw the corner of the roof of the lodge house, where Martha lived, at the far end. But there was a tall wall and high hedge surrounding Martha's garden, so it didn't seem as if anyone could see into her grounds. The small garden at the back of their annexe would never be private, but when would she and Craig have time to sit out there anyway?

Rona pulled her tape measure out, hung it over the width of the first window and wrote the measurements in her notebook. Some residents might want their own curtains, but it would look better if they all had curtains when relatives came to inspect a room. Yes, this was a nice room, the size of it was ideal and that view would be fabulous once the overgrown garden had been dealt with. There were a couple of well-established apple trees but at the moment the rest of the garden was a mess. Rona had already been in touch with a local gardening company and they were due to visit on the first dry day this week. At the moment it was pouring outside and the house felt even colder and damper. She pulled her woollen scarf tight around her neck.

'How're you getting on?' She leant round the door of the next room where Craig was on his knees in the corner.

'Okay, I'm just seeing if this carpet's going to be easy to rip up or whether I should ask the decorators to do it.'

'And?'

'Think I'll just leave it to the professionals,' he said, getting to his feet. 'I'll get on with clearing stuff – I've got to return the hire van at the weekend. Can you give me a hand in the attic for a minute?'

'No problem. A hand with what?'

'Remember I said there was an ancient pram up there?'

'Oh God, yes.'

'I'll need you to come up too. The pram's huge, can't manage to get it down the steps myself.'

They walked along the corridor and Craig pulled stairs down from a hatchway in the ceiling. They held onto the narrow rail as they climbed the steps.

At the top, they crouched down and looked around. The wooden gables criss-crossing the attic made it feel cramped. Craig wandered around, head stooped under the low beams and Rona followed.

'It's so cold up here. Thought heat was meant to rise?'

'It is a bit chilly, isn't it?' Craig frowned. 'Can't see that pram anywhere. It wasn't in the cellar, was it?'

Rona shook her head. 'Don't think so.'

'That's odd. The estate agents must've removed it. No idea why, though. Okay, let's get back down. Is it time for coffee? We can use the new percolator.'

Rona looked at her watch. 'Suppose so. I don't feel like coffee though, my stomach's not quite right. But I'm up for a cup of weak tea.'

✕

Later that afternoon, Rona was in the kitchen peeling potatoes when she heard a yell. She ran out to the hall and noticed the cellar door wide open.

'Craig? Are you down there?' She heard a muffled, indistinct voice. 'Where are you?'

'Come down here!'

Rona stepped down the dingy stairs and onto the bare cellar floor. Craig was nowhere to be seen.

'In here.'

She turned around and saw Craig's head pop out from the little red door on the right-hand wall.

'What's in there?' That strange, musty smell was still lingering.

'You need to crouch down, the roof's really low.'

Rona bent down and crept through the door. She used the large measuring tape from her pocket to jam the door open. She didn't want to be trapped in here.

Inside was a small area, no bigger than a large cupboard, with a very low ceiling.

'Reckon this would've been a coal cellar, but it's not black or sooty, must've been painted over. Is there a chute over there?' He pointed to the sloping ceiling at the back of the little room. 'This torch isn't bright enough. I'll come back in with the heavy-duty torch and look properly down there.' Something caught Craig's eye. He pointed the torch towards the back of the door. 'Come and see this.'

Rona was beginning to feel claustrophobic. She checked the door was still jammed open, then edged forward. She peered at marks on the wooden panel.

'What is it?'

'Letters, someone's carved into the wood.'

'W. I. N. Z. I. E. Winzie. What does that mean?'

Rona shrugged. 'No idea, maybe someone's name. Maybe an old Scots word – I'll ask Mum.'

Rona stood up and banged her head on the low ceiling. 'Ow,' she said, rubbing her forehead, 'I'm getting out of here.' She brushed her hands over her face. 'Ugh. Cobwebs. This place gives me the creeps.'

Rona stepped back into the cellar. In the dingy light she had to screw up her eyes to focus on something on the opposite wall.

Craig emerged from the small door and he joined her in the middle of the room.

'What are you looking at?'

'I don't remember seeing that when we were down here a couple of days ago, do you?'

There, in the dim light beside the wall, was a huge old-fashioned black pram.

'I could have sworn it was in the attic.' Craig peered inside the pram. 'What's that?'

Rona saw what he was pointing at. There was a square footwell in the solid structure of the pram.

'Somewhere to hide another baby?' Craig raised his eyebrows.

'Hang on, I remember Mum's godmother, Auntie Jean, had one of these prams. Not as ancient as this one looks, mind you, Jean's was from the 1930s. She kept insisting it was called a baby carriage. Anyway, hers had the same square hole. She told me there were no pushchairs in those days so when the baby was older it'd sit up in the pram. They just removed the mattress-base-thing and the toddler's little legs would dangle in there. Clever, really.' Rona looked under the pram. 'Look, here's the mattress, it fits over the footwell.' She placed it inside. 'But how did we miss it last time we were in the cellar?'

They both turned round at a noise.

'Was that the bell?' Craig asked.

'Think so, I'll get it, love.' Rona turned and strode towards the stairs. 'Get rid of the pram, would you? Creepy old thing.'

Upstairs, Rona crossed the hall and opened the door. Martha stood there, again dressed in black, with an emerald-green scarf.

'Oh, hi, Martha.' Rona opened the door wide. Was this woman going to make a habit of calling round every day?

'Hi, honey, I've brought you a cake.' She handed over a cake tin and stood on the doormat, smiling. 'It's an apple dapple cake, think you'll like it.'

'D'you want to come in?'

'Only if you're not too busy.'

'I was just going to put the kettle on. Come on through.'

'Thanks. I'd love a look around too?'

Rona sighed. 'Okay, tour starts here.'

Chapter 6

1898

Jessie turned over on the narrow mattress and prodded Bertha in the ribs.

'Are you awake? Can you hear that?'

Bertha grunted but did not move. Jessie lifted her head up a little and looked around, her eyes adjusting to the dark. The twelve mattresses – which Matron called palliasses – were all crammed close together in this small dormitory. There were two long wooden sleeping platforms raised up along the central corridor. Along each platform were six straw-filled mattresses covered in coarse jute sackcloth. On each mattress slept at least two bodies, lying under thin scratchy blankets. None had pillows, but Jessie was used to that from her own home, although there she at least shared a proper bed, not just a straw mattress. She had to stop calling it her home, Molly had told her off about that. Wardie House was now her home – this huge, cold, dingy building with bars on the windows and strange noises and unfamiliar smells. There was no way of getting out of this place. She was resigned to being there forever.

Jessie told herself she was far luckier than the other girls – at least she was allowed outside into the garden once a day. The pale skin and wan pallor of the others showed that they never saw sunlight. Jessie had to go out every morning, whether it was sunny and bright or freezing cold with thick heavy frost covering the ground. Her first morning chore after breakfast was to get Molly her vegetables from the garden for the dinnertime soup. It was there, digging up tatties and onions or kail and looking up at the vastness of the stone house, where she felt alive. Indoors, she felt she was just functioning, not living.

It was the second time Jessie had heard noises in the middle of the night. No one else had mentioned them. But Jessie was the one in her family with the keen hearing. She was always first to hear the foghorns out on the Forth when the haar came in. She'd wake up her mother who would fret and worry until the men all came back safe from the sea. Until that day, of course, when they never came back and it was all her fault.

She missed the sea, the fresh, salty tang of it, the feel of the wind buffeting her and all the other fisherlassies as they sat alongside the harbour wall helping with the mending. They repaired the nets while their mothers went off with their laden baskets, selling fish to places as far as Leith and even up to the city of Edinburgh. They came back reeking of sweat from carrying the heavy creel suspended from a band round their foreheads.

In this big, cold house the only smells were stale odours from the poor folk who never saw the outside and who looked like walking ghosts.

Jessie listened again. She was sure she heard wheels, a soft creaking of wheels being turned, back and forth. Jessie bit her lip and laid her head back down on the hard mattress. Then came another sound she knew well – the foghorn, booming out along the Forth, warning the boats and ships of the North Sea haar rolling in. Her father used to say the wailing sound of the foghorn was like the deep moaning noise he'd heard once from a whale stranded on the beach. It was a sound of distress. She had heard many tales of the dangers of being stuck out on the sea in the fog.

Jessie bit her lip harder as she thought of her father. Dead, with her brother and eight others in that terrible storm, and all because of her. Her curse had caused their deaths. She felt a tear trickle down her cheek and snuggled into Bertha's back for warmth.

✖

'What d'you mean, they grind up dead babies' bones?'

Jessie turned to the tall boy who was holding out his tin bowl for porridge. He had just told her he was now old enough to be working with the men, even though he was only fifteen, and their job today was to crush babies' bones.

The boy leant in towards her. He smelled funny so she wanted to draw back, but he started whispering. Jessie glanced round to where Molly was talking to Matron at the door. They were no doubt discussing whatever delicacy Molly had for Matron and the Governor today. Molly said Matron seemed to take little interest in food, whereas the Governor enjoyed both food and drink. His red nose reminded Jessie of Old Tom who was to be found every day at The Stone Pier Inn opposite the harbour. In summer, he was given a chair outside. He always had a tankard of ale in his hand. Jessie's mum used to say not to go near him – he would lash out at the children nearby the more he had to drink. The one time she and Dorrie had no choice but to pass close by, the stink of him was enough to make them want to vomit.

'The dead babies have their bones all hacked up then pounded up into dust and made into porridge.' The boy nodded at the pot in front of her. 'That porridge.'

'That's not true. It can't be true.' Molly waddled back over to the serving table, so Jessie asked, 'This isn't made from dead babies' bones, is it?'

'Billy, is that you telling tales again? Of course not, Jessie. Now get on with your work. And you, Billy Muir, be on your way.' Molly thumped down the ladle and said to Jessie, 'You've been here a good few months now. You know that boy's trouble. Ignore him. Stay clear of all those boys.'

Once the last bowl of porridge had been ladled out, Jessie looked over the dining room where the Governor had finished morning prayers and was sweeping past them with his usual scowl.

Squashed side by side on rickety benches at four long tables were the residents, heads bent low over the thin porridge. Two tables were for men and boys, two for women and girls. There was no conversation – no talking was allowed. Everyone had their heads bent low, concentrating on eating. Jessie started clearing the serving table ready to take the pan and ladle back to the kitchen.

'I'm setting up Matron's breakfast tray in her room. You stay here till they're finished, then bring their bowls and start on the washing up,' Molly said, heading for the door.

Jessie scraped the last dollop of porridge off the ladle into a bowl for herself, gobbled it down, then went to the kitchen with the porridge pot. She was heading back for the bowls when she stopped at the door. In the corridor was a tall girl, her back to Jessie, standing looking up at one of the portraits. Her long plait swung as she tossed her head to and fro. How had she left the dining room so early? They were never allowed to leave until dismissed by Matron. Jessie was fascinated by the girl's hair which was tied in a straggly pigtail that reached down her back to her waist. Jessie stared at the bare feet then up again at the swaying plait, trying to work out who she was. The girl turned around, slowly, and Jessie blinked in surprise. The face was not young and smooth, but wizened and lined; there was greying hair around her receding forehead. Jessie now saw she was not a girl, but an old woman, almost the same age as her granny. She darted back in to the kitchen and shivered as she plunged her hands into the water in the sink.

'They did grind up the bones.'

Jessie jumped and looked round. The woman with the pigtail was standing behind her. Jessie realised this must be Effie and smiled at the woman everyone said was 'a poor soul'. Jessie felt a pang of sadness looking at her, thinking of how she was sometimes called Mad Effie. Effie stood there, pulling at her tattered young girl's dress and scratching at her head.

'Did you miss your porridge, Effie? I might have a bit left here.'

Jessie scraped at the bottom of the pan.

'Cows and pigs, all their bones were ground up, but 'twas mainly the babies,' said Effie, nodding. She wandered off towards the door. Jessie watched her skip over the hall towards the stairs, her long pigtail bouncing up and down. From the back she looked young. All older girls and women had their hair up in tight buns. Bertha had told Jessie that Effie was very old – in her forties. Effie's lined face was testament to the fact she'd had a troubled life. Molly had told Jessie to just ignore poor Effie who never slept at night and that was what made her mad. You become an imbecile if you don't sleep, the girls had told Jessie. Effie hadn't always been like that, someone had said. Well, Jessie felt sorry for her. Jessie knew how it felt to be picked on, to be laughed at.

Jessie went into the dining room to fetch the bowls. Back in the kitchen, Molly was decanting some raspberry jam into a dainty little dish for Matron's tray.

'So it's not true about the bones then? Not even cows?'

Molly sighed and put down the jam jar. 'Some other poor-houses used to grind up bones a long time ago. Never here. They were from cattle and pigs, then they used the dust as fertiliser, on the fields – not in porridge. And they certainly never used dead babies!' Molly motioned with her hand. 'Now move along. I don't want to hear anything more about this.'

Molly bustled out with the tray. Jessie darted into the larder and straight over to the sack of oatmeal on the floor. She opened it and looked inside. She plunged in her hand and felt the gritty meal run through her fingers. This was oatmeal, it was exactly like the meal in her mother's scullery. And Molly's porridge smelt sweet and nutty as it cooked in gallons of water on the stove. Babies' bones – what nonsense! She returned to the kitchen, thrust the plug into the sink and started to pile in the dishes.

Chapter 7

1981

Rona sat in her kitchen listening to the sound of hammering and banging. Even with their door shut, the noise was deafening. The dust was settling throughout their annexe, seeping under the door. She'd just wiped a thick layer from the kitchen table.

Craig and the workmen had started on the bathrooms and today they were working upstairs. They had estimated they'd take three to four weeks to fit the en suites, provided they worked seven days a week. Today was Sunday and they'd been at it since eight o'clock. Rona's devout Hebridean family would be horrified if they knew they were working on the Sabbath. She glanced at the clock – it was nearly time to take them a tray of coffee and biscuits.

Rona leant back against the chair and smiled. Gone were the days she had a secretary to make her coffee, when she was a lawyer in Dundee. Here she was embarking on a project which would cost them so much time and effort, a venture that was risky yet exciting. She and Craig were convinced that care homes were the way forward and they both knew it would be hard work but hopefully, in time, it would become a money-spinner. The concept of a residential home for elderly people that was less like an institution, more like a hotel, was novel. It would be expensive to run, but it would all be worth it. It had to be a success. She no longer had her dad to help bail them out financially. The money from his estate was almost gone, but the bank was lending till the care home was up and running. It would all be fine. It irritated Rona that Craig didn't take a little more interest in the finances. Though perhaps one person worrying about whether they'd overstretched themselves was enough.

Rona opened the lid of one of the saggy cardboard boxes on the kitchen table. It was from one of the wardrobes in the cellar. Craig was going to take the wardrobes and that pram to the dump while the workmen were here with their vans. Rona had been scouring the Yellow Pages for a company that would hire out a dehumidifier to try to make the cellar less musty after Craig had cleared everything.

Rona peered inside the box and pulled out a couple of paintings. One was of a vase of flowers – garish, not attractive at all, although the frame was perhaps salvageable. The other, slightly larger one, was a portrait of a woman, again in a good frame. It was not as amateurish as the flowers, but at first sight, not remarkable. Though the more she gazed at it, the more she was drawn to it. The sitter's head was tilted slightly to the side and she was unsmiling, in fact she seemed to lack any expression. She had dark hair, with clumsy brushstrokes of auburn through it. Her lips were crimson and her eyes chestnut brown. She wore a high black collar but there was a line of white as if she wore a white blouse underneath. Both hands were loosely clasped under her chin and swathed in pale fawn gloves which looked soft. Rona remembered her mother's godmother had similar gloves which were made of kidskin. The woman in the painting held something silvery grey between the gloves.

Rona held it at arm's length and gazed. She thought it must be Victorian. Could this be the lady of the house from the 1860s or 1870s when it was built? Rona set the painting on the table. The picture of flowers would go to the dump. This portrait she might hang in the hall.

Rona delved into the carton again and took out a jewellery box of dark wood and brass. She tried to open it, before realising there was a tiny keyhole in an ornate clasp. Rona removed all the other things from the carton, looking for a tiny key, but found nothing apart from old newspapers and books. She opened one of the books; it had a dark green leather cover and gold-edged pages. It was a Bible and inserted into the first page was a slip of paper stuck with glue. It read: 'Sabbath School Lesson Scheme'. The date given was 1865. Rona turned a page and inscribed in beautiful flowery script was a name: Isabella W. Ramsay.

Rona opened a tiny book called *Daily Light*. It appeared to contain Bible readings for each day of the year. Written in a neat hand, in black ink, was, 'To Isabella, with fondest love, E. M. R., October 1870.' She flicked through the book and noticed pencil jottings throughout. She picked out a similar book, another *Daily Light*, this time inscribed by Isabella Ramsay, again in 1870, and another couple of tattered books, without inscriptions, which she put back into the box. Rona was about to open the old newspapers when she looked up at the clock. These would have to wait, there was too much to do. She went over to the sink to fill the kettle.

X

Bringing the coffee tray back down the stairs, Rona looked at the plate of crumbs. She'd put out some of Martha's cookies that morning and they'd all been eaten. She certainly was a good cook – the casserole, cake and cookies she had given them were all delicious. When Rona asked her if she had been a professional cook or chef in a former life, Martha had snorted with laughter.

It was kind of Martha to be a friendly neighbour, supplying them with food, but Rona hoped that was the end of it. There was something about Martha she couldn't quite pin down. She thought that sometimes the woman looked at Craig in a strange, almost flirty way. Rona never felt quite comfortable with her.

Rona loaded the dishwasher then picked up the two empty cake tins. She'd given Martha back her casserole dish when she delivered the cookies, so instead of giving Martha an excuse to call again, Rona would pop round to her house. Apart from one massive food-shopping trip to Willie Low's, she had been stuck inside Wardie House all week and it would be good to get out. She grabbed her bag and headed for the door.

When Rona went out, she realised she didn't know exactly how to get to Martha's gate. She turned right, expecting to find an entrance, but there was none. She could see the roof of the little lodge house, but where was the door in? She walked round the block and eventually found a narrow black door, a gate, with a small letterbox, underneath some dangling ivy growing along the wall. She flicked it aside and turned the handle. It didn't give, so she pushed her weight against it and shoved. The gate swung open and she was in a small garden, the grey stone lodge house straight ahead of her. She turned round to shut the gate but it had already swung itself shut.

Rona walked along the path, glancing back up towards her own house. She could just make out the top lintels of the bedroom windows of the back wing from here. Compared to this small lodge, their house looked grand and imposing. The building stone was different – the lodge looked older. It was probably pre-Victorian. Rona looked around at the small patch of straggly lawn and at the one sad, dying rose bush by the door; it was obvious Martha wasn't a gardener. Apart from that it was all earth, dark and thick, some of it mounded up into little hillocks. There was not a flower or green plant to be seen.

Rona knocked on the front door and waited, noticing that all the curtains were pulled shut. She thought she saw a curtain twitching. As she stood on the doorstep, she began to feel slightly queasy. She shouldn't have eaten that soup at lunchtime. Craig had insisted it'd be fine even though it had been made five days before. What could possibly go off in lentil soup, he'd joked.

The main door opened a fraction and Martha's head peeked out. 'Hi, Rona, good of you to come over. How're you doing?'

'Fine, thanks. I brought your cake tins back.'

'Oh, okay.' Martha reached out to take the tins. Rona noticed she was standing with one foot firmly wedged against the door so it could not open any more. Rona waited to be invited in. Martha's usual bonhomie was gone; they stood and stared at each other.

Rona attempted conversation. 'Is your house older than ours? Looks like different stone. I presumed they were both built together.'

'Yeah, this one's older, from the early 1800s I think. Or even earlier. Anyway, thanks for these.' Martha was about to shut the door.

Rona turned to go. A wave of nausea rushed over her. She felt the colour drain from her and knew she was about to be sick. Rona rushed over towards a mound of churned earth and vomited all over the dark soil. Martha was suddenly behind her, rubbing her back. 'D'you need any help? Shall I take you home?'

Rona shook her head and stood up straight. 'I'm okay now. Could do with a glass of water.'

'Wait here,' said Martha, rushing off into the house and returning within seconds with a glass.

Rona sipped it and looked up at Martha standing like a barrier between her and the house. Why on earth did she not invite her in? Martha had been in Wardie House for numerous cups of tea and drinks. Rona handed the glass back to Martha. She still felt a little bilious. She teetered towards the small gate in the wall. She stopped at the wall and turned round to see Martha standing in front of the door which was pulled to behind her.

Rona took a deep gulp of fresh air. 'It's a perfectly formed little garden isn't it? So secluded. The house looks really cute too.'

'It suits me.' Martha waved. 'Bye then, hope you feel better soon.' She went inside and slammed the door.

Rona shook her head. What was wrong with some people? When she was growing up in the Hebrides, you'd always ask someone in. It was simply good manners and would be so insulting to leave them standing on the doorstep. But Edinburgh was a little more stand-offish, so perhaps Martha, as an American, presumed that was the norm.

Rona went out the narrow gate onto the main street, thinking that she needed to go and lie down, yet that was hardly likely to be peaceful with all those men banging and clattering in the house. She plodded wearily round the corner and headed up the drive- way to Wardie House. She looked up at the ivy creeping along the tops of the windows. It was green with white edges, variegated ivy, just like Martha's.

Part 2

Chapter 8

1899

'Bertha, come on, you need to get up. Matron'll be here soon for inspection.'

Jessie poked her bed-mate in the back. She'd just splashed her face with freezing cold water from the basin and was now back by the mattress, finishing dressing. Bertha stretched and yawned. 'She was late yesterday,' she mumbled, keeping her eyes shut.

'That was just because of Mattie Thomson. She got the Itch so Matron put a mattress in the cellar for her to sleep. It'll be even colder down there.' Jessie shivered. 'Annie Rae'll get it next.'

'Why's that, Jessie?'

'They share a bed. Remember? Matron gave us all that talk and said if we didn't clean ourselves properly we'd all get it.'

'It's horrible,' Mattie had told her. 'You're just itching all the time and you get red and sore. Even that ointment Matron rubs all over you – sulphur, it's called – doesn't help much.'

'Anyway, Bertha, you're not ill, you need to get up, or we'll all get a row.' Jessie tucked her hair into the small cap on her head and sat down to pull on her boots.

'Can you get me my shift, Jessie?' asked Bertha. 'I'm cold, I'll dress under the blanket.'

Jessie glanced towards the door. 'Hurry up. Matron'll be here soon.' She flung the grubby brown dress at Bertha. 'What're you doing in the workroom today then?'

'Same as usual. The knitting. It's all they'll let me do, I'm so bad at sewing. But even with knitting, I still can't cast on right.' Jessie smiled. Bertha was often punished for being slow at the chores they had to do. But she was slow at everything, both physically and mentally. She couldn't even write her name easily, which was unusual for her age. 'How many hours did you say we sat there knitting yesterday, Jessie?'

'Twelve. You started after breakfast at eight then worked on till nine at night, with a break for dinner and tea.'

'When's it Sunday again, Jessie?'

'Tomorrow. You'll have to practise your hymn, remember I taught you it last week?'

Bertha shut her eyes tight. 'Forgotten it, Jessie, sorry.'

Jessie shook her head. 'I'll teach you it tonight once we're in bed. The minister said last week we were going to learn a new one tomorrow. I love singing.'

'And you sound so nice when you sing, Jessie,' said Bertha, pushing her straggly hair up under her cap.

'Here, let me do that.' Jessie pushed a clasp under Bertha's hair to keep it in place.

'Like a bird, that's how you sound. Though I've never seen a bird.'

'Don't be daft. You must have seen a bird, they're in the garden all the time. You can see them out the window if you stand on a chair.'

'I'd like to touch a bird. It would be so soft wouldn't it, Jessie?'

The door flew open and Matron stormed in.

Bertha jumped down from the wooden platform and yanked on her boots. She fumbled frantically with her laces while Jessie hurried to make the bed. The inspection started at the other end of the room. Both the girls and their bed had to be presentable by the time Matron arrived. Bertha's hair kept tumbling down from the clasp.

'Bertha Davidson,' Matron yelled. 'You look a mess as usual. Come over here.' Matron brought out a long pair of scissors from the deep pockets of her starched white pinafore.

'No, please, I …'

'I've warned you before.' She pointed her finger directly at Bertha then turned round. 'You two. Jessie Mack and Annie Rae. Come here both of you and hold her down.' The two girls sat Bertha on the chair as they had done before. She struggled, her frizzy hair tossing from side to side.

'Bertha, just let her do it or you'll get cut,' whispered Jessie, who was staring, wide-eyed, at the gleaming scissors.

Bertha sat still. She screwed up her eyes till they were shut tight. The other girls in the dormitory all huddled round to watch as Matron approached, brandishing her scissors. Matron pulled a clump of Bertha's hair up and yanked her head upwards. 'If you cannot keep your hair tidy, then it will be shorn. How many times have I told you that?' Matron's thumb and fingers snapped together as she snipped Bertha's hair, one clump at a time.

When she had finished, Matron pointed to the floor which was strewn with hair. 'You! Sweep it up!' Matron gestured at Jessie, pushed the scissors back into her pocket and stood up tall. Jessie fetched the brush as Matron stalked back along the narrow corridor between the wooden platforms. At the door, she looked back at them all. 'I will cut the hair from every single one of you tomorrow if I see any one girl with loose hair. What is it I say?'

'Loose hair means loose morals, Matron,' the girls mumbled, all staring down at their feet.

'You have five minutes to be downstairs for prayers and breakfast, girls.'

Annie was whispering into Bertha's ear when Jessie returned with the broom. She helped Bertha wedge her cap tight on her head with hair grips. Bertha patted her hair and sniffed. 'It's your fault, Jessie Mack,' she said as Jessie began sweeping the hair beside her.

'What d'you mean?'

'You and your curse, I never got in trouble before you came.'

Jessie shook her head. 'That's a lie. We all get punished, you

know that. You told me you used to get the tawse every week, have
you forgotten?'

Jessie took the dustpan and brush over to the corner and
returned to see Annie Rae whispering again to Bertha. Then
Annie ran towards the door, smirking. Jessie glowered at her then
went to help Bertha up from the seat.

'Annie says you're a Winzie and you bring bad luck to everyone,
not just me.'

Jessie's whole body stiffened. She had not been called a Winzie
for a long time, ever since she was flung out of Newhaven village
after the fishwives – including her own mother – had accused her
of causing the accident that made ten men drown. And all because
she was the only female ever to have set foot on her father's boat.
Jessie had gone aboard just before they set off into that storm
which devastated the fishing community. It had been her mother
who had told Jessie to run and take the dinnertime pieces to the
men on the boat just as they were about to throw off the mooring
rope. They'd forgotten them and had to have the bread and jam
pieces, there was nothing else for them to eat all day. They were
all busy on board and she couldn't just fling the pieces onto the
boat, so her brother who was untying ropes on the harbour told
her to take them on board, but to be quick. Jessie had scrambled
down the ladder attached to the harbour wall, gone aboard and
put the food tied up in a cloth down below. Then she had leapt
off, nimbly, back onto the harbour just as Johnnie pulled the rope
off its moorings and jumped back onto the boat with a cheeky
grin and a wave. How could anyone have foretold one of the most
devastating storms to hit the east coast of Scotland was brewing?

'Jessie Mack, Winzie!' Annie Rae called from the door before
she bolted off down the stairs.

Bertha looked up and stared at the birthmark on her face. 'She
says you're marked, Jessie, you bring bad things and what will you
do next?'

Chapter 9

1982

Rona sat at the desk in the office and looked up at the clock. It was four o'clock. She'd been working all day putting the folders and files in order in new filing cabinets. It was only a week till their first residents arrived and the bedrooms were all finished, en suites gleaming, beds decked in crisp new bed linen. She kept thinking of her granny and what she would have wanted if she had been in a home and not in their house for her final years. The only old folks' homes around were awful; Rona used to visit them with the school choir and sing to the residents. As well as the dark corridors and air of sadness, she also remembered the smell: cabbage and disinfectant. Wardie House would be fresh and light and the only smell would be freshly baked cake.

Everything was going according to plan except that she still had a shortage of carers. Rona had signed up three nurses, which she hoped would work well initially, one being on duty overnight. Any nursing shortfall, Craig could deal with. He'd been only two terms away from graduating as a doctor before that incident they never talked about. But they needed at least eight carers, enough to cover night duty, and she only had six. She was interviewing another man at 4.30 p.m. Hopefully he'd be suitable even though he had little experience of working with the elderly.

Rona went out into the corridor and admired the dark panelled walls and carpeted floors and the lifts with their shiny stainless-steel doors. She couldn't help but feel proud. They had worked so hard over the past four months and now it was almost ready. She'd be glad to get rid of the workmen after all this time; she was forever making them teas and coffees and enduring the constant hammering and banging. And even though they stored their paints and equipment in the cellar, there had been debris and dust everywhere in the main house for months. And then, over Christmas, the pipes had frozen so they had a water leak which was another expense and more disruption.

But now it was all finished. At last everything was ready, still smelling of fresh paint and everywhere spotless. They had eight residents arriving the following week. This would leave them four spare rooms which they would fill when they were fully up and running as Wardie House Care Home. Theirs was still a new concept, placing the elderly in a home that was more like a luxury hotel with nurses and carers. In addition to medical care and support to dress and bathe and the provision of all sorts of activities, it was Rona's intention to make residents' entire experience excellent. All the meals would be special, served on crisp, white tablecloths with flowers on the tables, delicious food and wine or sherry for those who wanted. These were people nearing the end of their lives – why not make it joyful? Of course, it meant they had to charge hefty fees, so only wealthy residents could move in, but hopefully when the council saw how successful it was, they'd allocate grants for people less well-off.

Rona had hired a cook the week before and she seemed very good. The housekeeper in charge of cleaning and laundry came highly recommended from the local school which surely boded well.

Rona stood staring at a patch of wall. Had she hung the Victorian portrait too high? Some of the old folk might have difficulty craning their necks. She was stretching up to remove the picture when the phone rang. She dashed back into the office.

'Hello, Wardie House Care Home?'

'Hi Rona. I'm not going to make it home tonight after all. Sorry.'
It was Craig.

'Why not?'

'The weather's really bad in Inverness, snow everywhere. What's it like down with you?'

Rona looked out of the window at the light dusting of snow on the lawn. 'Nothing much at all. So when will you get home?'

'As soon as I can. Been a good day up here though, really interesting course. I've learned loads about running a care home.'

'Suppose it's worth it, then.' Rona looked outside at the darkening winter sky. 'I thought I might leave some lights on overnight.'

'Why?'

'Well, remember the security man's not coming to fit the burglar alarm till tomorrow morning.'

'God, yeah, I'd forgotten. You could do, but you'll be fine in the annexe. Anyway, you're a country girl. Intrepid. Frightened of nothing.'

'It's not me I'm worried about, it's all the expensive equipment we've got in here.'

'Don't be daft, Rona. Any burglar attempting to remove a bath hoist deserves a medal. Not exactly easy stuff to steal.'

'I suppose so. And we won't have any medicine to steal till the nurses start next week. Let me know how you get on tomorrow.'

'Will do.'

'What'll you do tonight?'

'I'll be heading for the bar soon. Nothing else to do.'

'Craig, don't drink too much. Please.'

''Course not. And Rona, you're the one who's to look after yourself. No lifting anything heavy.'

'Yes, doc.'

'Love you.'

Rona went back into the corridor and into Room 1. There was the bed, chest of drawers and wardrobe. It could almost have passed for a hotel until she walked into the shower room and there were safety rails and hand grips everywhere. They had followed all the guidelines and had already had an initial inspection so hopefully everything would run smoothly. She wished she had a little more energy, but another early night would help. She could have a nice relaxing bath, then bed at nine. She was so sleepy at the moment, she felt she'd like to hibernate.

The doorbell rang. Rona rushed along the corridor to open the door to the man who was here for the interview.

'Hello there. Mr Devine? Come into the reception room.'

✳

Rona thought about the interview as she lay in the bath. It had gone pretty well: Ian Devine was nicely turned out, articulate and obviously intelligent. He had been a gardener and a labourer in the past and had worked as a hospital auxiliary, though only for a year. But he seemed not only caring and genuine, he was also well-built, strong enough to help with lifting any elderly residents if some of the younger girls were unable. She had provisionally taken him on, although she still needed to see the references he said he'd tried to obtain that morning without success. Surely he could just start meantime, no harm in that.

'I'm willing to try my hand at anything,' he had said.

'Toilet duties, serving teas, leading exercises classes?' she asked.

'Sure, why not? I don't understand the way some people treat old folk as second-class citizens, they've got to be treated with respect. We're all the same. Just that some need a little bit more looking after.'

Rona got out of the bath, dried herself, then made a mug of milky cocoa. She opened the door of their annexe into the main building where everything was pitch dark and felt reassured by the silence. The main building was all locked up. Rona closed the annexe door and locked it too. She gulped down the cocoa, brushed her teeth then went through to the bedroom and into bed. She flicked through a magazine for a couple of minutes then put the light out.

Rona fell asleep almost immediately but woke with a start to a grinding noise. Was it a key in the lock? She pushed herself up onto her elbows to listen.

'Craig?' Her voice was a whisper.

There was no way he could have got home in the snow. She slipped out of bed and peered round the bedroom door. The main room was still. Through the gloom she could see that the front annexe door was locked as she had left it. She must have been dreaming. No one apart from Craig had a key. 'Pull yourself together, Rona.' She went back to bed and to sleep.

Some time later in the night Rona awoke from another dream in which there was the intermittent sound of foghorns booming. Was it actual foghorns down on the Forth? There was a woman in her dream, with long auburn hair, dressed in old-fashioned clothes, all in black. She had said nothing but had flitted in and out of vision as she chased a large freewheeling pram in the fog. Rona patted to her right for the bedside light then squinted at the clock. 2.15 a.m. She tilted her head to one side on hearing another noise, an indistinct, faint sound – unless it was just the gentle flurry of the wind against the windows?

Rona got out of bed, pulled on her dressing gown and reached up to shut the top window in their bedroom. She was freezing. She went to the main door of the annexe, unlocked it and went into the main hall, patting the wall for the light switch. She looked up at the high window above the door to a narrow shaft of moonlight and shivered. She strode across the hall to the main building. It was bitterly cold, the wind outside whipping blasts of chilly air under the doorway. She made a mental note to get draft excluders and adjust the timer on the heating to stay on all night when the residents moved in. She should have put something on her feet but didn't want to go back till she found out what the noise was.

As Rona padded along the corridor, putting on all the lights, the noise seemed to grow louder, though it was still indecipherable. Was it a clicking noise? A creaking noise? Or was it the sound of wheels? Grasping the banister, Rona climbed the stairs to the top landing. She stopped for breath. She was so unfit – no chance of a daily run these days. The wind was battering the windows upstairs and shadows moved across her path. She looked out from the large window on the landing at clouds dancing across the moon.

Rona thought back to the phone call with her mum earlier that evening. She'd asked her to check in Granny's Scots dictionary for the word 'Winzie'. It turned out it was an obsolete word meaning 'cursed'. In the chill of the night, as she crept along the corridor of a huge, deserted house, it was something she wished she hadn't learned.

Rona continued switching on all the lights and headed for the end room where the noise seemed to be getting louder. She pushed open the door to Room 12 and headed for the window which was being hammered by the wind. Why had she heard so little wind in the annexe? Of course, it must be protected by the high walls. She peered out the window at the back garden where the snow had disappeared and everything looked dark. There was little sign of fog; it was more of a wet mist. Perhaps the foghorns had been part of her dream. She stood on her tiptoes and tried to see into Martha's garden. Was that where the noise was coming from? It now sounded like wheels, creaking wheels that needed to be oiled. She couldn't see into the garden but as her eyes adjusted to the dark she thought she saw a faint light from somewhere, perhaps it was a torch in the mist. She blinked and it was gone.

Rona pulled her dressing-gown collar up high round her neck. Her teeth were chattering with the cold. She went out of the room, shutting the door and putting off all the lights as she went back along the corridor and downstairs. She'd ask Martha about the strange noise the next time she called round. Rona crossed the hall, heading for the annexe. She glanced up at the portrait on the wall and realised the auburn-haired woman had been in her dream. Who was she? Was she the woman whose husband had the house built over a century before? She was turning away when she noticed the cellar door was slightly ajar. The workmen had definitely closed it after they left that morning; the wind must have blown it open. She closed the cellar door firmly, then walked back to the annexe, locked herself in and pushed an armchair up against the door. Rona headed for the bedroom and tried to shake the word 'Winzie' from her brain.

Chapter 10

1899

Jessie stood up straight and stretched her back. She clapped her hands together to try to warm them up. She had done many hard tasks when she was growing up in her fishing village on the shore but she had never had to tackle vegetables in a hard frost. She was standing in the back garden picking off the last of the kail. Molly had said there wasn't much left on the stalks but enough to use in the dinnertime broth. Her basket was only half full but there was no more green to be seen. Molly would have to eke out the broth with more onions from the store in the larder. One beef bone for that huge soup pan never gave enough flavour but it was all she was allocated by the butcher. Molly used to grumble after the butcher's visit every Monday. He brought beef steaks and lamb chops for Matron and the Governor's dinners, but no more than seven bones, one for each day, for the residents' dinnertime soup.

Having been accustomed to fish every day of her life, Jessie was fascinated to see the bones, different shapes and sizes, lined up on the ashet in the larder. Some even had tiny scraps of red flesh on them which Molly said became the brown meat when cooked. Jessie was only familiar with herring and mackerel – and her Ma's fish soup made from the bones of fish gutted at Newhaven market. There had been quite a to-do when the Granton fisherfolk built an ice-house beside the market the year before she left home. Ma had said it was so that the boats could stay away at sea longer and the fish wouldn't go off. But the ice-house increased the rivalry between the fishing villages; they wanted one in Newhaven too.

Ma had sometimes cooked a crab that got stuck in the nets. She said they were served as special treats in the big houses and taverns, but they were just a nuisance for the common fisherfolk. Jessie liked the taste of the creamy brown flesh, and even more delicious was the sweet white meat from the claws. They sometimes had oysters too. Her Pa used to bring home oysters to eat as no one else wanted them and she remembered the wonderful smell from The Peacock Inn along the shore on the day they were cooking their beef and oyster pie. She had dreamed of one day going in there and tasting it. But now she never would. She was stuck in this place forever. And though herring was not a treat – they ate it nearly every day – she was now salivating at the very thought of it, dipped in oatmeal and fried in butter for tea.

As she looked around at the fine layer of frosty white over the solid earth she realised how much she missed home with its familiar smell and taste of fish. Here the smells she'd become used to were Molly's broth or porridge, nothing else. There was never fish in the kitchen, which was curious since the sea was not that far away. One day she'd been told to go up to the men's dormitories to find Old Sandy Grant, the only one who could fix the gas lamps. Having checked there was no one about, she went right through the dormitory which was at the other end of the corridor to the women's and girls' dormitories. She headed for one of the tiny high windows, pulled over a chair then climbed up on her tiptoes. There, through the solid bars, she could see the sea, the wide Firth of Forth stretching over to Fife. There were a couple of tiny black dots which she realised were fishing boats. At the sight of them, she felt her eyes prick. She was blinking away the tears when she heard Old Sandy Grant's stick striking the wooden floor. She knew she would get into trouble if she was found at the window so she jumped down, gave him the message and ran downstairs, the old man tap-tapping behind.

Jessie was about to take the basket of kail back into the kitchen when she heard a noise and turned around. It was coming from round the back of the little lodge house, where the Governor and Matron lived. It was the sound of someone sniggering, then there was a yelping noise then silence. Jessie picked up her basket and headed over towards the lodge. As she stepped onto the path, her footsteps crunched on the thick frost. She stood still for a moment then a figure emerged from the back of the lodge and sped along the wall, heading for the main building. Jessie couldn't see clearly enough but it was one of the boys, one of the taller ones. She was about to head back to the kitchen when she saw Bertha come round the front of the lodge house, glance furtively back, then run towards the back door.

'Bertha,' Jessie hissed. 'What were you doing?'

Bertha looked round, startled. 'Oh it's only you, Jessie. Billy said I'd not to tell.' She lowered her head.

'Tell what, Bertha?'

Bertha shook her head and shuffled her dress around her. 'Nothing.' Bertha looked around again, then bolted for the back door.

✳

'Stir the soup while I'm along at Matron's with her tea.' Molly stood at the door, a tray in her hands. 'And add a tiny bit more salt if it needs it. Only a little, mind, I've already put a bit in.'

Jessie nodded and picked up the long wooden spoon. She stirred the soup then tasted. She screwed up her face. It was a bit sour, but it was maybe all the onions. Molly had been muttering all morning about the fact the kail was over now. What on earth was she going to put in her soup?

Jessie reached over to the salt bowl and took a couple of pinches then stirred and tasted again. Yes, that was a little bit better, but still too oniony.

Jessie got the bowls out and was clanking the soup spoons onto the tray when Molly rushed in. 'Matron says we've to have dinner soon as the minister's coming this afternoon. So hurry up and take everything along. I'll give you a hand, then we'll come back and carry in the soup pan together.'

Jessie and Molly carried everything along to the dining room and set up the serving table as usual, before coming back for the soup pot and ladles. One pan handle each, they marched out of the kitchen into the corridor as the dinner gong clanged. As Jessie and Molly set the pan on the table, Jessie noticed Annie Rae slink into the room first. Soon everyone else was rushing in from the workroom to queue up in front of the serving table. After the Governor had stood in front of them to say prayers as usual he commanded everyone to eat, then swept past them all. Jessie was listening to the thud of his heavy footsteps disappearing along the corridor when she heard the first person gasp.

She and Molly looked over towards the tables where people were pushing their bowls away. Usually not allowed to speak, someone whispered, 'Can't eat this.' Others joined in with complaints.

Matron, who had been striding up and down between the tables, yelled, 'Silence!' She pointed her finger at one of the men who had started the grumbling. 'What, pray, is the problem?'

'Can't eat the broth, Matron. It's far too salty.'

'Nonsense.' She spat out the word as she tramped towards the serving table.

'Ladle some out for me.' She picked up a spoon. Everyone was straining round to watch.

The last time someone had complained about the food was when one of the girls had found a slug on her plate. Matron had called over the Governor who had picked up the slug, tilted his head back, dropped it into his mouth, and swallowed. He had then roared at the girl, 'You will eat every morsel on your plate, you ingrate!'

Matron supped from the spoon then screwed up her eyes. She

poured a beaker of water from the table and downed it. She leant
in towards Molly and Jessie, towering above them.

'If they eat this they will all be ill. It has far too much salt.' She
gulped from her water glass. 'It is like sea water.' She glowered at
Jessie, pointing at her mole. 'Have you hexed the broth?'

Jessie stood, her mouth open, shaking her head. 'I did nothing,
Matron, nothing.'

'I let her add the salt while I brought you your tea. She maybe
just overdid it a bit,' Molly said, looking straight at Matron. 'It's not
her fault.'

'I see.'

'I added a pinch, not much at all, someone else must have added
more.' Jessie looked around, panic in her eyes. Everyone was staring at her, anxious; Annie Rae was smirking.

Matron put up her hand. She addressed the dining room: 'Do
not eat this, return the contents of your bowl to the pan. You will
go hungry until teatime.' Matron turned to Jessie. 'Follow me,
Jessie Mack,' and she strode out the door.

Jessie could hear mutterings and grumblings as she ran after
Matron, across the corridor, heading for the cellar door. Matron
opened the door and went down the steps. Jessie followed, her
hand patting the rough, cold wall to help her make her way down
into the gloomy cellar.

Matron removed a bunch of keys from her pocket and bent
down at a little door and unlocked it. She threw open the door,
grabbed Jessie by the shoulder and flung her in. 'You may stay
in the coal cellar until you stop the witchcraft. Remember what
I told you.' Jessie crumpled onto the floor. 'You have one more
chance, Winzie!'

Matron slammed the door and Jessie heard the key turn in the
lock. She heard Matron's footsteps resounding on the stone floor
then fading up the stairs.

Chapter 11

1982

'Thanks for calling round. I'd love a hand actually.' Rona took Martha into the office and watched as she hung up her thick coat. Rona sniffed; the coat smelled fusty, of damp wool or mildew. How odd, the musty smell certainly did not go with Martha's glamorous image.

Martha slumped onto the chair. 'I knew Craig wouldn't make it back so thought you could use some help. When is it the first resident arrives?'

'Saturday. Only four more days.'

Rona picked up a sheet of paper from the desk then glanced up at Martha, the nagging doubts returning. 'How did you know Craig wouldn't make it back?'

'Oh, the TV news was full of the snow up north. Looked terrible. But you know, I used to live in a place that had really heavy snowfalls every year and they coped. This country grinds to a halt.' Martha smiled.

'You're not talking about California, obviously. Where was that you lived, then?'

'Aspen. When I was a cool rock chick.' Martha snorted with laughter. 'Okay, put me to work.'

Rona handed her a sheet of paper and some photos. 'I need these sheets of fire instructions photocopied and stuck on the back of all the residents' doors. And photos of the carers alongside. It helps them know who's looking after them.'

'Okay.'

'Thanks.' Rona frowned. 'Sure you're not missing out on your own work? Is there a job you have to go to or are you a housewife?'

A smile played across Martha's face. 'Housewife without the wife thing.'

'You've never been married then?'

Martha stood up and went to the photocopier. 'Not my thing. But you know, calling me a housewife makes me sound dull. I used to do … well, other things.' Martha set the photocopier at twelve copies and shouted over the noise of the machine. 'How about you, Rona, d'you still have anything to do with your old job as a lawyer?'

Rona shook her head. 'This is enough work at the moment.'

'And Craig, did you say he trained to be a doctor?'

Rona looked up from her folder. 'Something like that. Right now he's a care home manager. I'm gasping for a cup of tea. Want one?'

'Sure,' Martha said, tapping the sheets of paper on the desk into a neat pile. 'I'll go and pop these into the rooms.'

✕

'I thought I heard a funny noise last night, so I went upstairs and along to Room 12.' Rona pointed upstairs from the residents' sitting room where she and Martha sat, nursing mugs of tea.

'Yeah?'

Rona pushed the biscuit barrel towards Martha but she declined. 'I meant to bake some more cookies for you. I'll bring some tomorrow, to welcome the residents.'

Rona picked up her mug. 'Won't be allowed. The cook officially starts on Friday. She's the only one who'll be able to provide food for the residents.' Rona glanced back up at Martha. 'So you didn't hear anything?'

Martha shook her head. 'What kind of noise?'

'Sort of a creaking. Like it could almost have been wheels.'

'You can't see into my messy old garden from up there, can you?

I took a look the other day from Room 12's window.'

'Can't see a thing. The walls and trees hide everything. They must make your house quite dark inside.'

Martha shrugged. 'It's an old house, got small windows. It was really windy last night, maybe the noise was something flying across the garden.'

Rona nibbled on a Rich Tea biscuit. 'You don't like gardening much, do you?'

'No, I reckon it's a complete waste of time. If I want flowers I can buy them from a shop.' Martha swivelled round. 'Talking of which, d'you need any flower vases? Residents are bound to get visitors bringing them flowers. I've got a few old ones I don't need.'

'Good idea. Thanks.'

'Oh, you know that keypad at the door, I presume you'll let the residents and their families know what numbers to tap in?'

Rona hesitated before answering, 'No, just the nurses and carers. And we'll probably have to change it every so often. I know some residents will get in a flap that they're not allowed access, but it's all for security and safety. A member of staff will ensure that no resident determined to escape could get out when the door's open.'

'Can't see they'd ever want to leave here, it's like a luxury hotel. And you said they can have meals in their rooms if they don't fancy coming down to the dining room?'

'Yeah, some of them will probably prefer breakfast in their rooms and we'll just see how it goes. It's all a learning curve.'

Martha swept back her thick, jet-black hair and Rona noticed her heavy make-up creasing into the lines on her forehead. Perhaps Martha was older than she had thought. 'You still planning on putting goldfish over there?' Martha pointed at a high table near the window.

'Yes, that's on Craig's list of chores for tomorrow.'

'There's a pet shop along on Granton Road, but I am sure he knows that.'

Rona looked out the window. 'Hope he gets home soon.'

'What about other pets? Old folk like seeing cats around. Or even a dog.'

'Nice idea. Craig really wanted us to get a puppy when we moved in but puppies are so much extra work. Also, with the baby coming, it'd be …' Rona kicked herself. Idiot, why did she say that?

'What? Are you pregnant, Rona?' Martha raised an eyebrow.

'It's meant to be a secret. It's still early days, not had a scan yet, so I shouldn't have said a thing, but yes. We're delighted.'

Martha drained the tea from her mug. 'Wow, you're sure going to have your work cut out.' She smiled. 'I can help out in this place whenever you like. I've done admin and stuff.'

'Thanks, Martha, I will keep that in mind.' Rona got to her feet.

'Hey, you can use that big old pram, I am sure it'll scrub up fine.'

'What big old pram?'

'You know, the one in the cellar? I saw Craig loading it into that van one day, heading for the dump. But I said you should keep it. So he said he would put it back.'

Rona frowned. 'Why should we keep it?'

'I've been to an old people's home where they had a pram and some residents – the ones who're losing it a bit – liked to wheel it around. Reminded them of their younger days when they had babies. Therapeutic.'

'Craig told me he'd taken it to the dump.'

Martha shrugged. 'Not what he told me.' She headed for the door. 'Shall I carry on printing off the menu cards?'

Rona nodded and went into the hall. Why on earth had Craig listened to Martha when she told him they should hang on to that spooky old pram? Rona crossed towards their annexe then turned to check the cellar door was shut and looked up at the portrait on the wall. The woman had those eyes that followed you wherever you went, left or right. She had an expression that Rona hadn't noticed before – she was not smiling, but neither did she look stern. Instead, with her eyes narrowing as they followed Rona from left to right, she looked wily, calculating. It was as if she, too, had a secret.

Chapter 12

1899

Jessie tried to stand up but her head bumped against the ceiling. She crouched down and proceeded along the narrow room, patting her hands against the cold, rough walls to try to feel her way. There was a little light ahead but it was still dim. She stopped at what she realised was a huge pile of coal. She had no idea how much farther the narrow cellar extended. She wiped the soot from her hands on her skirt and returned to the door where the ceiling was slightly less low. Here she sat down, her legs extended. It was dark and murky, but a little light streamed in from the far end and as her eyes adjusted, she saw daylight on top of the coal. This was obviously where the coal was tipped into the cellar. There were also a couple of cracks of light coming through the slats in the wooden door, but that would fade later as it was still dinnertime, the middle of the day. Surely Matron wouldn't leave her in here all day and all night?

Jessie began to sing. Singing had been a way of life at home in Newhaven, perhaps that would help her now. She tried the first lines of 'Caller Herrin''.

> *Wha'll buy my caller herrin'*
> *They're bonny fish and ...*

Jessie started to sob as memories of home came flooding back and a deep sadness swept over her. She rested her head on the stone step. It was cold, so she wrapped her arms round her shoulders and shut her eyes. She hated this place. How could her mother have sent her here? It was a prison, it had bars on the windows and no one could ever leave, unless they died. That's what Annie Rae said. Either they carried you out in a box or you went mad, like Effie.

What would she be doing now if she had been allowed to stay at home? She'd be down at Newhaven harbour, legs dangling over the harbour wall, mending the nets. And singing with the other fishergirls as they worked. Jessie took a deep breath and tried to remember the salty taste of sea spray on her face and lips. She coughed as sooty air filled her lungs.

When the first girl saw the boats coming back into the harbour, they'd all jump down from the wall and would gather round the boats. Then they'd help unload the fish before sorting it into different baskets for the men to take to the market and for their mothers and elder sisters to lug around the big houses in the city. Jessie never thought that she would miss it. How could she miss the smell, the hard graft, as they gutted the fish for hours on end? And before they started to work with the gutting knife, they'd to tie up their fingers – sometimes just one finger but often all of them, to protect against the knife slipping. They'd use cotton or linen cloth, usually material cut from the baker's flour bags or sometimes rags from servants' smocks handed in by ladies from the big houses through the church. They would wash the rags and then bleach them, tear them into strips and tie them tight round their fingers to last all day. Then they could start work, slitting the short knife along the belly of the fish as fast as possible and pulling out the guts. The girls would all compete against each other to see who gutted more fish. At night, Ma always checked Jessie's and Dorrie's fingers. If any were festering, she'd make a bread poultice with sugar in it and that cured it.

It seemed strange, but Jessie even missed the smell of fish that lingered. This was the smell that persisted even on a Sunday morning when they washed in the big basin in the scullery before walking along the shore to church. She missed the harsh squawking of the herring gulls as they swooped low over Newhaven harbour. In the dark silence of the cellar, Jessie hugged herself once more and, dreaming of the sea, drifted off to sleep.

⋇

A grating noise woke Jessie. She jolted up and banged her head, forgetting where she was. She rubbed her crown. It had become much darker. How long had she slept? Was there someone at the other side of the door? 'Hello?' she whispered through the cracks in the door. 'Is there anyone there?'

Silence, then there was more scratching. It sounded like fingernails against the other side of the door. She was sure there was someone near.

Jessie moved away a little from the door and waited. The scratching stopped and there was a clink as a key was inserted into the lock. The keyhole shook as the key was turned and turned, but obviously did not work. Another key was inserted then two more. Jessie was trembling now. Who was at the other side of the door with a set of keys? It was obviously not Matron.

Another key was thrust in. This time the handle turned slowly. There, crouched down on her hunkers, was Effie, smiling. She removed the key and put the bunch deep into her pocket.

'Effie,' whispered Jessie. 'Where did you get the keys? Are they Matron's?'

'No, they're mine.' She beamed once more, revealing blackened teeth.

Effie wriggled inside the coal cellar and sat beside Jessie who stared at her, taking in the long, thick fingernails and black teeth. Effie's dark hair was, as usual, greasy, her long straggly pigtail hanging down from her greying scalp. She was the one person Matron made an exception for during her inspections, partly because she was never in the dormitory in the mornings, as she never slept. Both Matron and the Governor let Effie wander around wherever she liked, undisciplined unless she was scratching at the walls with her fingernails, which she did often. Mad Effie, everyone would say, shaking their heads. Leave her be, it's just Mad Effie.

'Effie, I'll get into trouble if Matron sees me out of here. I can't walk out with you, I'll have to wait till she comes and unlocks the door.'

'Not wanting to get you out. I just brought you something, a collation.'

'A what?'

Jessie watched Effie take out a pair of scissors from the folds of her skirt. They looked like embroidery scissors, they were ornate and gilded. How had she got those? Effie reached under her skirts again and brought out a hunk of bread. She thrust the bread and the scissors at Jessie and smiled again.

'Oh, Effie, thank you, I'm really hungry. But you'd better go. If Matron catches you, you'll get a row. So will I.'

Effie used the scissors to snip the crust of bread into two thick slices then dropped them onto Jessie's lap. She handed Jessie the bread then got up onto her knees to leave. She turned round to look straight at Jessie, her dark eyes watery. 'It's because you and I are both Winzies. Don't worry, they can't harm us. We've got special gifts, you and I.' She stretched over to Jessie's lap and grabbed the scissors.

Jessie shrunk back, but Effie took them in her long fingers and pushed the door to. They were both shut inside now. She gripped the filigree scissors like a pen and began to chisel away on the wooden panels of the door. First there was a large W, then an I, then an N. Jessie watched her finish etching the word, fearful at the sight of Mad Effie with a pair of scissors in her hand. She had never been in such close proximity for so long. Considering Effie was nowhere to be seen at bath time, she didn't smell bad at all. Certainly not as bad as most of the women her age, whatever that was. Jessie looked at her close up and remembered someone said she was forty-something, which was very old, about the age her Granny M was when she'd died the year before. But Effie had something youthful about her, because of her strange childish ways. She watched Effie screw up her red-rimmed eyes in concentration as she continued etching the wood. Once she had finished the final letter E with a flourish, Effie turned round and smiled at Jessie who smiled back but said nothing.

Effie pushed the scissors into her pocket then crept out of the little room and began to pull the door shut.

'Thank you for the bread, Effie,' said Jessie, gazing at the door as it was shut. The key was inserted into the lock once more and it was locked. Jessie began to sob once more, not because she was cold and frightened, as before, but because the only person in this horrid place to be kind and help her was Mad Effie. She picked up a slice of bread and rammed it in her mouth then sat staring at the six letters on the door. WINZIE. The curse was still very much with her.

Chapter 13

1982

'Ian, can you show Mrs Bell into her room, please? Room 5, along at the end of the corridor.'

'You know I can't manage stairs well, but can I take the lift should I want to walk around upstairs?' Mrs Bell asked.

'Of course, Mrs Bell. Treat the entire house as your home. And anything else you need, just let me know. I'll pop round and see you later, check you've settled in.'

Ian Devine picked up Mrs Bell's capacious handbag and guided her out of the lounge, her stick thumping on the carpet as they walked. Rona watched Ian take her slowly along the corridor, chatting all the way. Even though one of the nurses said she had reservations about Ian, Rona knew better. His manner with their elderly residents was excellent. He didn't talk down to them, just spoke normally, and the day before the usually reserved Mr Benson had been chuckling away at his jokes. He was going to fit in just fine.

Rona sat at her desk, sorting through the files, then looked up at the clock. It was eleven o'clock so the tea trolley should be going around. She went to the door and peered out. Good, there was Mercy at the end of the corridor, pushing the trolley laden with tea, coffee and home-baked shortbread. The staff seemed to be following Rona's requests for everything to be on time, as much as possible.

There was one more resident due that morning and then that was the first eight rooms occupied. The first day had gone well, with the cook excelling herself and everyone enjoying the food even though most of them had small appetites. She and Craig would have to help during some mealtimes as a couple of residents needed a hand with cutting up their food, but that was all part of the job. Thankfully Rona no longer felt sick in the mornings. Those early weeks of her pregnancy were awful; she was constantly tired and felt nauseous, but she had to keep working – there was so much to do. But now, at four months, she felt she had more energy. Hopefully the sickness was over and she could just enjoy growing fat.

'Rona, Mrs Bell says, can you go and speak to her, please?'

It was the Australian nurse, Fay, looking smart in her starched blue uniform. 'I think she wanted a little reassurance from you. She didn't like that new carer calling her by her first name.'

Rona sighed. She had briefed the staff on the first day about how to address residents. If someone wanted to be called by their first name, that was fine, otherwise it was Mr or Mrs. Or Miss. The last woman due to arrive was a Miss.

Rona strolled along the corridor to Room 5 and knocked at the door.

'Come in.'

Rona went in and sat beside Mrs Bell who was perched at the window on a hand chair.

'Mrs Bell, that chair doesn't look very comfortable. Why don't I have this armchair moved to the window for you and you can keep this chair for visitors?'

'I don't expect I shall have too many visitors. My husband was the sociable one, I was more the stay-at-home one.'

'Your husband died only three months ago, Mrs Bell, didn't he? Are you managing all right?'

'Yes, fine. He had what I believe is termed a "good death". She sighed. 'And it was the right move for me to come here. The sheltered housing was fine for us both but not for me by myself.'

'Is everything to your liking here?'

'Yes, apart from a couple of things. First of all, I do not wish to be called by my Christian name.'

'Of course, that was a mistake. Charlotte said she was sorry, she was tired as she'd been on a difficult night shift. I apologise for my staff. That won't happen again.'

Mrs Bell turned back to the window. 'Also, I did wonder if there was a room upstairs instead of this one?'

'Yes, there is one, but it's further along. You won't have the same view over the garden.'

Mrs Bell nodded. 'It's that, well, I've not told you yet, but my husband and I used to live in the big house opposite and I hoped to be able to see it so that I can relive the memories of the wonderful time we had there. Can you see the house from upstairs?'

'Of course, you lived in that house. I remember someone telling me. Let me nip upstairs and check if Room 12 has a view towards it. It's a corner room and has two windows so I think you can see over the road and also over to the lodge house. I'm pretty sure, anyway.' Rona went to the door. 'It's just come to me, it was Martha who told me you and your husband lived there, for many years. It must have been such a wrench to leave it.'

Mrs Bell scowled. 'Is that Yank still around?'

'Martha? Yes, she lives in the lodge house.'

Mrs Bell turned away and stared out of the window.

✳

'So that's everything unpacked into your wardrobe and drawers now, Mrs Bell. Is that all right?' Rona shut a cupboard door in the upstairs room.

'I think so.' Mrs Bell looked out the left-hand window. 'What a difference to be able to see over to my old house. And I can still see the garden down below.' She pointed at the back of the door.

'Whose photograph is that on the door?'

'That's Mercy, she's your named carer.'

Mrs Bell frowned. 'I should so prefer that nice young man Ian as my named carer. Is that possible?'

Rona shrugged. 'I think that should be all right. Let me look at my staff lists later. Now, is everything else all right?'

'The safe. I am still not sure why you have to know the code too?'

Rona took a deep breath. She had a huge pile of admin on her desk needing her attention. 'As I said, Mrs Bell, I won't actually know the code. You write it down here and it goes into your file in an envelope which you will have sealed yourself. It's for emergencies only.'

'You mean, when I die?'

Rona smiled. This woman was sharp as tacks. 'Not at all. In case, say, you're ill and need something.'

'I see, very well.' She drummed her fingers on the arm of her chair.

'There is one final thing.'

Rona checked her watch. It was nearly suppertime, she had so much to do.

'That American. I presume you have little to do with her?'

'Martha? Well, she's helped us out in here sometimes. And she is our only neighbour really. We've never set eyes on the couple in your old house.'

Mrs Bell nodded. 'I see.'

'See you in the dining room in an hour then, Mrs Bell.'

Mrs Bell turned back to the window.

Chapter 14

1899

'Come and sit down at the table for a minute, Jessie. I'm sorry you got into trouble.'

Jessie sat down in the warm kitchen and looked up at Molly who had never spoken to her in such a kindly way before.

She sat shivering, still chilled from the afternoon in the cellar. Matron had come to let her out just before supper, saying nothing other than she had to get straight to work. Molly handed her a cup of hot tea and reached for the sugar bowl. Jessie's eyes opened wide as she watched the cook stir two spoonfuls into the tea and push it in front of her. She was never allowed tea in the kitchen and never more than half a teaspoon of sugar. She wrapped her hands round the cup.

'The thing is, Jessie, Annie Rae got away with it. She must have come in here when we were setting up at dinnertime and put all that salt into the soup. When I realised it must have been her, I went to tell Matron but she still left you in the cellar for hours.'

'Thank you.' Jessie took a sip of the tea and shut her eyes. She had never tasted anything so delicious. It was sweet, hot and comforting.

'Have you ever been down there?' Jessie asked.

'What, in the coal cellar? No. It's not very big is it?'

'The ceiling's low but I think it goes back quite a long way. There was too much coal – I couldn't see the end.'

'The coalman just delivered yesterday morning, that's why.'

Jessie glanced over her cup at Molly who was hanging up cloths along the range. 'Molly, how long has Effie been in here?'

Molly shrugged. 'She's certainly been here ever since I arrived. Why?'

'Just wondered. And why do Matron and the Governor just ignore her?'

'She's not quite right in the head, poor soul. You've seen how she scratches things with her nails. And she never sleeps.'

'Does she sleep in the women's dormitory then?'

Molly stood still for a moment without turning round. 'Yes, though she's never there.' She began bustling at the stove with the last cloths. 'Now, we need to be getting on. There's the supper dishes to wash. Has that drink warmed you up?'

Jessie nodded. 'Thanks, Molly,' she said, heading for the sink.

'Just try to keep out of trouble, Jessie Mack. Matron said she'd only give you one more chance then you'd be out. She's convinced you're cursed.'

Jessie touched the brown mark above her lip. 'But Ma won't take me back. Where would I go?'

'Let's not think about that. Just do everything she says. And stay well away from Annie Rae. She's trouble.'

⁂

Jessie went out the back door and took in a deep breath of air. She had finished all the dishes and Molly was taking Matron and the Governor their supper in the Governor's office. She had watched, amazed, as Molly had fried two beef steaks in a frying pan with butter. Butter was something they only ever had on a Sunday with their bread, the thinnest scraping, otherwise it was dry bread. She had boiled potatoes and put them on their plates with some cabbage. Jessie felt her mouth go all moist as she looked at the dishes and the smell of the beef while it was cooking had been almost too much to bear. Molly had added a couple of shakes of something from a small bottle to the pan which she then stirred with a wooden spoon into the buttery juices before pouring this liquid over the beef on the warm plates. Molly told her this was called a sauce and the bottle contained mushroom ketchup which gave it a nice taste. How could Molly bear to cook food like that every night after a day cooking watery porridge and thin broth for the inmates?

Jessie looked towards the little lodge house to the left. She walked down the steps and looked back up at Wardie House. The two buildings were built in different stone, the big house was far grander and looked much newer. She stepped round the back, wondering where the coalman tipped the coal into the cellar. She had already made up her mind that, if she was sent down there again, she would somehow find her way out, then escape. She was fourteen – old enough to look after herself.

For the first time, Jessie noticed a small door low down along the wall, not far from the back door of the lodge house. She turned the handle and the door opened and she noticed a wide chute which was filled with coal. The chute did not look big enough to go down, perhaps a small child would manage it. So that was where the light in the coal cellar came from. The cellar was very near the lodge house, perhaps it shared the coal cellar with the big house.

Jessie's eyes darted back to the kitchen door which was still shut, so she walked towards the lodge house. This was something she had never done before, but Matron and the Governor would be in his study for at least half an hour, eating their delicious supper with a glass of something from the sparkling crystal decanter. Molly told Jessie the dark red liquid was called claret. Well, it seemed that the Governor had more than just the one glass: when Jessie went in to clear the table every evening, the entire decanter of purple drink was gone. There were dregs in the bottom of his glass; Matron's glass was clean. Matron replenished the sparkling decanter twice a day.

Jessie peered in one of the windows of the lodge house. It was difficult to see as the lamps were not yet lit, but she made out chairs and, by the window, a desk with some books. There was a picture hanging on the wall, a woman she thought, but it was too dark to see clearly. Jessie continued round the back and stopped in her tracks. In the dim light, she could make out two figures, very close to each other, up against the wall. She retreated, sure they had not seen her, and sped over to the wall near the back garden door.

Soon, a figure ran from behind the lodge house to the back door. It was one of the boys. Then another figure followed, walking fast across the vegetable patch and up the steps where she was standing.

'Bertha, what were you doing round there?'

Bertha's eyes widened as she noticed Jessie.

'Nothing.'

'You'll get into trouble if you're caught. And how d'you get out the back door? It's always locked.'

'It's Matron and the Governor's suppertime.' Bertha smiled. 'Anyway, he knows how to get out.'

'Who? Who was that with you, Bertha?'

'Billy Muir.' She smiled. 'He loves me, Jessie, he told me.'

Jessie grabbed Bertha's arm, pulled her into the larder then shut the door. Bertha was a big girl, but her arms were soft and smooth, like a baby's. 'Bertha, you'll get into so much trouble. They'll send you to work down at the docks in Leith. That's what I heard Matron tell Elsie Wilson last week when she caught her. And Elsie was with her own husband. Matron won't have any of that kissing stuff around here.'

'We weren't doing anything, Jessie. Honest.'

'Just be careful, Bertha. Don't trust that Billy Muir.'

'I'll do what I like.' Bertha opened the larder door. 'Winzie!' she called as she ran towards the kitchen door.

Jessie shut her eyes tight. Bertha was seldom like the others, pointing at the mark on her face and calling her names; she had never spoken to her like that. But she was so simple, she believed whoever was speaking to her at the time and did what she was told. Billy Muir was no good and he obviously wanted something from Bertha. She hoped she wouldn't get into trouble.

Chapter 15

1982

Rona parked the car and walked up the path to Wardie House. She tapped in the keypad code and pushed open the door. It was quiet, mid afternoon, and most residents were resting in their rooms after lunch. It was a good opportunity to have some time for herself. She'd just been to Willie Low's for the weekly shop and was ready to sit down.

Rona pushed open the door to the annexe and heard something. Was it giggling? She traipsed into the kitchen.

Martha and Craig were standing close together by the stove. Martha was touching Craig's hair. What the hell was going on?

'Oh, hi Rona.' Craig went over to give her a peck on the cheek. As usual, he smelled minty; he was constantly sucking peppermints. 'You're early. Thought your doctor's appointment was at three?'

'No, four. I had time to come home from the supermarket first.' Had they expected her an hour later?

'Give me your car keys. I'll bring the stuff in. Martha's just made a pot of tea. Grab a cup.'

So the woman was now making herself at home in Rona's kitchen? Rona looked over at Martha who was smirking as she poured the tea.

'Were you inspecting Craig's hair for lice or something?'

'Very funny. No, I was telling your husband what good thick hair he has.' She flicked her own glossy locks. 'No chance he'll go bald like so many other men not that much older than him.' She looked Rona up and down. 'You can definitely see you're pregnant now. Love the dungarees.'

'Yes, well, it's all I can get into. Craig hates them.' Rona stared at Martha's slim figure. She wasn't about to tell Martha that Craig also hated the thought of his wife all fat. 'Were you two not meant to be setting up the lounge for Alex's birthday party tonight?'

'We were just about to start. Weren't we, Craig?' Martha's voice was now simpering.

Craig had just arrived back into the kitchen and was putting the supermarket bags on the table. 'The party?' He nodded. 'Just about to get onto that. I've got all the balloons and streamers and things. Oh, the cook wanted to see you about how she should decorate Alex's cake.'

'I've already told her to ice 'Alex' and '100'.' Rona gulped her tea then looked at her watch. 'I'll go and speak to her. See you in the party room later.'

Rona stood up, headed for the hall and slammed the door behind her. She was fuming. Who did Martha think she was? There was definitely something sly and calculating about her.

She looked over to the other side of the hall and noticed Mrs Bell standing by the cellar door, staring at the portrait of the Victorian lady.

'Hello, Mrs Bell.' Rona forced a smile.

The elderly woman turned, slowly, both gnarled hands clasped together on the handle of her walking stick.

'Hello, Rona.' She looked her up and down. 'Do you know, today's the first day I can actually see you are expecting? Remind me how many months you have to go?'

'The baby's due in July, so another three months.' Rona smiled as she patted her bump. 'Do you like that painting? I found it downstairs in the cellar.'

'It's a little amateurish but also rather charming. Have you noticed, she has those eyes that follow you when you move from side to side?'

'Yes. I wonder if she might be the owner of the house before it became a poorhouse?'

'I suppose so.' Mrs Bell thought a moment. 'I think I might have some information on who used to own the house in one of my drawers upstairs. Shall I try to find out who they were?'

'That'd be great, yes please, Mrs Bell.'

The door to the annexe swung open and Martha and Craig came out, carrying boxes of balloons. Craig stopped beside them. 'How are you, Mrs Bell? Is your headache better now?'

'Yes, thank you, young man.' Mrs Bell gazed at Martha who had continued on towards the sitting room; Craig followed on. Mrs Bell turned to Rona and whispered, 'Horrid cheap perfume she wears.' She crinkled up her nose. 'Watch that Yank, keep an eye on her. I saw her snooping around in the big linen cupboard earlier.'

'Maybe she was getting some sheets or towels for one of the carers.' Though that seemed unlikely.

'She reminds me of Lady Macbeth, you know.'

'Really?'

'Yes, but without a husband to do her bidding. I always thought she might be capable of evildoings.' Mrs Bell stood up straight and started walking towards the lift, her stick tapping across the floor.

✳

After she'd spoken to the cook, Rona went to the office and started to tidy up her notes. She had so many assessment documents to file. Once each of the twelve residents' folders was complete things would be in much better order.

Rona stopped and listened. She heard the sound of wheels, slow, creaking, turning wheels. It was similar to the noise that night when Craig was stuck up north in the snow, when she had gone round the rooms trying to find where it was coming from. The noise was becoming louder and now she could hear a voice so she opened the door and went into the corridor.

There, halfway along, was Mr Burnside, with his usual beatific smile, pushing the old pram towards her, mumbling to himself.

Rona had remonstrated with Craig that it had to go, but he had insisted Martha was right, some elderly people with dementia liked to push a pram, perhaps reminding them of when they were younger. Rona had presumed it would be mothers who would have memories of taking a stroll with their baby. Rona recalled, at Mr Burnside's assessment, reading that he'd never married so presumably had never taken his own children out in a pram.

Mr Burnside looked up and saw Rona standing there. He came to a stop, rocking the pram up and down.

'How are you, Mr Burnside? Is that a nice walk you're having?'

'What's that?'

'A nice walk with the pram?' She had forgotten he was very deaf.

'Yes, it's a good size isn't it? Very big.' He looked down at Rona's expanding waistline. 'Plenty room for another baby in here.' He stopped rocking and started to push the pram away.

'It's only ten minutes until Alex's birthday party, Mr Burnside. Shall we come and get you?'

'Yes, and I'll bring the baby.'

Rona sighed. Mr Burnside's mild form of dementia was not obvious to most people and he was never aggressive, but the nurse said she locked his door at nights in case he wandered about the home in the dark and hurt himself. Bless him, thought Rona, his smile would break your heart.

The lift door opened and Mrs Bell emerged, teetering on her stick.

'Rona, I found that information I was looking out for you. Shall I leave it with you? I'm in no rush to have it back.'

Rona wanted to start reading straight away but there was a birthday to attend. 'Thanks very much, Mrs Bell. Now, are you ready to go into the party room?'

Chapter 16

1899

Jessie was scrubbing the wooden table in the kitchen when she heard a tap on the door. She looked up to see one of the younger girls standing there, Jean, who was always getting into trouble from Matron for wetting her bed. Though she was only six, that morning Jean had been whipped and beaten and not allowed to drink anything all day after breakfast. She had been in Wardie House since she was a baby. Molly said her mother had abandoned her on the doorstep one cold winter's morning and so Matron and the Governor had little option but to take her in. A foundling, Molly said she was called. Sometimes the mothers came back for their babies after they abandoned them and Jean told everyone who would listen that her mother would come back, but no one believed her. It was such a shame.

'Is there something you want, Jean?' Jessie laid the scrubbing brush down and smiled at the thin, wan face.

'It's Matron. She wants to see you.'

'Does she?' Jessie bit her lip. 'Did she say why?' Jessie had behaved impeccably since she had been flung in the cellar, even though it had not been her fault, and over the past few weeks had worked even harder, if that were possible.

'Dunno, but she just called out to me in the corridor and said to fetch you.' Jean stood at the door gazing at the pitcher of water beside the stove. 'Can I have a drink, Jessie?'

'You're not meant to, Jean, you know that.'

'But I'm so thirsty. I've had nothing to drink since my porridge.'

Jessie headed for the door and looked into the corridor, which was empty. She pulled Jean inside the kitchen and reached into the cupboard for a small tumbler. She poured out some water and handed it to the girl who downed it in three long gulps. She handed Jessie back the glass and smiled. 'Thank you. That was fine.'

'Don't you be telling anyone I gave you a drink. And try to get up and use the pot if you need in the night. Wake me up if you need any help.' Jessie ruffled the girl's hair. 'Off you go now. I'll get along to see Matron.'

Jessie wiped her hands on her apron then walked along the corridor to Matron's room, looking up again at the portraits lit by the flickering light from the wall lamps. The first picture was of the Governor and then there were those other gentlemen, all dressed in black, none smiling. Jessie ran her hands over her hair, ensuring every last wisp of loose hair was tucked up under her cap, and knocked.

'Enter!'

Jessie walked towards the desk where Matron sat, a long, black pen in her hand.

'Ah yes, Jessie Mack. I wanted to see you.' Matron put down the pen and looked directly at Jessie.

'Your sister was here earlier and she had some news.'

'Dorrie? Dorrie was here? Have I missed her? Why couldn't I see her?'

'You were busy with your chores. Besides, this is a poorhouse, not a residential home where visitors are permitted.'

'But, I ...'

'Enough.' Matron raised her pointed chin. 'The news she gave was from your home. Your grandmother – "Granny B" she said you called her – died last Sunday and was buried yesterday.' Matron paused to look at Jessie, whose eyes had filled with tears. 'It would not have been appropriate for you to have gone to the funeral so your sister only came with the news this morning.'

Jessie lowered her head as she began to sniffle. She wiped her nose on the back of her hand and looked up at Matron, imploring. 'Can't I go home and see them all?'

'Out of the question. This is not somewhere you can please yourself.' She flicked her right hand at Jessie as if swatting a fly. 'And now I must get on.'

The girl turned round slowly and trudged back towards the kitchen where she sat down on a chair, put her head in her hands and shook with silent sobs.

✕

Bertha turned on the stiff mattress and prodded Jessie in the back. She had tried to cheer her friend up after Jessie had told her about her Granny. Granny B who was always smiling. Granny B, who was angry with Jessie's mother for taking the decision to send her away after the accident. Granny B had been the only person, apart from Dorrie, who didn't believe Jessie's father and brother dying had anything to do with Jessie and her curse. And now she was gone.

'Jessie, wake up, there's something I want to tell you.'

Jessie was already awake, lying there thinking about home and her lovely, warm Granny and her sister and realising how much she missed them all.

'What?'

'Remember you were cross with me for forgetting to wash out my rags?'

'What rags?'

'You know, the ones for the blood. You told me how to use them and wash them every morning.'

'Yes.' Because Dorrie was so much older than Jessie, she had seen her sister washing out special rags once every four weeks and her sister had explained what happened every month to a woman.

'I don't need them any more, Jessie. I don't bleed any more, so I don't need to remember. That's good isn't it?'

Jessie turned to face Bertha, whose smile she could just make out in the half light.

'What d'you mean, you don't bleed any more?'

'I don't need the rags. There's no blood. It's all fine. I'm like you again, a normal girl again.' Bertha beamed then started to turn over.

'Bertha,' Jessie hissed. 'When did it stop?'

Bertha shrugged. 'Soon after you were in the cellar. Don't know when that was.'

Jessie knew exactly when that was. It was three months ago. She had counted each day as she continued to plot how to escape. 'Bertha, do you feel anything else different?'

Bertha shook her head then tipped her head back in a big yawn. Jessie knew, from her sister, what happened when you started needing the rags as an older girl, then stopped. Unless you were an old woman, like her Granny or Great Auntie Maggie, it meant you were going to have a baby.

'Turn back over, Bertha,' Jessie whispered. 'Let me feel your tummy.'

Bertha lay on her back and giggled as Jessie touched her over her belly.

'It's tickly, Jessie.'

Jessie had seen her mum's younger sister's expanding waistline when she was expecting Jessie's cousins, and she knew what signs to look for.

'Bertha, remember when you and Billy Muir were together, round the back of the lodge house. What were you doing?'

Bertha turned back over and curled herself up, her knees into her chest. 'I told you, nothing. Now go to sleep. And don't be sad about your Granny any more.'

Jessie opened her mouth to speak then rolled back to her side of the bed. If what she thought was true, Bertha would be in a lot of trouble soon. She must try to think what she could do to help; otherwise Bertha would be sent to the docks at Leith. Bertha would not survive alone, and certainly not with a baby.

Chapter 17

1982

The doorbell rang once, a shrill, short blast, as if the person at the other side of the door did not want to disturb. Rona put down the letter she was reading and went to answer the door. As she crossed the hall, Rona passed an elderly man sat on a chair in the hall, walking stick by his side, his tartan cap perched on top of his snowy white hair.

'Morning, Mr Wilson, how are you?'

'Grand, thanks, Rona.' He pointed over to the portrait. 'That's a fine picture over there. Is it your granny?'

Rona smiled. 'No, I don't know who she is. Nice, isn't it?'

'She's got a look about her, as if she's got a secret, you know, like the Mona Lisa.' He turned to look up at Rona, blinking his rheumy eyes. 'Don't you think?'

'I know what you mean. Sorry, you'll need to excuse me while I get the door.'

The bell rang again as she reached for the handle.

It was the garrulous postman. 'Oh, hello, sorry to ring twice, I didn't know if you could hear. How's it all going? The old folk behaving themselves?' The man at the door peered at her through his thick glasses. Rona had had many chats with Donnie. It still amazed her that he got his deliveries done on time, he loved to stop and talk so much.

'Got something here to show you.' He handed her an

official-looking brown envelope.

Rona frowned. 'But it's not for Wardie House, it's for Wardie Lodge House. D'you not usually go there first?'

'She wasn't in and I didn't like to leave it in the letterbox at the gate. My reckoning is, they've got the wrong address. Looks like it's for one of your residents?'

Rona looked again at the name. Miss Janet McCallister.

'We don't have anyone with that name. Sorry.'

'You sure?'

'We've got twelve residents, only seven of them are women and I know everyone's names. That's my job.'

'My oh my. I'll have to go back round with it, then. But that's not the American lady's name.'

'Maybe someone who used to live there?'

'Oh, right, never thought of that. I could ask the lady up in Trinity Cottage. I think she might've known the folk who used to live in the lodge house. She told me it was where the Governor and Matron lived when it was a poorhouse. Quite a history.'

'Yes,' said Rona, reaching for the door handle. She was keen to get back to the office. 'Look, why don't I hang on to the letter? Martha's coming in later, I can give it to her.'

'That'd be grand, thanks.' He looked at his watch. 'My oh my, I'm already running late. They keep telling me off. I'm late for the second delivery. It's not my fault if folk like to chat to me.'

Rona smiled and waved goodbye.

Ж

Rona wheeled Betty Chalmers out of the dining room towards her room. 'That was a delicious lunch today. The soup had such a good flavour. When I asked the butler he said it was the home-made stock that gave it that excellent taste.'

Rona grinned. The 'butler' was one of the male carers whose duties included helping serve meals and assisting residents who couldn't feed themselves. Betty called the female carers house-maids.

'That nice young man told me.' She turned round to point an arthritic finger at one of the carers. 'And he said the pudding was made with rhubarb from the garden. Splendid. My cook used to do many puddings with the rhubarb the gardener forced under pots. Marvellous.'

Betty Chalmers had come to Wardie House from a stately home in the Borders and had settled in well, although she still insisted on ringing the bell for everything from yet another cup of tea ('Milk in second, never first!') to help squeezing out her toothpaste. She had a wonderful appetite, unlike most of the other residents who needed to be coaxed to finish their platefuls.

Rona wheeled her into her room then emerged to find Ian Devine waiting for her.

'Okay if I use the photocopier in the office, Rona? Mr Benson wanted me to copy a picture of his grandson in the paper. There's a photo of his school football team and he wants to send it to his niece in New Zealand.'

'Of course, help yourself.'

'Oh, Rona, remember you gave me the key for the cellar yester-day to look for the spare bath hoist? Well, I thought I'd better tell you, Martha was down there.'

'Where? In the cellar? How'd she get a key?'

Ian shrugged. 'She said she was checking something for Fay but the minute she saw me, she ran back up the steps.'

'Odd. Can't think what the nurses would want from down there. Anyway, I'll leave you to it.' Rona then headed along the corridor. At the far end she noticed Craig, chatting to someone she couldn't see round the corner in the hall. Rona saw him tip his head back as if finding something hilarious, then step away out of view.

Rona strode along to the hall and found Martha and Craig hud-dled together, far too close. Martha was whispering something and Craig was shaking with laughter. What was it about the woman?

'Hi,' Rona snapped. Was something going on between the two of them?

'I'm just off to change the plug on the projector before it fuses the whole house.' Craig ruffled Rona's hair as he passed.

'Oh, hi Rona, I was just telling Craig about my morning at yoga. The class ain't as good as the one I went to back home, but pretty good. So funny, the positions you have to contort your legs into, in fact your entire body.'

So that was why she had a glow about her today, Rona thought, she'd been exerting herself and a shimmer of sweat glistened across her forehead.

'Was that in Aspen, your yoga class back home?'

'Nope, the Prairies.'

'As in, *Little House on the Prairie*?'

'That's the one.'

'Thought you lived in Aspen – or in fact, wasn't it San Francisco?'

Martha smiled. 'A wanderer, that's me.'

'Well, can you wander into the office with me? I've got something for you.'

'Sure. I promised Craig I'd help him set up for the old movies night tonight, but that can wait.'

Ian was just leaving the office, two bits of paper in his hand, as the women entered. He nodded a greeting and held the door open.

Rona went to her desk and picked up the brown envelope. She handed it to Martha. 'This came in the post. Donnie gave it to me. I presumed the name was a mistake and it must be addressed to someone who lived in the lodge house previously?'

Rona watched Martha as she studied the envelope in silence.

'Maybe, yeah.' Her drawl was slower than usual. 'I'll take it and give it back to Donnie tomorrow.' She rammed it into her coat pocket.

'Have you got a forwarding address?'

Martha took out a handkerchief from her other pocket and dabbed her brow. 'Yeah, I'll deal with it, don't worry.' Martha wiped off most of her foundation from her forehead, leaving a beige streak across her eyebrows. 'In fact, I'll just nip home with this now. Tell Craig I'll be back in ten minutes, will you?'

Rona watched as Martha padded out from the office in her plimsolls and tapped in the code on the keypad by the door. Goodness knows who gave her the new code. Martha removed the envelope from her pocket, stared at it, then walked out, slamming the door behind her.

Chapter 18

1899

'Will you look at the state of this child!'

Jessie turned from the sink where she was washing the dishes after dinner to see Matron holding Jean by her collar. The little girl was covered in scratches.

'Jean, what happened?' Jessie dried her hands on her skirt and rushed to the door.

'She has obviously used her fingernails to scratch herself in a foolish protest.' Matron's brows were furrowed in anger. 'She was down in the cellar. The place with which you too have been acquainted, Jessie Mack. Her punishment for the vile bed-wetting. After two hours in there, she looks like this.' Matron swept her hand in the air with a flourish. 'Clean her up then return her to the school room.'

Matron's footsteps faded as she stormed off along the corridor. Jessie took the girl's hand. 'What happened in there, Jean?' The little girl continued to hang her head, staring at the floor. Jessie lifted up her chin so she could see the scratches all over her face. The red grazes were also all along her bare arms and hands. 'Come on, sit down here and tell me what happened and I'll bathe them in some warm water.'

Jessie led the girl to a stool and lifted her onto it then went to fetch some water in a bowl. As she dabbed at the affected areas, the girl flinched. Jessie stopped and crouched down so she was eye-to-eye with Jean. 'Was it scary in there? Was it awful dark? Did you scratch yourself?'

Jean shook her head and swallowed. 'It wasn't all dark, there was a light down the passage.'

'What passage, Jean? Was there not a big pile of coal in there?'

'Coal?'

'Yes, coal. Sooty and black?'

'Only a bit, but behind there was a light so I went past the coal to follow it, see if I could get away from her, from Matron.'

Jean started to whimper.

'Oh, of course, I think it's tomorrow the coalman does his delivery,' said Jessie, swabbing Jean's elbows. 'So today there'd be almost none left in there. What happened then?'

'I went along the little passage. It was low but I could still stand up.' Jessie continued to clean the little girl's arms. 'Then suddenly it was steep and I fell and I slithered down the dark path and was tumbling and then I landed in some scratchy bushes.'

Jessie inspected Jean's forearm and teased out something stuck in the skin with her thumb and forefinger. It was a thorn, prickly to touch.

'That's whin. Where were those bushes, Jean?'

Jean shrugged. 'They were all prickly and I fell into them so I got myself out of the bushes and scrambled straight back up the slope, up the steep path to the coal again. And I sat and waited for Matron.'

'But I don't see how there was a path. Was it not dark at all?'

'Not really, not at the bottom, there was some light at the end and when I tumbled into the bushes, I could see sun.'

Jessie was very still. 'Did you hear anything, Jean?'

'Just some noisy birds, you know those big squawky ones we see sometimes from the window.'

'Herring gulls.' Jessie nodded and dabbed at the girl's face with the cloth. The only place she knew there were gorse bushes – called whin in her village – was along the shore. Was there a tunnel down to the sea?

X

Jessie finished scrubbing down the large table in the kitchen then peeked out from the door where she saw the lamps had just been lit. There was still a dim light coming in through the bars on the windows. She saw Matron and Effie standing close together at the foot of the stairs. Matron smoothed Effie's pigtail back over her shoulders and was smiling. Jessie had only ever seen Matron smile once and that was when the Governor had announced it was her birthday and they all had to sing a special hymn for her at morning prayers. Jessie watched as Matron then touched Effie's cheek and nodded, then continued along the corridor towards her room.

'Effie!' Jessie hissed.

Effie turned round, the pale, wrinkled face breaking into a smile on seeing Jessie. She came scuttling over.

'Matron's being really nice to you. Lucky you.'

Effie shrugged and followed Jessie into the kitchen. Then she stood, pulling at her skirt, looking around. 'How are you, Winzie?'

When anyone else said that word, Jessie flinched. But from Effie's mouth, it was somehow all right.

'I'm fine. Effie, remember when you came to see me in the cellar you had some keys with you? One of them was for the little door. Do you still have them?'

Effie shook her head and clawed at the table with her long fingernails. 'But I could acquire them.'

'Could you?'

'Yes.'

'This evening?'

'Yes. You want me to unlock the door?'

'Yes. Would you do that?'

'Yes.' Effie stopped scratching and looked into Jessie's eyes. Her dark eyes looked huge in her pale, gaunt face. Then Effie jumped at a noise behind her.

Molly bustled into the kitchen. 'What are you doing in here,

Effie? Are you after a wee piece of Matron's cake again?'

Jessie could not believe what she was hearing, Molly giving away Matron's cake. Molly picked up a knife and a small plate and went into the larder, returning with a piece of Madeira cake. Jessie knew it was called that as Molly only ever made two types of cake. One was yellow and was called Madeira cake, the other one was flecked with black bits and was called seed cake. These were only ever eaten by Matron and the Governor, dainty slices laid out on plates on their tea tray.

Effie rammed the cake into her mouth, swallowed, then cackled with laughter before running out the door and down the corridor.

'Why do you give Effie cake when no one else gets it?' Jessie looked at the open larder door. 'Can I have a bit?'

'No you cannot. It's not for the likes of you. Nor me.'

'Why does Effie get some? And also, why is she allowed those long fingernails?' The other residents had to have their nails cut once a week and Matron cut them down to the quick so they hurt.

'Get on with your work, Jessie Mack,' Molly growled, turning towards the stove.

✳

That night, Jessie lay in bed wondering when she should go and find Effie. She must have been in bed for an hour or so. Bertha was snoring, a light whistling sound that Jessie always found reassuring.

Jessie swung her legs off the mattress and pulled a shawl round her shoulders, then tiptoed, barefoot, out of the dormitory and into the darkness of the hall. She tilted her head to one side at the noise she thought she had heard before, but less distinctly. It was wheels, a slow, rhythmic creaking sound. Jessie crept downstairs, following the noise.

None of the lamps were lit but there was moonlight shining in between the bars on the high windows and enough dingy light to be able to see. The hall was empty, so Jessie continued towards the cellar door which was ajar. She listened at the door, before stepping down onto the first stair. It was dark so she stood still for a moment as her eyes adjusted. The creaking noise was louder now and she peered into the gloom to see a figure walk slowly across the cellar floor, pushing something. Jessie stepped down the steps, keeping her hand flat against the rough stone wall for support. She looked again and there was a figure, arms outstretched, shoving something large. It was Effie, pushing a big black pram, her head bobbing up and down with each bounce of the pram.

'Effie? Effie. It's me, Jessie.'

The wheels stopped. Effie looked up, fear in her eyes. Jessie crossed the cold stone floor and came towards her. A shaft of moonlight from a tiny high window shone down onto Effie who resembled a ghost, pale and wan.

'Effie, remember you were going to see if you could get the keys?'

Effie patted her hand along the base of the pram. She lifted up a narrow mattress with one hand and thrust her other hand down, into the deep, square footwell and fumbled around. She removed something rectangular, like a wooden frame, and an ornate, rectangular box. Where did she get these things, Jessie wondered. She hoped Effie wasn't stealing from Matron, or she would get into serious trouble.

Jessie watched as Effie lifted something that glinted in the dim light. It was the set of keys she had before. She must have hidden them underneath the pram mattress.

'Thanks Effie. Does Matron know you've got these?'

'It is not her concern.'

Jessie glanced up at Effie whose expression was more focused than she had ever seen.

'Can you open the coal cellar door? Please?'

Effie patted the pram handles so the pram bounced a little on its springs then she turned towards the coal cellar. She selected one of the keys on the key ring, pushed it into the lock and turned the handle.

'Thanks, Effie. Are you coming in with me?'

Effie shook her head then turned away.

Jessie bent down to go into the cellar then stopped. 'You won't lock me in, will you? You'll leave the door open, won't you, Effie?'

Effie nodded then held up her hand.

'Wait, Winzie, wait! Illumination.'

Effie sped off up the stairs and Jessie waited. What was 'illumination'? Jessie stared into the darkness, and wondered whether to return to bed. Soon, she heard footsteps on the stairs and she looked up to see Effie's face, beaming, a lit candle in her hand.

'Thanks, Effie. Hope you're not going to get into trouble for this.'

Effie shook her head and walked back towards the pram. She pushed the handle again, the large wheels creaking in a steady rhythm as they moved slowly across the cold stone floor.

Chapter 19

1982

Rona went to the window in the annexe and pulled open the curtain. She could see nothing. The fog was so dense, she couldn't even see the garden wall a few feet away. It was thick and still, silent like heavy snowfall without wind, a hushed curtain falling from the sky.

Rona felt a twinge and realised it was the baby. She had begun to feel it moving recently. She held her hand low down on her belly, feeling the rhythmic twitch. She smiled. The baby must have hiccups. Rona was looking out at the eerie fog but not really seeing it, concentrating more on the comforting movement in her belly. Then there was a sudden booming noise and she jolted. It was only the foghorn out on the Forth; the fog must be just as thick down on the water. Even though she was brought up in the country and she was never frightened of the dark nor bothered about strong winds or gales, she always felt uneasy when it was foggy. She knew it was irrational, for it was nothing but thick mist. And there had been plenty of that on Lewis, where she had grown up.

There was a light rap on the door. Rona pulled the curtains shut and went to open it. It was Ian.

'Really sorry to bother you, Rona. I know it's your night off, but Mrs Bell wants to see you. I said you weren't working but she insisted.'

Rona sighed and followed Ian out the door.

'She kept ringing her bell, then refused to stop till I got you. Sorry.'

'It's okay, Ian. I was just going to look at her husband's folders actually.'

'Her husband's folders?'

As they climbed the stairs, the foghorn boomed again.

'Yes, he wrote a history of Newhaven. Apparently he was some kind of amateur historian. I thought we might find out about the history of this house.'

'Bet that'd be worth a read.' Ian stopped outside Room 12 and knocked.

'Come in!' an imperious voice shouted.

'I'll leave you to her, then. I'll be bringing round the tea trolley soon.'

'Thanks, Ian.' Rona went in and stood beside Mrs Bell who was at the window in her pink, quilted dressing gown. She seemed to be looking for something outside.

'Rona, I know you aren't working tonight but I had to call you now. This has happened before, you see.'

'What has?'

'Do you recall, a week or so after I moved in here, there was a similarly foggy night, with the foghorn sounding too?' As if on cue, the horn sounded on the Forth. It was louder from here, as Mrs Bell's room was on the other side of the house. 'Then a couple of weeks ago, the same thing.'

It had been unusually foggy these past few weeks. 'So what happened?'

Mrs Bell put a finger up to her lips and bent her ear to the window. 'Listen.'

Rona leant into the window and listened. There was a creaking sound, slow and rhythmic. God, it was that noise she had heard weeks ago, also on a foggy night.

'You hear it? Now you see why I had to call you. I believe this noise only occurs when there is fog. I think it's a cover for someone up to no good, so they can't be seen.'

Rona grinned. Mrs Bell was always reading crime fiction; Agatha Christie was her favourite author. 'I don't think so. Look, we can't see anything out there and even if it was a clear night, it's only the garden out there and it's all enclosed.'

'Precisely. But I had a thought. I think that were you to go up to the attic and open the window, you would actually see into her garden.'

Rona frowned.

'The Yank's. During the day, I can see across your lovely garden and down to the sea. But within those high walls is her garden and no one can see a thing.' Mrs Bell pointed at Rona's belly. 'Obviously you cannot, in your state, go up that ladder, but is that husband of yours at home?'

Rona shook her head. Craig had taken to going to the pub on their nights off, to play darts, he said. But his clothes never smelt of smoke when he came home, so was he actually at the pub? And if he wasn't, where was he?

'I think that something is going on in her garden at nights but only when it's foggy. Listen!' Mrs Bell scowled and bent her head again.

It was definitely the same sound, as if wheels were being pushed, slowly, somewhere down beneath them.

Rona looked at her watch. This was her only night off this week, she had no intention of spending it up in Room 12 with Mrs Bell. 'I'll see if Craig will go up to the attic next time it's foggy. Right now, there's nothing we can do. Sorry.' Rona smiled. 'Now, the tea trolley will be coming round soon. Why don't you get back in your chair and put the television on?'

Mrs Bell tapped her stick on the carpet then walked over to the armchair to sit down. 'She's up to something, I'm sure of it.'

✻

Half an hour later, Rona slumped onto the sofa and took a sip
from her mug of tea. She swivelled round. Was that a noise at the
annexe door? She peered over to check she had locked it then
turned back, shivering. Rona wrapped her hands round her mug.
Why did she have this feeling of uneasiness? Malaise, her mum
used to call it. Everything was going well. She was going to have
a baby in a couple of months, the care home was up and running,
the residents and relatives seemed happy and they had done well
in their first inspection. But she was exhausted. Was it because
she worried about Craig? Rona had no idea if he was getting as
much satisfaction as she was from running the home. He'd been a
little strange lately. Actually, he had been a bit odd since she found
out she was pregnant. Not distant, but just a little distracted and
instead of enjoying their nights off together, Craig used them as an
opportunity to go to the pub. Or so he said. When she'd asked him
why he didn't stink of smoke from the pub, he muttered something about the sea breeze blowing it off him on the walk home.

Craig did put in the hours during the day helping the nursing
staff when needed and organising all the work around the home.
And thankfully she had excellent staff who worked well in a team.
She'd only had a couple of problems, including young Charlotte
who kept forgetting to address Mrs Bell by her surname and had
the audacity to called her Jane. Rona chuckled when Ian told her
about that. Ian was a good worker, reliable and always on time, so
good with the residents, patient and kind. He had offered yesterday to help her with the admin in his lunch hour. Craig had sat
reading the paper in his break, even though he had a long list of
things to do around the care home.

After checking again that the annexe door was locked, Rona
put her mug down and picked up the heavy folder from Mrs Bell.
Her husband's history of Newhaven was, according to Mrs Bell,
his life's great opus and was certainly a hefty volume. Rona had
been told that he was a lawyer but spent all his free time research-
ing local history. Rona had been instructed to be careful with it.

Now he was gone, it was Mrs Bell's prized possession. She flicked through the pages and noticed that, though mostly typewritten, there were many pencilled notes written in the margins in spidery hand.

Rona started reading about Newhaven being renowned as a fishing port. The local fisherlassies travelled far and wide selling their fish, wearing the traditional outfits of striped petticoats and aprons. They also wore patterned paisley shawls on their heads and a thick band over their foreheads to carry the sturdy baskets on their back as they trudged round the city of Edinburgh and even as far west as Cramond. The fishing community was very tight, with marriage outside the village frowned upon. Even a girl marrying someone from Leith, just along the coast, was discouraged.

This was all fascinating, but she'd be here all night if she read every detail. Rona flicked to the back and noticed there was an index. She was scrolling down to Wardie House, so that she could read more about the people who built the house and first lived here, when she noticed an asterisk at the word 'Smugglers'. She'd always loved hearing stories about smugglers when she was growing up, so, her curiosity aroused, she turned to page 47.

Mr Bell had written that smuggling was part and parcel of many fishermen's professions during the seventeenth and eighteenth centuries. The merchants provided the cargo – tobacco, tea, brandy, wine – but it was the fisherfolk who supplied the boats and men to work as both crew and lookout. After the Union with England in 1707, when taxes increased hugely, smuggling became even more widespread. At some time during the eighteenth century, smugglers' tunnels were built from Wardie down to the sea at Newhaven. And the customs men were invariably outwitted as the entrances to the tunnels along the shore were hidden behind the cover of prickly, dense gorse bushes. How the smugglers managed to get through their thorny blockade was a mystery, but they were able to unload their cargo to waiting men who dragged it uphill to the end of the tunnels situated within the grounds of respectable houses at the top.

There was, Mr Bell said, no record of when the practice stopped, but during the early twentieth century, solid stone walls were built along the shoreline from Newhaven to Granton and the gorse bushes all removed. The smugglers' tunnels, he surmised, were still there, but no longer in use and most entrances had been bricked up. Perhaps some houses, he wrote, still had passageways out to the sea, tenuous links to times past.

Mr Bell went on to write about two particular houses having had tunnels down to the sea, though there could be more unrecorded. These two were documented because it was in these tunnels that fishermen and smugglers were caught by excisemen and punished – often by death. The houses were some of the oldest in the area and one was in Primrose Bank Road and called Inchcolm Lodge. She'd never heard of that one, but she read on. The other was in Wardie and was called Wardie Lodge House. Martha's house.

Chapter 20

1899

Jessie got down on her knees and lifted the candle level with her head. She felt upwards with the other hand and touched the low ceiling above. The stone was cold and damp. She shuffled along a short way then held out the candle in front. She was conscious of taking short rapid breaths so she didn't blow out the light. The ceiling was just above her head and she tried not to think of getting trapped inside here, crushed and squashed under the low ceiling. She looked ahead and saw something to her left. It was another passageway coming in from the side, presumably a tunnel to another place. She stretched out her hand and the candlelight shone a little way but she could see no further.

Jessie shuffled on down the main passage, feeling her knees get wetter and wetter as the ground beneath her became damp. It was pebbly earth below and cold stone all around. She continued on then stopped as she felt the ground slope down a little. That must have been where Jean tumbled towards the bushes. She could still see very little, even with the candle held out in front, so she got up off her knees onto her feet, squatting down low. She continued to drag herself along on her hunkers, stopping every few yards to try to get a grip with her toes on the cold damp earth.

Jessie turned her head and looked back towards the door which was scarcely visible now in the candlelight. She listened. What could she hear? She hoped it wasn't rats or mice. She was used to them, of course, both in her home and now in Wardie House, but she hated to feel them on her bare feet. Only last week when she was in the larder, a large rat had run across her boots while she was in there getting the oatmeal for Molly. She had screamed and run out to tell her but the cook was already beating its head with a broom. Molly might be fat and slow on her feet, but she had sharp eyes.

Jessie continued to edge down the slope, one hand gripped onto the candle, the other running along the rough stone wall. She stopped once more. There was that noise again. She held her breath and listened. It was the sound of gentle, rolling water. Jessie took a deep breath and smiled. She could hear the soft sloshing of water onto the sand, the gentle lapping of the waves. That sweet familiar music was the sound of the sea; she was nearly down at the seashore.

Jessie stretched out the candle and saw gorse bushes ahead. How on earth would she get through those? She staggered on, turning her body a little, preparing to protect her face from the thorns ahead. She felt like a crab, the ones that they used to watch scuttling across the pier at the harbour when her dad landed his catch.

The bushes were huge. Jessie remembered seeing them from the other side, tall and round with spiky branches and bright yellow flowers. The ground was level now. She just had to get through the bushes. She pulled her shawl up high round her neck and, head down, pushed through the branches with her shoulder, thrusting her body against the prickly gorse. She pressed against the thorns, protecting her head with her raised elbows, then rushed through, emerging at the other side and yanking her shawl off a branch where it had become entangled. Jessie looked out ahead at the moon shining bright over the sea and smiled. She breathed in deeply, feeling the salty tang of the air filling her lungs. She looked down at her left arm, which had some scratches, but the shawl had taken most of the thorns. She looked at her right hand. The candle was out. She would find her way back up the tunnel all right, but what should she do now?

Jessie planted the candle in the sand in front of the gorse bushes so she would recognise the tunnel entrance amidst the row of whin. She walked along the shore, revelling in the feel of cold wet sand on her bare feet. She headed for the harbour where a beam of moonlight cut through high clouds onto the fishing boats. The single-masted yawls, like her father's vessel, were all tied up to the pier and she walked alongside, letting her fingers run along the mesh of the nets drying along the harbour rail.

Jessie walked along the harbour wall. She was familiar with every stone, so hardly needed the moonlight to find her way. She gazed down at the water on the other side of the wall, remembering how she and the other girls would watch an occasional lone seal dive and roll, its glossy back emerging from the waves as it swam towards the harbour in the hope of being thrown a fish.

She came to the place where the barrels were stored against the solid stone wall. This was where the fisherlassies sat, dangling their legs down over the wall, gutting the fish while singing the songs they had learned from their mothers and grandmothers. Jessie hummed 'The Boatie Rows' as she stepped over the coiled, heavy ropes towards the lighthouse at the mouth of the harbour. She turned and looked back towards the village with its rows of tiny cottages all along the shore. The gas lamp by the Lyle family house cast an eerie shadow along the main street. Three houses further along was her own cottage. After six months away, she thought it would look different, but it looked just the same. Why should it have changed? Life here had gone on the same. Only Jessie's had altered forever.

Jessie walked back from the lighthouse, scratching at her itchy arm. When she came to the barrels she stopped and looked again at the only house she had lived in and at her granny's house beside it. Who lived in Granny B's tiny cottage now?

Jessie shifted her gaze to her own house. There was no point in her going home. Her mother would be livid and send her back to the poorhouse. And though her sister would make a fuss of her, Jessie knew she couldn't go home – she couldn't abandon Bertha. Now Jessie had found the tunnel, she had discovered a way out. She remembered now her dad speaking about smugglers' tunnels; it must be one of those.

Her decision made, she peered down between the barrels, feeling with her nimble fingers for something. Jessie patted her hand in between the wooden staves then eventually pulled out a cloth and unwrapped it. It was a gutting knife. Even though the girls were meant to take their knives home every night, some left them hidden between the barrels so that they didn't have to queue along at Old Jimmy Noble's house to have them sharpened on his sharpening stone. It meant you could get to bed earlier – and you didn't have to put up with his stories or his horrible smell.

Jessie squinted at the knife in the half light, stretching her hand towards the lighthouse to see better. She had no idea whose knife it was, but lassies had their knives taken all the time. She once lost hers when she was about ten, and her mother beat her so hard that Jessie was unable to work for two whole days, she was so sore and bruised.

Jessie walked towards the gas lamp and on to her own house. She peered over the half-curtain across the window but could see nothing inside – it was too dark. She took a deep breath and turned round. The gutting knife clutched to her chest, she headed back to the beach and the dark tunnel awaiting.

Chapter 21

1982

'Rona, is it okay if I nip out for a quick ten minutes? Just need to get some fresh air. Mr Wilson's fine now. He's watching television in the lounge.' Ian grinned. 'He and Miss Grant are holding hands watching *Dangermouse* together. Myra's getting the tea trolley ready. I'll be back to help her.'

Rona smiled. 'Of course, Ian. See you in a bit.' She picked up the post from the doormat and headed across the hall towards the office. Charlotte was in there, her arm around Mrs Craigie's shoulders.

'Everything okay?'

'Yes, Rona, thanks. I was just telling Mrs Craigie that she doesn't need to help you with the photocopying today.'

Rona smiled. This wasn't the first time the elderly lady had tiptoed into the office and started tapping the buttons on the photocopier. 'Thanks anyway, Mrs Craigie. You'd better get back in your room – the tea trolley's due.' The elderly woman nodded and allowed herself to be guided out by the gentle hand of the carer.

Rona placed the pile of letters on her desk and sat down. She lifted off the top one and was ripping it open with a paper knife when, out of the corner of her eye, she noticed something glinting, by the phone. It was an earring. She picked it up and held it up to the light. It was one of Martha's. She couldn't remember seeing anyone else wearing dangly hoops. Rona pushed the letters aside and stood up. She could do with some fresh air too; the care home felt stuffy. They needed to keep the radiators on full blast for the residents. She'd open a few windows later.

Rona went across the hall, pressed the numbers into the keypad and opened the door wide. She breathed deeply; it was so good to be out in the fresh air. She walked round the corner to the entrance to Martha's garden, remembering she'd only ever been once, that day when she'd been sick. Considering all the times Martha had been in their annexe and the care home, it was extraordinary she'd never invited them into her house.

Rona pushed open the narrow gate and began to walk along the path, when she noticed someone standing at a window at the side of the lodge house, palms flat against the panes, trying to peer in. It was Ian Devine.

Rona opened her mouth to speak, then decided against it. Instead, she headed for the front door, pretending she had not seen him.

She was about to ring the bell when Ian appeared behind her.

'Hello again!' He was flushed.

'Hi. I'm just returning Martha's earring.' Rona looked at Ian, expectant. 'You?'

'Oh, I could have brought it over. I thought I'd call and see if Martha had finished the list of stuff we need for Maisie's ninetieth birthday party.'

He was obviously lying. But why? Ian was red-faced and there were beads of sweat on his forehead. Rona rang the doorbell and they waited. The door opened a fraction and Martha's head appeared.

'Hi, Rona.' She noticed Ian and grinned. 'And Ian! Well, isn't this cosy?' Martha swept her hair back and tilted her head as if trying to find her best angle. Good God, was she flirting with Ian?

'Here's your earring. You left it by the phone.'

Martha lifted her hand to her left ear. 'Oh, thanks, I can't speak on the phone with earrings on. They clang into the receiver.' She tipped her head. 'See, I've still got the other one on.' She smiled at them both.

Rona turned to Ian. She wanted to witness him give his excuse before she left.

'Martha,' he mumbled. 'I was wondering how you're getting on with the list for Maisie's party.'

'You asked me that earlier, Ian. I said I'd go to the post office for those special balloons. I meant to go half an hour ago in fact but something came up.'

'Okay.' Ian nodded. 'Bye then. See you later, Rona.'

The two women watched Ian bolt up the garden path and out the gate.

'Nice guy, so good with the patients.'

'Residents, Martha, not patients.'

'Gee, sorry, I keep saying that.'

There was a low noise from behind Martha. It sounded like a faint voice.

'Have you got visitors?'

'What? No, it's the television. I always like to have it on when I'm home alone. It's company for me.' She looked at her watch. 'Sorry, Rona, gotta go, I need to get to the post office before it closes. Thanks again!' She slammed the door shut.

Rona walked back along the path, taking in once more the messy state of the garden, the straggly lawn and the earth dug into little mounds. There must be a problem with moles, but if so, why didn't her garden next door suffer? Rona shut the garden gate and thought about Ian looking in the window. What was that about? And the way he blushed … was there something going on between them? Surely not, she was twice his age. But at least Martha didn't seem to be flirting quite as much with Craig.

Martha was a mystery and certainly gave nothing away about her life now or in her past. Did she have a reason not to invite anyone into her house? Perhaps, like her garden, inside the house was a mess and she was ashamed. Yes, that was probably it. She was so smart and well dressed, perhaps an untidy house would be a shock. How strange some people were, as if that was important.

✕

There was a squeak of wheels as Mr Burnside passed Rona's office with the pram. She smiled and went out to see him. He had a t-shirt on today and she could see his dark tattoo prominent on his forearm. She didn't like to peer at it but one of the carers had said there was a name in small writing amidst the heart and the anchor.

'Are you having a nice walk?'

'Yes, the baby seems to be sleeping nicely. I got her off to sleep.' Mr Burnside beamed and rocked the pram handle gently. Rona peered in and saw a doll covered in a blanket. The doll had been the idea of one of the night nurses. And they had put the solid pram mattress in, to cover the deep footwell, so the blanket fitted nicely along the flat base.

'It'll be grand to take your own baby for a walk, Rona, just like Morag here.'

'I think I'll get a different pram for our baby, Mr Burnside, let you use that one.' She looked at her watch. 'You know it's only half an hour till supper. Why don't you wheel the pram along to the end of the corridor and then back into the dining room?'

Mr Burnside manoeuvred the pram around and headed back along the corridor. Rona felt the baby move and laid her hand on her belly. She hoped Mr Burnside wouldn't cause problems once the baby was born. There was no way her baby was going into that creepy old pram.

Rona was about to go back into the office when Ian emerged from the lift with the tea trolley. He saw her and came over. He parked the trolley. 'Rona, you were probably wondering why I was round at Martha's.'

Rona shrugged.

'I realised you maybe thought there was something going on and I wanted to tell you what it was about.'

'Ok. Why were you there?'

Ian sighed and looked down at the carpet. 'The thing is, Mrs Bell asked me to check out Martha's house when she was out. Well, when she was supposed to be out.'

'What d'you mean, 'check out her house'?'

'See if Martha was living by herself. Mrs Bell wouldn't take no for an answer. She is sure Martha has some fancy man – those are Mrs Bell's words – living with her. In sin, as she says.'

Rona burst out laughing. 'And did you see any evidence of some fancy man?'

Ian shook his head. 'The curtains were all drawn, which is weird since it's the middle of the afternoon. I'm really sorry I wasn't honest about it, Rona. I was embarrassed you'd found me there.'

'It's fine. At least it's not you having a fling with her!'

Ian laughed, then clicked off the trolley brake. 'Must get this back to the kitchen. It'll be suppertime soon.'

Chapter 22

1899

Jessie picked up the candle and tucked it under one arm. She hacked away at a low gorse branch with the gutting knife. She did not want to remove too much, for fear the tunnel would be discovered, but if she was going to get Bertha through here she would have to make some sort of passageway. The branch dropped onto the sand, some of its pretty yellow flowers scattering at her feet. After one final breath of sea air and a quick look up at the dark sky, Jessie bent down, slipped underneath and into the mouth of the tunnel, pulling the branch through. She propped it up against the bush so the hole was fully covered.

Jessie got down onto her hunkers and began to crawl back up the tunnel. It was more difficult scrambling up the hill since the soil underneath was damp and slippy. She tucked the knife under the same arm as the candle and used her free arm to guide her along the passage. She lifted her head high but there was no light at all: she was in pitch darkness. Suddenly she felt something sweep across her face and she shook her head and tried to brush it away. It was light and floaty – a spider's web. Unlike rats and mice, she had no fear of spiders. The fisherlassies were used to spiders becoming entangled in the nets; the spiders weaved their silky webs on the nets drying overnight.

Jessie continued on up the slope then stopped as she realised she had come to the level ground again. She looked ahead into the blackness. Not long now, surely. She was hoping to have a glimpse of the door soon. She can't have been gone too long. Hopefully Effie would still be there or at least have left the door unlocked for her. If not, she would have no choice but to go back down to the village.

Jessie continued to pat the wall as she crawled along on the earth. She was beginning to feel panicky. What if the door was locked? She couldn't see a thing, what would she do? Her hand soon touched something solid and she tapped her fingers all around, pressed her palm against it and pushed. Was it the door? It felt like wood, but why was it not open? Surely Effie would not have shut it? She lifted her hand to her nose and sniffed. It smelt like soot, but she didn't remember any coal here earlier. She sat down and felt around her with her fingers. High up, there seemed to be a sort of ledge and she patted her fingers all along, hoping perhaps to find a key.

Her fingers alighted on something soft. Jessie withdrew her hand at once. Was it a baby rat? No, it was too high, impossible for a rat to get up here. She lifted it down. It was made of wool. As she stroked it against her cheek, Jessie remembered that not far from the entrance where Effie had let her in, just beyond where the coal usually piled up, she had seen another passageway, linking to the main tunnel. She had perhaps taken that one instead of the correct one in the dark.

Jessie shuffled backwards along the passageway, clutching the woollen bundle, trying to feel her way back. She came to a section of wall which seemed to turn right instead of going straight down towards the slope. She continued along this and, at last, there was a sliver of light. Jessie stretched forward and tapped what she hoped was the door. She let out a sigh of relief as it creaked open a fraction. She could just make out the word 'Winzie' carved on the wooden panels. Thank goodness, she was back in the cellar. That link in the tunnel was a way to somewhere else, another house. Of course, she thought, it must be the coal cellar for the lodge house where Matron and the Governor lived. The two cellars were obviously joined. She pushed the wooden door fully open and listened. There was no sound. Effie must have moved on, but thankfully she'd not locked the door.

Jessie stepped out into the main cellar, stood up tall and stretched her back. She pulled the little door fully shut. She hoped no one would notice that it was shut, not locked. She climbed the cold stone steps up to the cellar door and opened it. There was a little light from one of the high windows, moonlight piercing through the solid bars. She looked down at herself; she was covered in soot and earth. She'd have to get out of these filthy clothes and put on clean ones before anyone noticed. She would run along to the laundry room before heading back upstairs to bed.

But first, Jessie laid the knife and candle on the ground and examined the little woollen thing. She saw it was a tiny little sock, a knitted baby's bootee, made from soft white wool. It had flecks of black on it, probably from the sooty coal below. She blew these away. The bootee had a little drawstring, a narrow ribbon, for tightening around a tiny ankle. Jessie pulled this open and poked her fingers around. She felt something inside. She pulled it out. Jessie's eyes opened wide as she saw what she held in her hand.

Chapter 23

1982

Craig set down the teapot and pushed a mug of tea over to Rona.

'Rona, love, we've been fully up and running, what, three months now? Are you happy with everything? It's just, you seem a bit, kind of, stressed.'

Rona lifted her tea and sipped. 'I'm fine. It's just sometimes I wonder if we've taken on too much. Not just financially, but our workloads – I mean, it's only eight weeks till the baby's due and ...'

'I know. Great, isn't it?' He bent back down over his newspaper.

Was he actually looking forward to the baby coming along? Rona had no idea. He rarely asked her how she was feeling. She hoped he'd show her some more affection. Admittedly, she must look like one of the seven dwarves, with these ugly maternity dungarees taut over her massive tummy, but there was little choice – the flowing maternity smocks made her look like a marquee. A pregnant woman was never going to be attractive to someone who'd often stated how much he loathed the sight of a fat woman.

She sighed. 'How on earth are we going to run this place if I'm busy in here with a little one? Mum can only come down from Stornoway for a couple of weeks. She can't stay forever.'

'I thought we'd agreed Martha would help more with the admin side of things?'

Rona glanced over the top of her mug at her husband. 'I'm not sure about that now. I'm not sure about her at all, to be honest.'

'What d'you mean?'

'We know nothing about her. Not a thing. She could be a crook or, I don't know, a murderer or ...'

'What? She's really efficient and gets stuff done and I think she's probably lonely, living in that house all by herself.'

'Mrs Bell reckons she's hiding a big secret. Has a fancy man living with her.'

Craig laughed. 'Ha, I don't think so. Why on earth would Mrs Bell think that?'

'She told Ian that Martha is flirty with every man she meets and she's convinced there's someone living there.'

'God, Rona, how'd that be possible?'

'Sometimes it looks like she's flirting with you.'

Craig burst out laughing. 'Don't be bloody ridiculous. She must be twice my age!'

'Hardly.'

Rona downed her tea and held out her mug for a refill.

Rona watched Craig head to the fridge for milk; she noticed two wine bottles in the fridge door. 'Where did that wine come from?'

'Oh, must've been Martha. She obviously doesn't approve of our choice of wine.'

As Craig topped up her tea Rona said, 'Why are there so many empty bottles out the back, by the way? The residents aren't drinking in their rooms, are they?'

'No idea. Ask the carers.' Craig pulled back his sleeve to look at his watch. 'God, look at the time, I said I'd help Mr Donaldson get dressed this morning. He doesn't like the female carers doing it. Ian's the only man on and Mrs Bell won't let him out of her sight!'

'Mrs Bell's becoming a bit of a busybody. She told Ian we got the house cheaply as there were some dodgy goings-on last century.'

Craig chuckled. 'Dodgy goings-on ... the woman's going a bit crazy, if you ask me.'

Rona wrapped her hands round the mug. 'True.' She glanced up at her husband. 'Craig, what d'you do in here when I go to bed at nine o'clock every night? I have no idea even what time you come to bed.'

He shrugged. 'Watch telly, read a book.'

Rona steeled herself. 'You're not drinking again, darling, are you?'

'Don't be daft.' He bent over to kiss the top of Rona's head then headed out of the room.

Rona gazed at the door Craig had just closed behind him. In the few years she had known Craig, she had never seen him read a book. Ever.

⋊

Rona emerged from the annexe to find Mrs Bell, leaning both hands on her stick, standing by the cellar door.

'Ah, Rona, just the person I'd hoped to find.' She pointed to the painting. 'I've just worked out who this portrait is of. Have you read the chapters on the original owners of the house yet?'

'Sorry, Mrs Bell, I meant to read it all last night but I had to go to bed early – I couldn't keep my eyes open. I plan to have a good look tonight.'

'Well, when you come to the part about the family, see if you agree: I think this is one of the daughters. I seem to recall they both liked to paint. Perhaps one of them painted this portrait. I've forgotten their names. Was one a Eugenie or something noble like that? Quite a grand family, well respected. Until the scandal, of course, then everything changed.'

Still unsettled by her conversation with Craig, Rona wasn't in the mood for one of Mrs Bell's stories. She heard the coffee trolley. 'Can I take you to the lounge? Would you like to sit there for your morning coffee?'

'Yes, that would be fine, thank you.'

Rona walked her to the lounge door and ushered her in. Betty Chalmers was already in the chair Mrs Bell liked to sit in, by the window.

'Ah, Mrs Bell, will you join me for morning coffee?'

Mrs Bell bristled. That woman with her airs and graces was sitting in her seat. She tapped her stick over towards the window. 'Thank you, Mrs Chalmers, I can allow myself a quick cup and a biscuit then must return to my knitting.'

'What are you knitting?'

'Baby bootees. I just started last night and they are coming along.'

'Bootees?' Rona asked.

'Yes, Rona. Someone must knit things for your baby's arrival, surely?'

Rona smiled then headed for the trolley. Ian was lifting up a piece of home-made shortbread with tongs outside Mr Burnside's room.

'Ian, you've still not given me that reference from your last job. We're really pleased with your work obviously, but I still need it for the admin file.'

'No problem, Rona, I'll get onto them again. I wonder if they've changed address, though. Maybe they're not getting my letters.'

'I see. Ian, I wanted to ask you something else.' She leant towards him and whispered, 'Have you noticed any of the residents drinking in their rooms? I mean, alcohol. There's an awful lot of empties round the back.'

Ian concentrated on pouring coffee. 'No, I don't think so. I thought it wasn't allowed?'

'It's not, really, which is why I was asking.'

'Apart from the sherry most of them have at supper, I haven't noticed any of them drinking.'

He stirred a teaspoon of sugar into the coffee and lifted the cup and saucer with the plate of shortbread. 'Mustn't let Mr Burnside's coffee get cold.'

Rona walked back along the corridor to the office, frowning. What on earth was niggling her? Craig was right, she was stressed about something but could not pin down what it was.

Chapter 24

1899

'Bertha, what were you speaking to Annie Rae about?'

'Nothing, Jessie.' Bertha looked away.

'Why did she have a pile of rags in her hand?'

'She was asking me why I don't need them any more.'

'And what did you say?'

Bertha hung her head low and mumbled something.

'Don't say anything to her, ever. She's trouble, Bertha.' Jessie patted her friend's chubby arm and handed her the soap. They were washing their faces at the basin of cold water. 'You didn't tell her why I told you that you don't need the rags any more, did you? You never mentioned a baby, did you?'

Bertha shook her head then splashed her face over and over with the water.

Jessie leant in towards her. 'I've got a plan, Bertha. I'll tell you about it once we're in bed.' She handed her the towel and turned round to find Annie Rae right behind her. She must have crept up when Bertha was splashing noisily in the water.

'What plan have you got, Winzie?' Annie Rae smirked.

'None of your business, Annie,' she said, trying to get past.

Annie Rae grabbed Jessie's wrist and leant in towards her. Her rotting breath made Jessie want to gag. Annie Rae sneered and tightened her grip. 'I don't think Matron would want to hear about your plan, would she?'

Jessie yanked her arm away and stomped off towards the mattress, turning to mutter to Bertha, 'Hurry up.'

Later, when the candle had been blown out and Jessie was sure Annie Rae was on her mattress at the other end of the dormitory and couldn't hear, she nudged Bertha. 'Right, are you listening?'

'Yes, Jessie.'

'I explained about how the baby is growing inside you and how Matron will send you to Leith to work down at the docks which would be the most horrible thing in the world. I've told you what happens to girls who end up there.'

Bertha started to snivel.

'So we've got to get you out of here.'

'But how can we? The gates are all locked, the wall's too high and … Anyway, where would I go?'

'Just listen. There's a tunnel from the coal cellar; it goes all the way down to the beach. I'll tell you where to go to get to my house. I'll give you a note for my sister Dorrie and …'

'No, Jessie, you have to come. I can't go all that way on my own.'

'But I'll give you something, something to tell Dorrie all about you. She'll see you all right and—'

'I can't go on my own,' Bertha hissed.

'Quiet.' Jessie put a hand over Bertha's mouth. 'This is what's going to happen. You'll go down the tunnel. I'll tell you exactly where to go once you're through the end.'

Bertha's hot breath puffed against Jessie's palm. She was panting fast. Jessie released her hand.

'Can't do it alone, Jessie, I can't.'

Jessie sighed. Bertha's narrow grey eyes were filled with tears. Bertha was right, she could not do this herself. Jessie would have to go with her. 'All right, Bertha, it's all right, we'll go together, but you know you have to leave, don't you? Otherwise you know what Matron will do to you?'

Bertha nodded.

'It's got to be soon. In the next couple of days. The coalman doesn't come till Friday so we'll get down the tunnel all right. I'll take you to Dorrie then I'll have to get back here.' She patted her friend's hair. 'It's going to be fine. Just don't say a thing at work tomorrow and if Annie Rae speaks to you, ignore her. D'you understand?'

'Yes, Jessie. I won't say a thing.' She yawned. 'I'm awful tired, Jessie. Can we go to sleep now?'

⋊

Jessie was at the kitchen sink, her back to the door, when she heard a noise. She turned round to see Matron standing there, a stern look on her face.

Jessie continued washing up while Molly put down the onion she was peeling. She and Jessie had just been joking about how onions always make you cry.

'Is there anything I can get you, Matron?' Molly wiped her hands on her apron.

'No, thank you, Molly.' She coughed. 'It is Jessie Mack I wish to speak to. Send her along to me, please.'

Jessie swallowed and lifted her wet hands from the washing-up water. She had just finished the last plate and still had to dry them all.

'You've not done anything wrong, Jessie?' Molly frowned.

Jessie shook her head. 'No. I've done everything properly since that last time. It's maybe news from home.'

'I hope it's not bad news again, Jessie. Off you go.'

Jessie walked along the corridor, gazing up through the bars in the high windows. She saw a cloud gust past in the fading early evening light. It didn't look like rain, but she could hear the wind getting up outside. As usual, inside was dingy and dim.

She knocked on Matron's door and waited.

'Enter.'

Jessie walked towards Matron who, unusually, was not at her desk but stood by the fire which was blazing in the grate. Apart from the Governor's room, this was the only room that had a fire in its grate. The kitchen was usually warm because of the stove, but everywhere else was frigid.

Matron examined Jessie who, even though only fourteen, was as tall as her. Despite the meagre food, she had grown much bigger since she had been here.

'Jessie Mack, I have heard some rumours about Bertha which have not pleased me. Before I speak to her, I need to know if there is any truth in the matter, which seems so improbable. For such a simple thing.'

Jessie gulped and fixed her gaze on the flickering flames by Matron's side.

'Do you know if Bertha continues to use rags every month?'

'No, I don't know. Sorry.'

'Is this not the kind of information you share, as bed-mates?'

Jessie shook her head. Matron's expression was still stern.

'So you have never discussed this matter with her?'

'No, Matron.' Jessie clasped her hands together tightly round her back.

'I see. Annie Rae believes you have some information on this subject and also have formulated some, as she calls it, "plan", to help Bertha.'

'I don't know anything about that.' Jessie's fingernails dug into the palms of her hands. 'Sorry, Matron.'

'I see. Well, since Annie Rae is not the most reliable of inform- ants, I shall interview Bertha myself as soon as possible.'

There was a knock at the door.

'Wait!' she bellowed, before drawing closer to Jessie. 'If, how- ever, I find out that either you or Bertha have been lying or cov- ering something up, then I do not need to spell out the conse- quences, do I?'

There was another knock.

'Come in,' Matron shouted crossly.

Molly stood there, a tray in her hands. 'Sorry to bother you,

Matron, but it's liver and onions tonight and I don't want it to get cold. Doesn't taste nice cold. I'll set it up in the Governor's room as usual, shall I?'

'Thank you, Molly.' Matron turned to Jessie. 'One more misdemeanour, Jessie Mack, and you know what will happen.' She stood up and swept off along the corridor, leaving Jessie standing all alone.

)(

Jessie wiped down the table at the end of her long day and ran her forearm over her brow. She kept thinking of Matron's talk with her and was mulling over whether she should risk everything by trying to get Bertha out. If she did manage to get Bertha down the tunnel to Dorrie for help, that would be the best solution for Bertha. Her belly was beginning to bulge so Matron would soon notice, even if Bertha managed to lie about the rags. But what would happen the following day when Matron realised she was missing? She would surely blame Bertha's only friend, Jessie. And how could Dorrie help Bertha? Perhaps Bertha could stay down in Newhaven and see if Dorrie could find her somewhere to live. Dorrie had that friend along in Granton. Maybe Bertha could go there, find a job. She could learn to gut fish, though she probably wouldn't be as fast as the other girls. Or Dorrie might come up with another plan, to send her somewhere far away.

A sound outside the door broke Jessie's train of thought. There was no one else around. Everyone was finishing their evening work in the workrooms and Molly had two hours off, having been allowed out to visit her sister who was ill. Jessie tiptoed towards the door and peeked out. In the dim light she could see two figures whispering. As her eyes adjusted to the light she saw that the one with her back to her had a long pigtail. Effie stood by the wall, scratching at it with her long fingernails, and Matron stood opposite her, one hand at the pearl choker at her neck and the other removing Effie's hand from the wall and placing it by her side each time she scratched.

'I'm not going to ask you again. Where is it? Tell me, where did you hide it? Surely you must remember.'

Effie said nothing, just shook her head, her plait quivering down her back.

Matron grasped Effie's hand as she tried to claw at the wall and leant in towards her. 'He is not going to hurt you. All we need is for you to tell me where you have hidden it.'

There was another noise at the far end of the corridor and Jessie peeked out to see the Governor storming towards them. His footsteps resounded loudly as he strode along. He stopped abruptly when he saw Effie standing behind Matron. The Governor stroked his pointed grey beard and Jessie noticed, not for the first time, how red and bulbous his nose was. Effie began to shake. Her entire body trembled.

'Euphemia, my dear, how are you tonight?'

Jessie's eyes widened. She had never heard the Governor speak in such a gentle manner, nor had she ever seen him smile. And why did he call her that name and not Effie? He stretched out his hand to her but Effie shook her head again, her pigtail swinging as she continued to stare at the floor.

Matron turned to him. 'She will not say. Perhaps you have forgotten where you hid it, Euphemia? Shall I fetch you some of Cook's tasty cake? Would that help your memory?'

There was a loud thud as Molly came crashing through the front door, locked it and placed the huge key in her apron pocket. She looked round. 'Oh, excuse me for interrupting.'

Molly was about to head for the kitchen when Matron held out her hand.

'The key, Molly.'

'Oh, yes, here it is,' she said, delving into her pocket.

Effie had slunk off along the corridor during the interruption. She made for the cellar door where she paused and looked back at them, eyes narrowing as if deep in thought.

Chapter 25

1982

'Come in, Doctor Bruce. I'm sure it's nothing to worry about, but I was just keen to have a second opinion on Mrs Bell. Her cough's been getting worse.'

Rona closed the door behind the doctor and guided him along the corridor. 'I'm sure it'll be fine but both the nurse and my husband think she might have a chest infection.'

'Your husband?'

'He was a medical student, but of course the nurse knows best.'

'Where does he practise now?'

'He doesn't, he went down another career route.' Rona ushered him up the stairs. As usual, when anyone asked about Craig's past, Rona became embarrassed. How could she explain that Craig had drunk so much in his final year that he hadn't attended ward clinics nor completed the coursework? He'd turned up on one ward clinic so drunk, he had almost dropped a baby in Maternity. The faculty refused to let him sit the exams and he left university without any degree at all. Craig said he wasn't drinking like he used to, but she was sure he was lying. That was what was niggling her. How could he possibly be a responsible father if he had a drink problem?

'Here we are, Doctor Bruce,' she said, opening the door. 'Oh, hello Ian.' She nodded at Ian who was reading to Mrs Bell, who was sitting in the chair by the window in her dressing gown. 'This is Doctor Bruce. I'll leave you to it. I'll be downstairs in the office.

Let me know if there's a prescription that needs collecting.'

Rona wandered back down the stairs, still thinking of her husband's past – the past she had thought was behind him for good. Her mum had never been keen on her marrying Craig, but then Granddad's illness worsened and she became embroiled in that. Her mum's father had been an alcoholic and she recognised the signs. She'd told Rona during a visit to their flat in Dundee how worried she was about their future if Craig refused to get help.

Rona headed for the office, passing Betty Chalmers being wheeled out of her room by one of the agency carers.

'How are you, Mrs Chalmers?'

'I am rather well, thank you. This pleasant young lady is dealing with all my needs. She is taking me along to the lounge so I can enjoy the view. What a beautiful day. I shall use those binoculars to look at the birds. I saw a chaffinch yesterday.'

'It is a lovely day, isn't it?'

'Oh, I meant to ask you, is that Canadian woman in here today? I had asked her about the place she used to live in Saskatoon and she was going to look in her old address book as my niece moved to Canada. It wasn't a large town, so perhaps they lived nearby.'

'Sorry, who's that?'

'Now, what's her name again? Margaret? Marian? Dark hair, smartly dressed.'

'You mean Martha? She's American. She said she lived somewhere in California. She never mentioned Canada.'

'No, she has a Canadian accent. It sounds less of a drawl than the American one.'

She turned round to the carer who had been waiting patiently. 'You may continue now, young lady. Goodbye, Rona.'

⚹

There was a knock on the door. Rona looked up from the pile of documents on her desk.

'Hello, doctor, come in.' She gestured for him to enter.

Doctor Bruce sat down and delved into his doctor's bag. 'I did find signs of a chest infection so have prescribed some antibiotics.' He handed over the prescription.

'Thanks, I'll nip out to the chemist for that myself. I could use some fresh air, in fact.' Rona lifted her hand to her mouth to cover a wide yawn.

'How are you keeping, Rona? Are you due for a visit to the midwife soon?'

'Not for a couple of weeks, but everything seems okay.' The doctor was looking closely at her. 'I'm fine.'

'Can I just check something? You look rather pale.' The doctor moved closer and pulled Rona's lower eyelid down with his finger. 'Yes, I think you might be a little anaemic. Are you sure you're not overdoing it?'

'No. I mean it's hard work, but I always get to bed early. I get plenty of sleep.'

'Okay. But I'd like you to make an appointment with the nurse. Come in for a blood test. Let's check your iron levels.'

'I'll pop in to the reception once I've done the chemist.'

'Right. And there's nothing else you're worrying about, is there?'

Rona shook her head and noticed the doctor's concerned frown. Mrs Bell probably told him about how Rona worked non-stop all day, including feeding some residents who needed help at mealtimes. 'I'm fine,' Rona replied, smiling. She hoped Mrs Bell hadn't mentioned to him that in comparison Craig did far less, refusing to start work till after nine some mornings and even then he didn't exactly push himself. At lunch, he always insisted on taking a full hour off. He kept trying to get Rona to join him in the annexe for lunch, but she invariably ended up having a rushed bowl of soup once she'd finished in the dining room. Why didn't she try to make him do more? It was better to keep the peace; she didn't want to push him. That monumental row they'd once had ended so badly.

'Sure?'

Rona nodded. How could she tell the doctor she lay awake at nights worrying about money? Their last bank statement wasn't good. Because of the extra work needed on the house after the pipes had burst at Christmas, they'd had to take out a loan, something that would have horrified her financially savvy dad. Nothing the doctor could prescribe would help with that.

The doctor snapped his bag shut and stood up.

'Is that you finished your lunchtime house calls then, Doctor Bruce?'

'One more to do, but it's right next door so I can just walk round.'

'Oh, who's that, then?'

'Miss McCallister. Lives at the lodge house.'

Rona chuckled. 'Oh, isn't that funny, all these months we've known Martha, I've never known her surname.'

The doctor took out a sheet of paper from his pocket. 'No, it's not Martha, it's Miss Janet McCallister.'

Chapter 26

1899

'Effie, it's me.' Jessie tiptoed down the steps into the cellar where she could just make out a figure walking to and fro, head bent low over the pram handles as she walked over the stone slabs. 'Effie,' she called again, her voice echoing around the cold stone walls.

Effie peered through the gloom and walked the pram towards her. 'Hello, Winzie.' She bent over the pram and smoothed down the blanket that covered the mattress. She bounced the handles up and down.

'Effie, are you all right? I saw you talking to Matron tonight. And the Governor.'

At the mention of his name, Effie shivered. 'All is well. Thank you kindly for your concern.'

'You know if you need any help, I'm here. I'm not sure I could do much but I could try.' Jessie slipped her hand into her pocket and was reassured to feel the cloth wrapped round the gutting knife.

'Thank you. You are too kind.'

Jessie smiled. Sometimes Effie's expressions were so proper. She often spoke like she was a lady, not just some mad old woman in a poorhouse.

'The door to the coal cellar's still unlocked, isn't it?'

'I do believe it is.'

'Thanks, Effie. I'll let you get on then.'

She watched as Effie wheeled the pram towards the other side of the cavernous room and strolled up and down, peeking into the pram as she walked. Jessie pushed the door of the coal cellar open a little to check it was unlocked then ran up the stairs.

Bertha stood at the top, clutching a knotted cloth holding her few belongings.

'Right, come down now, Bertha. It's safe. Be quiet though, so Effie doesn't hear you.'

Jessie stretched out her hand for Bertha who followed her down to the cellar floor.

'Can't she see us, Jessie?'

'She's lost in thought. Just be quiet. Get in here,' Jessie pushed the little red door open into the coal cellar.

Bertha had done all her crying as they crept down the stairs into the hall, with Jessie telling her once more she had no choice and trying to keep her quiet as she snuffled and snivelled. Bertha stepped in and banged her head.

'Ow.'

'You have to bend down. Get onto your knees.' She pulled Bertha in and shut the door behind them.

'I can't see, Jessie.' There was panic in Bertha's voice.

'I told you it'd be dark. Here, take my hand.'

'I don't like it.'

'Look, this is the only thing we can do. Keep holding my hand and we'll be out at the beach soon. Shall I sing to you?'

'Yes,' Bertha muttered as her grip tightened.

Jessie began to sing one of the fisherlassies' songs, soft and melodic. It was pitch dark, but she didn't want to ask Effie for another candle in case she got into trouble. Jessie just needed to remember where the start of the slope might be.

She pulled her hand away from Bertha's grip. 'Stop now, Bertha. This is where it goes downhill.' Jessie got down onto her hunkers. 'Get onto your feet, like this. Crouch as low as you can and just go slowly, behind me. I can't take your hand now.'

Bertha did what she was told. Jessie could hear Bertha's

breathing becoming short; she was panting.

'Now we need to take our time, so you don't slip.' Jessie continued to sing.

> *Wha'll buy my caller herrin'*
> *They're bonny fish and halesome fairin'*
> *Buy my caller herrin'*
> *New drawn frae the Forth*

'Jessie, how much longer?' Bertha sounded terrified. She had been in the poorhouse since she was about five years old so knew little of the outside world. Her mother had brought her into Wardie House then died within a few weeks. Jessie hoped she would be all right outside. She was so naïve; that was obviously how she became pregnant with Billy Muir's child.

'Jessie, I just felt something,' Bertha screeched. 'Something brushed across my face.'

'It'll just be a cobweb, it's nothing. Come on, we're nearly there.' Jessie could see a patch of dim light ahead.

They arrived at the gorse bushes. Jessie felt to her left, removing the large branch she had cut away. 'Bend your head down and follow me, Bertha.'

Jessie burrowed under the bush and pulled Bertha's larger body through. They both fell onto the damp sand with a thump then sat up on the beach and looked ahead.

'Here we are! We did it! Look at the sea, Bertha. Isn't it grand?'

They looked out at the grey water and the dark clouds rolling out east towards the North Sea. 'Listen to that sound, Bertha.' The waves sloshed onto the shore ahead of them and still Bertha said nothing.

Jessie leant towards her friend whose eyes were wide. 'It's all right, we're out now. You'll never have to go back to that horrible place. Unlike me.' Jessie sighed. 'Stand up, we've got to go and wake Dorrie.'

※

Jessie placed the knife back into the nook amongst the barrels and started along the harbour wall. She wouldn't need it any more and she didn't like to steal; the owner must've got into terrible trouble from her mother for losing it. The knife had served its purpose, helping cut down the gorse.

Jessie was mid stride when she stopped and looked down at her feeble body. Without the knife, she felt vulnerable, less strong. Perhaps, after all, she might need it. She had no idea what lay ahead. She felt bad for the lassie whose knife it was but she felt safer with it. Though she wouldn't kill for Bertha and her baby, she might need a knife as a threat. She returned to the barrels, slipped it out again, rewrapped it and tucked it back in her pocket. Once Bertha was safely away, she'd come down and return the knife when she'd no need of protection.

Jessie looked ahead and saw Bertha standing under the gas lamp, in exactly the same spot she had left her, her hands clasped tight together. The tension in her face eased a little when she saw Jessie approach and together they walked, hand in hand, along Main Street.

'Right, Bertha. Remember what I said. When we get to my house, you'll have to wait outside. I don't want Ma waking up and finding us. I'm just going to wake Dorrie.'

Bertha nodded. Jessie clasped her friend's hand tight.

They stepped over the cobbles until they came to the tiny cottage with its low narrow windows and whitewashed wall, and the outside stairs by the door that led up to the Carnies' house above. Jessie listened, checking if anyone was around. No one. She had seen there were very few boats in the harbour, but that was normal in the middle of the herring season, which meant that the men would be away every night. It was only the women who'd be at home with the children.

Jessie pulled Bertha round to the Carnies' wooden stairs and sat her down on the bottom step. 'Sit here and wait,' she whispered. 'Don't move or say a thing.'

Bertha nodded and in the dim light Jessie could see her face screw up, as if she was going to cry. 'I'll be as quick as I can.'

Jessie pushed open the wooden door under the stairs, hoping that the annoying old creak hadn't returned. Her father used to oil it and she presumed her Ma did things like that herself now. It was a good thing none of the villagers ever locked their doors. No one even had keys to the locks; everyone was so trusting. She entered the low-ceilinged room and looked around as if seeing it for the first time. Faint evening light came through the tiny, deep-set window and as her eyes adjusted she noticed the heap of tangled nets in the corner. There weren't many, so presumably the rest were out in someone's boat tonight. Perhaps Uncle Johnnie had stepped in to help her mother after her dad had died. There was the fireplace and the empty grate and a large blackened pan hung from the swee. Two pairs of thick woollen socks hung above the fire on the rail.

Jessie took a deep breath. The smell of fish, having eluded her for so long, was strangely welcoming. She turned to look at the bed set in the alcove where the gentle snoring was coming from. But before waking her sister, she tiptoed to the back room, a tiny airless recess with nothing but a bed in it. This was where her father and mother used to sleep. She and Dorrie slept together in the bed beside the fireplace and her brother had slept on the floor beside them. Jessie peeked round the door and at once recognised her mother's frizzy grey hair sticking out the top of the coarse brown blanket. It was strange to see her alone in this bed, without her father.

Jessie returned to the bed near the fireplace and peered in close. She saw the locks of thick dark hair lying over the blanket. There was Dorrie, sleeping as she always did, facing the wall, her body wedged close, as if still leaving plenty of space for the sister who used to sleep alongside. She crept towards the bed and sat down on the edge, watching her sister's body heave up and down. She smiled then stretched out her hand to her sister's shoulder.

Chapter 27

1982

'Martha, do you have a minute?'

Rona had watched her walk in the front door and cross the hall, heading for the cellar door. Rona looked enviously at Martha's hair, which as usual was shaped in its perfect bob and was silky and glossy. Rona twirled a curl round her finger and felt only its dry, brittle texture; pregnancy had not been kind to her hair.

'Sure,' she said, swivelling around. 'I said to Myra I'd help arrange those beautiful flowers she just brought in.'

'So why were you going to the cellar?'

'The cellar?' Martha scratched her head. 'Vases. Myra thought there was a big one down there.' She smiled. 'How are you feeling, Rona?'

'I'm fine.'

'You look pale,' Martha said, ambling into the office.

'The doctor thinks I might be anaemic. I've to go and see him in a day or two once the blood test comes back.'

'I keep telling Craig he should be helping you more, but he seems to like doing his own thing, doesn't he?'

Rona bristled. It was one thing for Rona to notice her husband's lack of motivation, it was not all right for Martha to mention it.

'He's fine. He does things in his own way.'

'He'll have to step up to the plate once the baby comes. How long now?'

'I'm thirty-six weeks, so another four weeks.' Rona rubbed her belly and felt a gentle kick.

'Anyway. I've been wondering, Martha. Betty Chalmers was saying something about you being from somewhere in Canada. How come you told us you were from California?'

Martha shrugged. 'So many English people don't get the difference.'

'What, you mean like when people call us English?'

'Oh yeah, Scots don't like being called English, do they?'

Rona snorted. 'No. We don't. Because we're not.' She sat up straight. 'Anyway, are you Canadian?'

'Lived in both Canada and the States. What's the problem?'

'Nothing. Just interested.' Why had Martha lied to them about where she actually came from?

'I'd better go now. I told Myra I was just nipping out for ten minutes.'

'Someone you're checking up on?'

'No.'

'You said you lived alone, but how come Doctor Bruce told me he was visiting a Miss Janet McCallister at the lodge house?'

Martha blinked a couple of times then stood up. 'No idea. Jeez, you'd think doctors would get things like names and addresses right.' Martha headed for the door. 'Can I bring you a cup of tea, Rona? I think the cook's baked my brownies again so I could bring you one of those.'

Rona would have killed for a brownie. Martha had given their cook her own recipe from America. Or perhaps Canada. Instead she said, 'No, I'm fine,' and swivelled round in her chair towards the pile of papers on her desk.

✳

Rona slumped back on the sofa. What an exhausting few days they'd had at Wardie House. Three nights previously, Miss Grant had died. She was their first resident to die since opening and they were relieved that all the procedures in place to deal with a death had gone according to plan. The staff kept her room locked and curtains closed and they then prepared the body by washing it and putting on a clean nightgown. Fay said she was relieved Miss Grant had her own teeth as sometimes it was difficult to get them back in. She'd died during the night, so when Rona contacted William Purves the undertakers first thing in the morning, she was able to organise for them to arrive during the early afternoon when most residents were having a nap. Only Mrs Bell sat by the window in the main lounge after lunch most days, so Ian had rushed in and pulled the curtains shut when he saw the black hearse turn into the drive. When Mrs Bell remonstrated, he told her it was because it was so sunny outside and the sunlight was bad for the goldfish.

The rest of the staff teased him about that later. 'Have the goldfish got their factor 20 suncream on, Ian?'

'I couldn't think what else to say,' he muttered. 'It's not like we've got a back door to park the hearse.'

Once the body had been taken away and the room deep-cleaned, Rona and Craig decided to give the news of the death only to Mrs Bell and Betty Chalmers, since they shared a table in the dining room with Miss Grant. Also, they read *The Scotsman* every day and the first section they both turned to was 'Obituaries and Death Notices'.

Rona reached forward to the coffee table and opened the folder of Mrs Bell's husband's notes. It was already nine o'clock and she was tired, but she really wanted to find out more. Craig was at the garage filling up the car with petrol. Or so he said. Was he in fact buying alcohol? Rona tried to dismiss the thought. She'd seen no evidence of his drinking recently and he never smelled of alcohol.

Rona flicked through the pages to 'Wardie House History', propped her feet up on the coffee table and leant back against the cushions to read.

David Seaton, retired naval captain, bought the land up the hill from Newhaven, beside a small lodge house which dated from the early 1800s. He chose that location to build Wardie House because of the elevation: there would be views from the upper floor windows down to the water and over to Fife. He had been ordered by naval doctors to retire because of his weak heart and he missed the sea.

The foundations of the house were laid in 1862 and the design was for a palatial building, featuring four public rooms and numerous bedrooms, even though he had no children. The captain's weak heart was the cause of his premature death in 1863, aged only forty-eight, when the house was still unfinished.

Seaton's widow had no desire to continue with what she considered her husband's folly and sold the land and uncompleted house to Andrew Ramsay. Mr Ramsay was Mrs Seaton's jeweller and, despite an age difference (Ramsay was in his mid twenties, Mrs Seaton late thirties), there was a not-unsubstantiated rumour of a liaison between the two. He certainly bought Wardie House for a low sum of money. Andrew Ramsay was in charge of the family jewellery business from an early age; his mother died giving birth to his younger sister and their father passed away a few years later of a broken heart.

Rona shook her head. None of this was exactly uplifting. Was there anything happy about the history of the house? Is that why she sometimes felt, late at night, some sort of brooding presence in the house? And that word 'Winzie' etched into the tiny cellar door – did that mean the house was cursed?

Mrs Seaton returned to her home in London after the sale to Andrew Ramsay, who had the house completed to the captain's design. By 1866, Andrew Ramsay was living there with his two younger sisters.

At the time, Ramsays the jeweller, in George Street, was one of the most prestigious and popular shops in the city. It had a loyal clientele, who shopped at Ramsays for clocks and silverware as well as jewels. They came to specialise in precious stones, the shop's commercial contacts sailing into the port of Leith with gemstones from South Africa where diamonds had recently been discovered.

The next piece of information we have about Wardie House dates from the mid 1870s, before it was converted into a poorhouse. The elder of the Ramsay sisters, Isabella, had found out that ...

'I'm back, darling,' came a voice from the hall.

Rona laid down the folder and smiled as Craig walked in and kissed her. 'How're you doing? Cup of tea?'

'That'd be lovely, thanks. Did you get the petrol?' She looked at the clock. Surely it can't have taken half an hour to get petrol.

'Yeah, but I had to go all the way along to Leith. That petrol station at Goldenacre shuts at 6 p.m. on weekdays.'

Craig opened the fridge door for the milk and Rona looked in again. 'Craig, I see there's no wine in the fridge or in the rack. Is that deliberate?'

Keeping his back to her, he muttered, 'Kind of.' He stirred the milk into the tea and brought it to her. 'I'm trying hard, Rona. I'm determined not to be an idiot again. I've been a bit distracted lately, sorry, darling, but I'm going to make it up to you. In fact ...' He looked around. 'God, I go to all these lengths to buy your favourite chocolates from the garage and I leave them in the bloody car.' He ran to the door. 'Be right back!'

✳

Rona finished her tea and looked at her watch. What could be taking him so long?

Craig crashed through the door.

'Quick! Phone the fire brigade. There's a fire in Martha's house.'

Rona rushed out after him to the hall where he was unclipping the fire extinguisher. 'I saw smoke when I came back earlier but presumed it was a bonfire. Thank God I forgot your Milk Tray. I just went round. The smoke's getting worse. There's a fire at the back of the house.'

'I'll phone the fire brigade then get Ian to give you a hand,' Rona said, running back inside towards the phone. 'Be careful!' she bellowed after him.

Rona dialled 999, gave the details, then dashed back into the hall and along the corridor, looking right and left, in case Ian was in one of the bedrooms. She saw him at the top of the stairs, chatting to the night nurse.

Rona stopped to catch her breath. 'Ian, can you come down quickly? There's a fire next door.'

'What?' Ian ripped off his plastic apron and ran down the stairs.

'Craig's there. I've phoned the fire brigade,' Rona shouted after him. 'Fay, ensure everyone here's kept calm. Don't mention a thing, please. I'll be back as soon as possible.'

'No worries, boss.'

Rona crossed the hall and opened the front door. Thank goodness it was unflappable Australian Fay who was in charge tonight. She would keep everything under control.

Rona slowed down as she walked round the corner, trying to keep calm herself. Any sense of panic would be bad for the baby. She opened the gate to Martha's garden and saw clouds of filthy grey smoke rising from the back of the house. At least she couldn't see any flames. Presumably that was a good sign? Rona looked all around in the fading evening light and realised there was no sign of Craig nor Ian. Oh God, they must have gone inside. This was not the time for heroics.

Rona went towards the front door. It was wide open. There was a strong smell of smoke but she couldn't see any sign of them in there. All the doors off the hall were shut. 'Craig? Ian?' She lifted her arm up to try to cover her nose with her sleeve. 'Where are you?'

Rona heard a noise from the end room: voices. They must be in there.

The door opened wide to reveal two figures and something being pushed in front of them. One of the figures pulled the door closed behind them.

'Get outside, Rona, we're okay!'

Rona rushed out the front door to the middle of the garden and waited. As she watched the figures emerge, she became aware of someone behind her in the shadows. She swivelled round.

'Martha! Are you okay? There's a fire at the back of your house. The fire brigade's on its way.'

Sirens announced the approach of a fire engine; Rona put a hand on Martha's shoulder. In the gloomy light, Rona saw her neighbour's eyes open wide as Craig and Ian – and was that some-one else with them? – emerged onto the doorstep, Craig shutting the door firmly behind him.

'You all right, Martha?'

Martha nodded but said nothing. Her stiff shoulders never moved an inch.

'Were you inside when the fire started?'

'No.' She slipped past Rona and headed for the house.

Rona watched Martha's back as she traipsed along the path. She must be in shock: she seemed devoid of any emotion. Rona turned round to see two firemen rush towards the house. She heard Craig and Ian tell them the fire was contained in the back bedroom and all doors were shut. She watched as long hoses were yanked in from the street.

'Get out into the street, please,' the fireman shouted at Rona and Martha, pointing at the gate. 'Quick as you can.'

Rona went out the gate and crossed to the other side of the road. Martha emerged from the gate then Craig came out and rushed over to Rona to give her a hug.

'You reek of smoke, are you okay?' Rona asked.

Craig nodded.

'Are Martha's things all okay?'

'No idea, but look …' Craig pointed over the road. Martha had disappeared but there was Ian, pushing a wheelchair with someone in it. He turned left towards Wardie House. The woman's head was bent low and both hands held a paisley scarf up against her face, covering it. A shock of curly white hair was visible above the scarf. Rona and Craig crossed the road and Ian crouched down beside the wheelchair.

'Don't worry, now,' Ian said in the soothing voice he used with the residents. 'You're safe – you're out in the fresh air. Everything's just fine now.'

Rona bent down and patted the old woman's bony shoulder.

'Let's take you next door and make you a nice cup of tea.' The old woman pulled the scarf down off her face, revealing watery brown eyes, wide with fear. Her face was pale and wrinkled. She nodded and looked up with a flicker of a smile. Rona smiled back and noticed that, above the old woman's lip, lined with age, was a distinctive birthmark, a large dark mole.

Part 3

Chapter 28

1899

Jessie pushed at the door and breathed a sigh of relief as it swung open. All the way through the tunnel, she'd worried Effie might have locked it again. She'd been away for much longer than anticipated, but Bertha had to be coaxed into staying with Dorrie, even after her sister's grand plan had been explained to her. When the three of them sat on the harbour wall, huddled together in the chill of the night to discuss what to do, Dorrie had told Jessie she must get back up to Wardie House before anyone suspected she was gone. They made a pact to try to meet up in a couple of weeks, just before the next coal delivery blocked the tunnel, and Dorrie would give her news of Bertha and tell her if the plan had worked.

Bertha had sobbed when Jessie hugged her goodbye, but she had eventually accepted the situation. It helped that Dorrie and Jessie looked so alike, apart from the curse evident on Jessie's face, of course.

Jessie crawled out through the door and shut it as quietly as possible. She waited until her eyes adjusted to the light, which was dim yet not as black as it had been inside the tunnel. There was no sign of Effie and she could just about make out the pram at the far end of the cellar. The silhouette was completely still and there was no creaking of the wheels.

Jessie looked down at her clothes and brushed them as best she could. She didn't want Matron to be suspicious, so she couldn't put on a clean smock from the laundry room. She rubbed at the bits of dust and dirt and then shrugged. There was nothing more to be done. She climbed the stairs, padding up each step barefoot, then continued along the corridor to the girls' dormitory. She stopped outside the door. Had she heard a noise? It was perhaps the sound of something outside, an owl maybe. Molly said she sometimes heard them outside in the big tree if she left late at night. There was no sign of anyone there, so Jessie crept into the room and stole over towards her mattress. She lifted the cold, rough blanket and lay down, shivering. She missed Bertha's warm body beside her. At least her friend was in a safe place now. Jessie knew Matron would blame her; thankfully, she had an alibi set up.

✳

'I repeat. Where is Bertha, Jessie Mack?' Matron's voice boomed the length of the dormitory as she glared at Jessie, her eyes blazing.

All the girls turned to look at Jessie who stood by her mattress, hair neatly tied up under her cap and arms straight by her side. Her back was stiff and she stared back at Matron, unblinking.

'I don't know, sorry,' she mumbled. 'All I know is that when I got up the second time to get Jean to use her pot, she wasn't there.'

'And when was this?'

'I don't know. I've been waking Jean twice in the night, like you told me to. The first time it was really dark and the next time there was just a bit of morning light I could see.'

'Jean, come here.'

The skinny girl in the ragged dress stepped forward, her head bent down.

'Did Jessie Mack take you two times – I repeat, two times – to use the pot last night?'

Jean nodded.

'Speak up, child!'

'Yes, she did, Matron. Two times.'

Jessie watched as Matron glowered and looked all around. 'Did anyone else see Jessie waken Jean Smith?'

They all shook their heads. Jessie's eyes widened as she noticed Annie Rae's hand go up and a sly expression cross her long thin face.

'Yes?' Matron barked.

'I didn't hear Jean get up at all, Matron. Not even once.'

'Come here, Annie Rae!'

Matron walked over to Jean, towering over the slight girl who cowered beside the bully. Would Jean waver from what she had been told to say?

'What do you say now, Jean Smith? Did Jessie Mack waken you twice to use the pot or not?'

Jessie watched the little girl blink then swallow. She turned her head away from Annie Rae, who was standing right beside her, leaning into her.

'Yes,' she mumbled. 'She did.'

'Go and fetch the pot from beside your mattress.' She was the only girl allowed to sleep alone, because of her bed-wetting, so if her pot was filled, it was from her, not from a bed-mate.

Jean stepped away from Annie Rae. She bent down and stretched her hands to the back of the mattress to retrieve her pot. She lifted it up in two hands and carried it over for Matron to inspect. Jessie could see the yellow liquid slosh around in it. There was far too much there for anyone to believe it was filled only once in the night.

Matron peered in then said, 'Put it down on the floor.' She poked her finger into Annie Rae's scrawny chest and leant in close. 'You are trouble, girl. So now you will empty this pot and in fact all the pots in the dormitory. Then you will scour them all clean. Every single one. You will then come and see me in my study once you have scrubbed your hands so clean they are red raw.'

There was a noise at the door and everyone turned to see who it was. Effie stood there, pulling at the pigtail down her back.

'Ah, I was looking for you.' Matron strode across the dormitory and joined Effie at the door. 'Let us walk downstairs together.' She turned and bellowed, 'Every one of you miserable children may be assured, we will find Bertha very soon and when we do, there will be trouble. There is no way that simpleton could have got away by herself. Do you understand?'

'Yes, Matron,' the girls chanted and moved back to their own beds.

Jessie checked that Annie Rae was not looking, then lifted the corner of her mattress and pulled out the bundle of sooty clothes. She looked over at Jean who stood by her mattress in her grubby nightdress and mouthed, 'Thank you.'

Chapter 29

1982

Rona stirred the second spoon of sugar into the tea, grabbed a couple of biscuits from the biscuit barrel and headed for the corridor. Ian and Craig were in the lounge with the old woman who had sat in complete silence as they wheeled her into Wardie House. Who was she? The poor woman was evidently in shock, having been stuck in that wheelchair, presumably thinking she was about to burn to death.

Rona tiptoed in to join them and sat down beside Ian. She handed the cup to the lady.

'I'll just go and speak to Fay, check everyone's all right upstairs.'

'Okay, Ian, but I don't think anyone would've been aware anything was going on. Only the rooms on this side would hear the sirens and they all have their hearing aids out after dinner. Unless Mrs Bell looked out of her window, no one else would have seen the fire.'

Ian shook his head. 'She was sound asleep when I looked earlier.' He headed for the door.

The old woman took a sip of the tea, then put the cup back down. She looked all around as if searching for someone or something. Her expression was inscrutable.

'Can you manage a biscuit? Or can I get you a sandwich or something else?' Rona took her bony hand and gave a gentle squeeze. Her skin felt delicate, like fine parchment, and her fingers were gnarled and bent.

'Are you warm enough? Can we get you a blanket?' Craig asked.

The woman shook her head and picked up the cup again. She'd said nothing to the firemen when they asked her where she'd been inside the house and if she was all right. Craig had told them where they found her and said they'd take her to Wardie House for some warmth. The firemen agreed and said they'd be back later and, once the fire was under control, they needed to speak to the house owner. Presumably Martha was still with them.

'Would you like to stay here tonight?' Rona asked. 'We've got a nice room you could have, if you want.'

'Excuse me,' Craig said to the old woman as he got up and walked round the back of the chair to whisper to his wife. 'What are you talking about? Where can she go?'

'We can put her in Miss Grant's old room. It's still all blank walls, but the bed is made up,' Rona whispered.

'I'd forgotten the family cleared her stuff yesterday.'

'Yes, everything's been cleaned – it certainly should all be ready now. But can you run along and check there are towels in the bathroom, please? Oh, and put on the kettle to fill a hot water bottle.'

'Okay,' said Craig, kissing the top of Rona's head. He still smelled of smoke, as did the old woman, but Rona didn't want to suggest washing her. She just wanted to keep her safe and comfortable.

Rona studied the pale, lined face with that distinctive mole that extended from her upper lip to below one nostril. Her brown eyes were no longer wide with fear yet her expression was still unfathomable.

Rona lifted the plate. 'Would you like a biscuit? Anything else to eat?'

The old woman stretched out her gnarled hand and took a digestive biscuit then patted Rona's hand. There was a flicker of a smile, then she nibbled on her biscuit and continued to stare around the room again as if something was familiar, but she couldn't quite place what.

✳

Ian wheeled the old woman out of the bathroom. She strained her neck to see out of the window.

'You've got a nice view over the south side. In the morning you'll see; it's too dark now,' he said, helping her into bed. She didn't seem to mind Ian lifting her, nor Rona tucking her in. He wheeled the chair to the other side of the room. 'I'll pop in during the night to check you're okay,' he said. 'Anything I can get you?'

She shook her head then rested it on the pillow.

Ian drew the curtains and she shook her head. 'D'you want me to leave the curtains open?'

She nodded and Ian pulled them wide open.

Rona filled a glass of water from the jug by her bed then slipped her hand under the blanket and removed the hot water bottle. 'I don't want this to burn your legs,' she said, smiling. 'Can you tell us your name yet?'

There was a sound at the door and the old woman opened her eyes wide.

'It's all right, it's just Craig, my husband. I'm Rona, by the way. He and I run this care home. Ian's the carer on your floor, so he's the one who'll look in during the night.'

The woman nodded.

'Any sign of Martha yet?' Rona glanced at the woman whose brow was furrowed.

Craig shook his head. 'No idea where she is. I'll nip round later. She must still be speaking to the fire brigade.'

Rona looked at the woman again and noticed her eyes were screwed up tight, like a child's if they were counting in Hide and Seek. Rona and Craig exchanged looks. 'There's a bell here. If you need anything, just ring and Ian'll come straight away. He's just along the corridor.'

The woman's face relaxed a little. As Rona stood up, she realised how odd it was not calling her by name, but they didn't know what to call her. Then it struck her: was she the Miss Janet McCallister whose letter the postman had delivered and who Doctor Bruce had been sent to visit?

Rona bent down.

'Is your name Janet?'

The old woman opened her eyes. She lifted herself up from the pillow and shook her head. Then she leant back against the pillow, shut her eyes and let out a long breath.

Chapter 30

1899

Jessie stood at the sink, scowling at the pile of dishes. She had been keeping her head down since the day before when Matron had accused her of helping Bertha leave. She picked up the brush and started scrubbing the plates and spoons clean. They were all almost spotless anyway; everyone was so hungry, they left nothing behind. The inmates didn't realise how lucky they were to have a cook like Molly who could make acceptable food from so little. Jessie had heard of other poorhouses with food that was almost inedible.

As she sloshed water over the plates, Jessie thought back to the night before. She hoped Bertha would be all right. She and Dorrie had come up with a plan, and unless something unforeseen had happened, then at this moment Bertha would be on a ship leaving the port of Leith and bound for Canada. Jessie smiled. Her friend and bed-mate was on a ship going somewhere so strange, so far away. She, who was so cautious and careful, was on her way to the other side of the world. What would she do there? What would happen to her baby? How would they live?

Dorrie's friend Bob worked down at the docks and knew all about the ships getting ready to sail. He had told her there was one sailing for somewhere called Halifax the next day at noon and he'd always boasted that he could easily get someone on board. Since he was sweet on Dorrie and would do anything for her, Dorrie was going to take Bertha along to Leith at dawn and turn on the charm with Bob. There would be no problem securing a passage, considering what Bertha had with her, carefully hidden in the baby's bootee in her underskirt pocket. Jessie worried that Dorrie might get into trouble with their mother, but she had been rising late recently because of her bad back and Dorrie said she could get home before she awoke.

After Jessie had explained everything to Bertha and managed to calm her down, Dorrie had taken her inside and said she could lie down on her bed for a couple of hours. Jessie had given her friend one last hug and wiped her tears away. 'You be sure to come back and see me with the bairn, Bertha. You'll be married to a rich fisherman in Canada by then, you'll see.' Jessie could see Bertha was trying to be brave, but there was no disguising the fact she was terrified. Even in the dim light of the kitchen, Bertha's eyes were wide with fear.

She'd be fine now, of that Jessie was sure. Dorrie was reliable, she would have sorted everything out. Jessie remembered the final hug with her big sister and Dorrie's words: 'Try to come back here soon to see me. I'll start talking to Ma about you coming back to live with us. She'll get over it. She's fallen out with Uncle Johnnie's bidie-in, Meg Rae. Meg was the one poisoning her all the time about your curse. She's a nasty piece of work. I'll see what I can do, Jessie. I miss you.'

Jessie had realised then that Meg was Annie Rae's mother. Her entire family was bad. Jessie plunged her hands back into the greasy cold water, pulled out the plug, and with her sleeve wiped away the tears trickling down her face.

✗

'Jessie, where were you last night? Matron's been asking me.'

Jessie swivelled round, the drying cloth in her hand, to see Molly standing at the door, scowling. Her fingers drummed on the side of the sink. 'Did you help Bertha get away? Is it true she's with child?'

Jessie shook her head and turned back to the plate in her hand which she rubbed over and over with the cloth.

'So how come Annie Rae told Matron that? Is she just making it up?'

'I don't know.' Jessie glanced round at Molly who was now over at the stove, tying her apron strings. 'But I think Annie's a nasty, spiteful lassie. She's got it in for everyone, not just me.'

'You could be right there.'

'Was Annie's mother in here too?'

Molly nodded. 'Yes, Meg Rae was a mean woman, but she got out of here somehow, so she went back down to Newhaven and she's biding with a fisherman now, I hear.' Molly sat down and pointed to a chair for Jessie to sit. 'You realise what would happen if Matron or the Governor find out you helped Bertha get out of here?'

'Got to be better than what would have happened to her if Matron had found out she was having a baby,' Jessie muttered.

'So it was true. She was having a bairn?' Molly leant back against the chair and folded her arms.

Jessie turned back to the sink. 'She might have mentioned there was a chance ...'

'Good God, lass, why did you not tell me? I helped Lizzie Smith last year when she was expecting. And MaryAnn Logan the year before. It happens. It happens in here more than it should but that's none of anyone's business.' Molly turned and looked Jessie in the eye. 'Well, until it shows, then the girl just has to get out of here. Fast.'

Jessie wiped her hands on her apron. 'Is it true Matron sends the girls down to the harbour at Leith if they're found with child?' Jessie looked straight at the cook and held her gaze. 'Why would she do that?'

'You know she's really strict, Jessie, morals and everything.

That's all there is to it.' Molly's eyes narrowed. 'Not so sure about him, mind.'

Molly stood up, pulling down the line of cloths from the rail above the range. She sat down again and began to fold them on the table in front of her.

'Matron's horrible and scary and …' Jessie stopped and looked up. 'Why's she so nice to Effie though, Molly? She never shouts at her like she does to us.'

Molly did not look up at Jessie but continued folding the cloths and stacking them into a pile. 'That's different.'

'Why? Why is that different?'

Molly slipped a hand underneath the cloths, placed her other hand on top and lifted them over to the linen drawer beside the sink.

'It's just how it is,' she said, speaking over her shoulder. 'Now, let's get started on the supper things. I need you to scrub those tatties.'

'But why is Effie treated like a different person? Matron never forces her to tie her hair or even wash. It can't be because she's a bit simple. Or older, Janette Smith's much older. Why is Effie treated differently?'

Molly's head bent low. 'Because she *is* different.'

'She wheels that pram around and wanders about all night. Matron lets her do anything she likes. Why? How is she different?'

Molly turned round, her face flushed. 'It's not for me to say, Jessie. You'll find out one day, maybe.'

'I want to know now.' Jessie's brows were knitted in indignation.

Molly sat down again beside Jessie. She leant in close. 'You are getting in a state about nothing. Like I said, it's none of your business.'

'Why can't you tell me, Molly? Please? I like Effie, she likes me. I want to help her but …'

Molly leant over and tugged Jessie's earlobe. She pulled Jessie towards her and hissed, 'You're not meant to know. No one is meant to know why she gets special treatment. Is it not obvious? Look at them both. Look at those eyes they've both got.'

'What about their eyes?' Jessie jerked her head away, squirming at the pain in her ear. 'Effie's got dark brown eyes, but I've no idea what Matron's are like.'

Molly bent down and looked straight at Jessie. She whispered, 'Matron is nice to Effie because Effie is not what you think. Her real name is Euphemia Ramsay and she is the sister of Isabella Ramsay.'

'Who's that?'

'Matron. Effie is Matron's sister.'

Chapter 31

1982

'Where the hell is Martha?' Rona was throwing Craig's clothes into the washing machine as he came through to the kitchen after his shower.

He shrugged. 'No idea, maybe the fire brigade needed her to stay at the house with them for a bit longer. It's all under control now. The chief fireman said it was fine and there'd just be smoke damage in that back room.'

'I put all your clothes in to wash, by the way. They stank of smoke. We'll get the new lady's clothes washed tomorrow once she's had a good night's sleep.'

Rona watched Craig as he opened the fridge door and pour himself a tall glass of milk. He'd been drinking a lot of milk recently, as if aligned with her pregnancy diet.

Craig took a couple of gulps then sat at the table. 'So who do you think the new lady is?'

Rona moved towards her husband and stroked his cheek. 'No idea, but thanks to you and Ian, she's alive and well, just a bit shocked.'

'What a horrible thing to go through, and at her age too.'

'I know. She must've been fully aware there was a fire but she wasn't able to get out of the room as she was stuck in her wheel-chair.'

Craig downed the rest of the milk. 'She couldn't have got out anyway, her door was locked.'

'What?'

'Yeah, Ian and I tried the handle, realised it was locked, and I was about to put my shoulder to the door when Ian saw the key hanging above the door on a hook.'

Rona frowned. 'Like we do here for our residents so the night staff can get in without disturbing them?'

'Suppose so.'

'Why would Martha lock an old woman in a room? And especially when there was no possibility of her getting out if there was something like a fire?'

'Beats me.' Craig scratched his head. 'Did she settle down all right?'

Rona nodded. 'I'll nip along later to check she's asleep. I asked her if she was Janet McCallister but she shook her head.'

'Is that the person you said the doctor was going to visit?'

'Yes. Oh, good point, I'll call Doctor Bruce the minute the surgery opens in the morning. See if he can call round.'

'And now, let's go to bed. It's late. There's loads to do tomorrow.' Craig stood up. 'Remember one of us has to go to Miss Grant's funeral.'

'Oh, I'd forgotten about that. It's all been so quick.'

'Miss Grant had everything prepared in advance. The undertakers had been given a list of her funeral plans ages ago apparently.'

'Ian's not on tomorrow – it's his day off – so could you go please, darling? Then I can take care of the new lady?'

'Okay. I'll go and look out my black tie.'

Ж

In the morning, Craig was out of the annexe early. Rona dressed quickly then headed for the office. It was 8.30 a.m. which was staff handover time. She saw Ian coming out of the lift having finished his night shift.

'Ian, how is the new lady? Did she sleep okay? Is she speaking yet?'

'I've just been in, but she's still sleeping. I thought I'd just leave her. I was about to brief Fay on everything, unless you want to?'

Rona shook her head. 'It's fine. You crack on. I don't suppose Martha's been around? No idea where she went last night.'

'Nope. Though the firemen said the house was okay, so she probably slept there.'

'Suppose so. Can't understand why she never came to see how the woman is, whoever she is.'

Ian shrugged. 'I'll be in later, by the way. I said I'd give the new carer a hand.'

'Thanks, Ian. What would we do without you?' said Rona, as she watched Ian stride along the corridor towards the nurses' station.

Rona dialled the surgery number and waited.

'Hello, Bangholm Loan Medical Practice.'

'Oh, hello, it's Rona from Wardie House Care Home here. Is it possible to have a quick word with Doctor Bruce please?'

'I'm sorry, Doctor Bruce is off on holiday for two weeks. We've got a locum, though. Doctor Henderson.'

'That's fine. Could Doctor Henderson come round as soon as possible, please?'

'Is it to see one of your residents?'

'Em … yes, it is, yes.'

'What's the name?'

Rona hesitated a moment, and then said, 'McCallister. Janet McCallister.'

'That's fine, she'll be there after morning surgery.'

'Thanks.'

Rona crossed the hall towards the front door and looked up at the portrait on the wall. The brown-eyed lady seemed to be looking down at her. Was she smiling? She was sure her expression had appeared more stern before. She peered at it and noticed the silvery thing between her fawn gloves. Was it a jewel? From where

Rona stood, it looked as if it could be a large diamond, though it wasn't shiny. Perhaps that was just the thick brushstrokes.

Rona grabbed her bag from the annexe and opened the front door to a beautiful summer morning. She sniffed the air. Had there really been a fire at the lodge house last night? It seemed like a dream. There was a strong breeze and all she could smell were the fragrant tea roses as she walked down the path to the gate. As she headed round the corner, she wondered what Martha was going to say. Martha had some explaining to do.

Chapter 32

1899

Jessie lay in bed, wide awake. She was churning over the news that Effie was Matron's sister. Her name was Euphemia Ramsay and she was not what she seemed. She was not a poor, mad, ordinary woman – she was a lady.

Jessie had wanted to ask Molly more about Effie but the Governor had knocked on the door asking Cook to bring him a hot toddy as he could feel a head cold coming on. 'And be generous with the whisky!' he had commanded.

Jessie had dashed back over to the sink and then turned to look at the Governor. She had seldom looked directly at his face. Jessie usually stared at her feet if he addressed her. His nose was red and his thinning hair and bushy moustache were tinged with grey. His eyes were dark. Like Effie's.

'What are you looking at, child?' He had scowled at her. 'Get on with your work.'

Jessie had plunged her hands into the cold greasy water and grasped the chain to pull the plug out. Only when she heard his footsteps disappear along the corridor had Jessie turned to Molly. 'Is the Governor …?'

'I've said enough, Jessie Mack. Don't you dare say a thing to anyone else. I've got to go and see if Matron wants her evening tea yet.'

Jessie wriggled down the mattress and opened her eyes wide

to stare at the high ceiling in the dim evening light. None of it made any sense. How could someone as obviously well bred as Effie be an inmate – like the other poor souls whose lives had been so hard, they had been forced to live in this horrible cold, dark poorhouse where they had to work their fingers to the bone?

Jessie lifted herself up onto an elbow and listened. She could hear the faint noise of wheels creaking. It must be Effie downstairs. Could Jessie ask her about her life or would she get angry? She slipped one leg off the mattress and then the other. She pulled her shawl round her shoulders, reached under the mattress and thrust the cloth deep into the pocket of her smock. Patting her pocket, now Jessie felt safe. She tiptoed out of the dormitory and headed for the stairs.

The door to the cellar was ajar so Jessie pushed it open and peered inside. There, at the far end, was Effie, her pigtail swinging to and fro as she walked up and down. As Jessie approached, she noticed Effie was pushing the huge pram with one hand; the other was clutching something. It looked like a frame.

'Effie,' she whispered. 'Effie, it's me, Jessie. Are you all right?'

Effie swivelled round. On seeing Jessie, her face relaxed and she smiled. 'Come and see, Winzie, see what I've got here.'

Jessie went nearer but still couldn't see well. 'I can't see, Effie, is there a candle?'

Effie nodded and thrust a wooden thing into Jessie's hands, then padded over to the stairs. Jessie turned the wooden thing over and saw it was a picture. She squinted to try to make out what it was but could only see the outline of a head. Effie walked towards her, carrying a lit candle, the light making her dark eyes huge, her wrinkled face ghostly white.

Effie held the candle beside the painting and Jessie stared at it. It was a young woman with long chestnut-brown hair and large dark eyes. She had a high-necked black collar with a line of white along the edge as if she wore a stiff-collared blouse underneath a high silk gown. There was something sparkly held between her two fawn gloves. She was looking directly at the painter and, though unsmiling, there was the flicker of something in her eyes. What was it – affection, tenderness? But there was also something familiar about the lady in the painting. Jessie stared at it again, then held it at arm's length. Effie moved the candle beside it and smiled encouragingly.

Jessie gasped. 'Effie, it's you!' She peered at it again. 'Look at you! What a lady you were.'

Effie set down the candle and snatched back the painting. She held it up high so that the portrait was beside her head. Even though Effie's greying hair was now yanked back in a tight pigtail and her eyes were surrounded by puffy purple bags through lack of sleep, the similarity was now obvious.

'Effie, you're so fine and beautiful. A real lady. What …'

'What happened to the lady, Winzie? Indeed.' Effie took the painting and moved towards the pram. She lifted the cover and delved into the footwell. She shuffled some things around then brought out something small, a piece of stiff paper. She handed it to Jessie, who realised it was one of those things called a photograph. The year before, she and Dorrie had been made to sit in the front row of the Newhaven Fisherlassies choir the day a man came to take their picture with his camera. They had to sit very still, not moving an inch, and wait while he disappeared under a vast black cloth and shouted a muffled 'Smile!' They had seen the picture later, after church one day. The minister had been delighted that his choir lassies were in this picture, since the lassies from the choir in Granton had not been asked to pose for the camera.

The photograph in Jessie's hand was a little faded, the brown colours dingy, but she could make out that it was a baby. The baby had short tufts of dark hair and had its eyes closed. It was lying on a blanket on a chair. It had a white sheet swaddled around its body and a crocheted shawl wrapped round its neck and tucked under its chin. There were two flowers laid on the chair beside it, their long stems the length of the baby's body.

'Who's the baby, Effie?'

Effie began to push the pram handles up and down as if pacifying a crying baby. She walked the pram gently across the back of the cellar and came back to Jessie, leaning in close. 'It's my baby, my little one.'

✳

Effie heard the noise before Jessie. She grabbed the photograph back. 'Go and hide, Winzie. Run!'

Jessie had just got to the coal cellar when she heard Matron's voice.

'Euphemia, I thought you said you were going to try to sleep in your bed, your own bed in our home. Why don't you come along? Andrew is out somewhere for the evening and we both know how that will end up. He will not bother us. Come, I need to ask you something.'

Jessie pulled the door shut but could still hear the sisters talking.

'I know you have something behind your back. Show me your hands. Both of them! Oh, for God's sake, are you still holding onto that photograph?'

'Give it back, Bella, give it back.'

'Come with me now to the house. We need to find where you put the diamond. Then, once you have remembered, then – and only then – might we be able to give up this God-forsaken poorhouse and live in comfort as we used to.'

Jessie had never heard a woman blaspheme before; she was surprised at Matron. Of course, down at the harbour the men and women swore, but she had never imagined a lady would.

Jessie heard a tussle as if they were pushing each other about. She then heard Effie gasp.

'If you don't come with me now and help me find it, I shall destroy this!'

'No!' she heard Effie cry. 'Not the photograph. Give it back, give it back!'

Jessie peeked out to see Matron hold the tiny photograph high above her head and Effie try to grab it.

'Then come with me to the lodge house. We shall look together. Then you might have this back. Come, Euphemia!'

Jessie saw Effie lunge at Matron, but Matron stepped aside and Effie stumbled and fell over.

'Get up now, you fool.' She saw Matron sigh and help Effie to her feet. 'Come along. You may return here later. Let's go and have a nice slice of cake.'

Jessie watched the two sisters pass nearby as they headed up the stairs for the door, Matron holding on firmly to the photograph and Effie running her hands up and down her legs as if scratching her skin through the folds of her flimsy dress. Her eyes were wide with fear.

Chapter 33

1982

Rona knocked on the door and looked around. The garden was a mess, full of mounds of earth. Martha was such a fastidious woman in her appearance, why did she not bother with the garden? There must be a company who could deal with the moles in a humane way?

Rona knocked again and waited. There was still no answer. She tried to peer in the front window, but as usual the curtains were all drawn. Rona gave one more loud, sharp knock then went round the back of the house, trying the back door, but it too was locked. There was obviously no one at home. Noticing a small door by the shed, Rona bent down to open it and saw it was a wide chute. This must have been a coal cellar; the walls were stained black, as if sooty. She pulled the door to and headed back round the front.

Rona wandered back along the road to Wardie House and stopped at the gate. The baby was moving. She smiled and spread her fingers wide over her belly. Not long now.

She looked over the road towards Mrs Bell's old house and wondered why no one ever saw the residents. Martha had said they were always at work or away at weekends, but it was still rather odd that there was never any sign of them, her nearest neighbours. She'd ask Mrs Bell who she and her husband had sold the house to. It must seem so strange for her to now live directly opposite the house she had lived in most of her married life.

✕

Rona was tapping in the entry code at the door when she noticed movement behind the glass panes. It was one of the residents and two carers. They'd been having some problems with Bob Campbell who was always trying to escape. She'd told Craig they should have kept the solid wooden door instead of the modern glass one, but he had argued the wood was rotting and glass let in so much more light.

Once, soon after he had arrived, Bob became violent and was trying to poke his stick through the glass. Now he was much calmer, though he still tried to make a break for freedom every few days. He had an important appointment at his bank, he would insist to anyone who cared to listen.

Rona watched as two carers came to calm Bob down. One hand on each of his scrawny arms, they walked Bob down the corridor. Rona opened the door and went inside. Frank Sinatra was belting out 'Fly Me To The Moon' from the dining room. Most of the residents loved it when the carers played cassettes from when they were young, though Mrs Bell and Betty Chalmers always stayed away. They obviously felt listening to American crooners was beneath them.

Rona took out the annexe key and paused at the door. Were there voices inside? She pushed open the door, tiptoed into the kitchen and gasped. There, at her kitchen table, sat Mr Burnside on his own, looking out of the window, muttering to himself. He had his sleeves rolled up and as Rona approached, she noticed again the tattoo on his forearm, the heart and anchor intertwined and some lettering in the middle she couldn't make out.

'Good morning, Mr Burnside. You're not really meant to be in here, you know. This is the house where Craig and I live.'

Mr Burnside smiled a gentle, benign smile and nodded. 'I know, but I wanted to see where the baby's going to be born.'

'Well, the baby will be born in hospital, but, yes, this is where he or she will live.'

'I brought something to show you.' He delved into his pocket and thrust an old photo at Rona. 'Thought you might like to see it since your baby will be here soon.'

Rona sat down and looked at it. There was a small boy, about two or three years old, wearing breeches and a little jacket. He stood on a small stool beside a large pram which had wheels with large narrow spokes. Inside the pram, propped up on several cushions, was a baby. Its eyes were shut and its head leant to one side. It wore a long embroidered gown that stretched down to the end of the pram and spilled over the end. There were a couple of long-stemmed roses tucked alongside, as if the boy had placed them there, straight from the garden. The baby had tiny curls of blonde hair, just like the little boy whose hand held the tiny hand of the baby in the pram.

'Who are they?'

Mr Burnside pointed at the little boy. 'That's me, Rona. That's me, can't you tell?' He beamed. 'Look, can you see the dimple on my chin? My mother always said I got the family dimple.'

Rona stared at the photo again. 'Yes, yes, I can see that now. Is that your little sister?'

Mr Burnside nodded. 'Morag, yes, that's Morag. I was to hold her hand for the man who took the photograph. Her hand was cold but I tried to warm it up. She loved me, Morag did. She ...'

There was a knock at the door and Rona stood up to open it.

Ian stood there. 'Sorry to bother you but ...' He realised Rona had a visitor.

Mr Burnside waved the photo in the air. 'I'm showing her the picture I showed you, Ian.'

Ian strode over to the table, turning to ask Rona, 'Is he meant to be in here?'

'I don't know how he got in. I must have forgotten to lock the door when I went round to Martha's.'

'Oh, right.' He turned to the old man and raised his voice. 'Mr

Burnside, I need you to help me with something next door. I'm going to oil the wheels of the new lady's wheelchair. Could you give me a hand, please?'

Mr Burnside sat up straight. 'At your service, young man.'

'Rona, d'you know where Craig put the WD40? I only noticed this morning how creaky the wheels were when I was helping the new lady out of the shower.'

'Is she any more talkative this morning?'

He shook his head. 'But she's smiling more.'

'I'll go and see her once I've had my tea.' Rona went to the sink to fill the kettle. 'Oh, I've no idea where the WD40 is, by the way. Try the cellar?'

They walked towards the door and Ian steered Mr Burnside gently out into the corridor. 'Wait for me over there, please. Take a seat by the cellar door. I've just got something to speak to Rona about.'

He turned back to Rona. 'That photo he showed you. Did you look closely?'

Rona shrugged.

'Notice anything odd?'

She shook her head.

'Did you not see there were some flowers in the pram beside the baby?'

'Yes, now you mention it.'

'The baby was dead, Rona. He was holding his dead sister's hand. For a bloody photograph. Bunch of weirdos, those Victorians. Really gave me the creeps. I told him to keep it in his cupboard and not to show it to anyone. He obviously forgot.'

Rona's eyes widened.

'Are you all right? It's horrible isn't it?' Ian put a hand on her shoulder.

'Why? Why would they do that? Take photos of dead babies?'

'I looked it up in the library after he showed me the photo. Apparently that was what a lot of people did at the end of the nineteenth century. It was the only way they had to remember their dead. So many died as infants, it was just accepted.'

Ian looked at his watch. 'I'd better go and find the WD40. See you later.'

'Okay.' Rona shut the door and headed for the kitchen. What a hideous photo. Why hadn't she realised the baby was dead? She looked down at her belly and stretched both hands over her bump, clasping her fingers together.

Chapter 34

1899

Jessie emerged from the coal cellar and headed for the stairs then stopped on the bottom step. That evil look on Matron's face and the fear on Effie's were not normal. Perhaps she should go and check Effie was all right. But how could she? It wasn't as if she could march up to the lodge house and demand to know what was going on. She was no one, a fisherlassie who had a curse.

Jessie started to climb the stairs then stopped again. Surely the other passageway in the coal cellar led to the lodge house? If she went past the place she'd found the little woollen bootee hidden, there must be an entrance into their house, just as there was one in this big house.

She ran upstairs to her bed and lifted the cloth bundle from under the mattress. Then, taking the stairs two at a time, Jessie headed back down into the cellar and through the tiny door into the coal cellar. For once she was glad of the blackness inside as she did not have to look at the word carved out by Effie's scissors. Of course, now she knew Effie was Matron's sister, it made sense why she had access to such things – and the bunch of keys too. Did Matron just give her the run of both houses? Was the diamond Matron had mentioned the one Jessie had found? If so, Jessie could be the reason Effie was in trouble.

Jessie crawled along the dirty floor until she came to a pile of coal. Thankfully the coal hadn't been there when Bertha and she had made their escape – her large, clumsy friend would never have been able to climb over the coals. Jessie, slender and nimble, clambered over the pile with ease and, when she came to where she thought the other tunnel was, she turned to the left instead of going straight down. There was a huge mound of coal here, even more than for the main house. Presumably Matron and the Governor kept their own little house cosy and warm while the inmates of the poorhouse shivered constantly from the cold. Jessie patted the walls around her and found the little shelf above her head where she had found the baby's bootee. She headed over the sooty coals and stretched her hand forward. A sliver of light cut through the gloom. This must be the door of the lodge house coal cellar. Jessie pushed it slightly open, then hunkered down at the entrance, brushing some of the soot from her shift. She listened. She could hear distant voices approach. It sounded as if Matron was telling Effie to come and sit in the kitchen; the coal cellar must be just off the kitchen. Jessie strained her neck forward to hear.

'Now, Euphemia, why don't you sit down here and I shall fetch you some of Cook's cake. It's a seed cake. You like that, don't you?'

Jessie imagined Effie ramming the cake into her mouth as she had done in the kitchen that day. She heard the noise of plates clattering.

'Do not eat like a peasant. You were not brought up to have the manners of one of the dreadful inmates in this vile place. You can do what you like over there but in this house you will eat like a lady.'

'May I have the photograph back now?' Effie mumbled.

'Do not speak with your mouth full. We will see about this picture. All in good time. Now then, my dear, let us—'

There was a noise of a plate smashing. Then a chair scraping. 'You are so clumsy, Euphemia. Look what you have done! It is because you never sleep. Why don't you sleep? Look at you, those great puffy bags under your eyes and your hair in that ridiculous childish plait. Why don't we go to your bedroom, and we shall brush out your hair and perhaps find another frock to wear. This one is so tattered. You used to be lovely and then ...' Matron sighed. 'Go and fetch the dustpan and sweep it up. And while you are on your feet, carry some more coal from the cellar. It is becoming cold in here.'

Jessie drew back as far as she could without disturbing anything or making a noise, then waited for the door to be swung open wide.

Effie stood at the entrance to the coal cellar with a brass-handled coal bucket in her hand. She took hold of the coal shovel and pushed the door, then must have noticed a bare foot for she peered slowly inside and saw Jessie, whose forefinger was at her lips. Effie opened her mouth to speak then scowled and shook her head. Jessie smiled and nodded her support.

'Hurry up with the coal! the fire is about to go out,' Matron called.

Effie shut the door a fraction and went back with the bucket. Jessie leant forward and peered through the door; she was now able to see inside. Matron's back was to her and she saw her toss the photograph from one hand to the other. Effie stoked the fire with coal and returned to sit beside her sister.

Effie stretched out her hand. 'Give it to me, Bella. It's mine.'

But the photograph was taken out of Effie's reach. 'When you have told me where it is. Where have you hidden the diamond?'

There was silence and Jessie could see Effie bend her head low and stare at the great stone slabs at her feet.

'All I have had to wear at my neck for years is our mother's pearl choker. As eldest, I ought to have been wearing her diamond, her beautiful sparkling diamond. But I cannot, since you removed it from my jewellery box. At first I thought it had been misplaced, but now I know for certain that you hid it. And now, I've had enough. That diamond is my one way out of this house of hell. Where is it, Euphemia?'

Jessie saw Effie scratch the back of her head as she continued to look down.

'Very well. I have no choice.' Matron stood up and opened a drawer in the dresser. She removed a pair of long, shiny scissors and held them in one hand, the photograph in the other. 'If you refuse to say where you hid it, then this photograph will be snipped into tiny bits and thrown into the fire. Do you hear me?' Matron's voice was raised. Jessie noticed that her cheeks were flushed.

'Why did you not save her, Bella? Could you not have saved my baby?' Effie began to wail.

'You were but eighteen, a child yourself. You had betrayed us both by entering into a liaison with that wastrel, that man who insinuated himself into our family with the feeble excuse that he was an artist. He could no more paint than—'

'He could, Bella. My portrait's fine and lovely and—'

'It is amateur and naïve. I could do better myself. So could you for that matter – he was a rogue. And that baby did not deserve to live.'

Effie thrust her hands over her ears and rocked from side to side.

'She was only little, she was beautiful. Why did she have to die, Bella? Why?'

Matron pulled Effie's hands away and leant in close.

'She died because she was a bastard. For God's sake, Euphemia.' Matron was breathing heavily now. 'You brought our name into disrepute and then there was the business with Andrew and that woman and – oh, we used to have such a fine life until you ruined it. You and our brother.'

Effie tilted her head from side to side, her pigtail swaying down her back. 'I used to have dreams in those days when I went to bed and could sleep. I dreamt that she was born and then I saw her and she was lovely and her little eyes opened and I was happy and then you took her from me and all I could hear was her crying and crying. And then nothing. Everything was still. Not a whimper.' Effie began to scratch at the wooden table with her long fingernails. The noise grated. 'And then I stopped going to sleep. I thought, if I do not sleep, I cannot dream and I shall forget the agony of her crying – and just remember the lovely baby.'

Jessie wanted to go and give Effie a hug to comfort her, she was so distraught. Her sister simply stood over her, taunting and gloating as she held the photograph high.

'Why did she die, Bella? Why?' Effie was now wailing. 'We had everything ready down in the cellar. There was the pram and I had knitted those tiny bootees, bonnets and matinee jackets – and then she died. Something happened, I'm sure of it.'

Matron flung the scissors on the table and slapped her sister across her cheek. 'She died because she was a bastard. She died because she had to. She did not deserve to live. She died because she was a disgrace.' Her eyes narrowed. 'It did not take long.'

Effie's head swivelled upwards. 'What d'you mean? I thought you said she had a sudden fit. That she died just after he'd taken the photograph, while I lay next door.'

'We should never have agreed to the photograph. But Andrew had the camera all set up on its stand. He insisted it would placate you after we told you the child was to be sent away. Why, for God's sake, did I agree to be kind to you and give you this?' She thrust the photograph at Effie's face then clenched it in her fist as if trying to destroy it with her fingers. 'Unless you tell me where the diamond is, this is going too – the last vestige of a memory of that hideous time. And that pram will be burned tomorrow.' Matron bent over Effie and shouted in her face. 'Tell me where you have hidden it.'

Jessie watched Effie as her eyes grew large and her mouth opened wide. She lunged towards her sister and scratched at her face with her long nails. 'You killed her, didn't you? She was so perfect, so healthy – and then I remember hearing her cry as if she was in pain, and then silence. You killed her and —'

Matron grabbed Effie's scrawny arms with one hand and rubbed the palm of her other hand down the side of her face. She inspected it. Jessie could see red; Matron's cheek was bleeding.

Matron held Effie's hands before her, her eyes blazing. 'Yes. I killed your bastard child. I killed her. Do you want to know why? Because she kept crying and crying and I could stand it no longer so I smothered her. It was easy. I just held her down with the blanket over her mouth and nose. That was how easy it was. Andrew even laughed as my hand held the squirming creature down. And I am about to do the same to you unless you —'

Jessie flung open the door and ran into the kitchen. 'Don't touch her! Leave her alone.' She reached into her pocket and pulled out the gutter's knife.

Chapter 35

1982

Rona dialled Martha's number, drumming her fingers on the desk as it rang out. She replaced the receiver. Where on earth was she? Had she disappeared after the fire because everyone now knew about the old woman who lived with her?

Ian had just taken the newly oiled wheelchair along to the old woman's room where the doctor was examining her. Hopefully, if the doctor said she was physically well, they could get her out into the garden.

The office door opened and Craig walked in, chin up as he eased his tie.

'I know I shouldn't say this since it's your funeral suit, but you look good in a suit.'

Craig grinned.

'How did it go?'

'There were very few people there, not many more than the handful of family members who were in her room clearing her things. Did you know Miss Grant had been a teacher at the Gaelic school? Her full name was Angusina Malcomina Grant. She was from somewhere way up north in the Highlands. Anyway, the minister said she dedicated herself to teaching children how to read and write Gaelic. Why did we not know that? Sad, really, so few people there.'

'Bless her.'

'What have I missed here, then?'

Rona told Craig about Martha's house being locked and coming back to find Mr Burnside in the annexe.

'How the hell did he get in? We always lock it. Hope he doesn't think he can just pop in any old time.'

'I'm a bit worried actually. You know how he's always walking that big pram around the place and I'd hoped we could get rid of it before our baby comes along? Well, I don't think we can now.' She explained about the photograph.

'Ghoulish. Let's make sure we lock our door every time we pop out, even for a few minutes.'

'Okay. No one else has this key, do they?'

Craig shook his head. 'Nope, unless you gave it to anyone?'

'No. Anyway, what about Martha? Where on earth can she have gone? Surely she'll come back to get her stuff?'

'She might have done that last night. There was very little in the house. I mean, Ian and I only ran in then straight out once we got the woman out, but I do remember thinking there was very little furniture or anything. Perhaps she's done a runner.'

'Why would she do that?'

There was a tap on the door.

'Come in.'

It was a young woman with a doctor's bag in her hand. 'Hi, I'm Doctor Henderson. Just been to see Miss McCallister in Room 10.'

'Hello, I'm Rona. Sorry I missed you earlier. This is Craig, my husband. We're the managers. How is she?'

'She's actually not too bad, considering. Your carer was telling me about the house fire. It's remarkable she's come out pretty unscathed. He told me she was sitting with her scarf wrapped round her head so no signs of smoke inhalation or anything.'

'Did she speak at all?'

The doctor shook her head. 'But I was having a look at her previous notes and saw that Doctor Bruce mentioned this too. She either doesn't speak or only speaks in a hoarse whisper. She didn't speak at all for me just now. There's nothing wrong, from what I can see, with her throat, so it could just be shock. She's been through a lot for someone her age.'

'How old is she?'

'Ninety-seven. Now, can I speak to Martha Sinclair please? I presume she's here too?'

'Well, no. That's the problem, we've no idea where she is. Ever since the fire no one's seen her.'

'She got out of the house all right?'

'Oh yes, she was at the gate with us but we were so busy helping the old woman, we didn't see where she went afterwards.' Rona stood up. 'So is the woman's name definitely Janet McCallister?'

'Yes, why?'

'Well,' said Rona frowning, 'when I asked her, she shook her head.'

'She's registered with the practice under that name. She responded when I called her that name even though she didn't talk to me. Maybe she has a nickname that she prefers or something. Because she won't or can't speak, I can't tell at this stage whether she's got some form of dementia. She's definitely still suffering from mild shock.'

'What happens now?'

'I'm sorry to say I'm not at liberty to discuss anything unless it's with her legal guardian. And if Martha Sinclair is missing, then that's a problem. Are you all right to keep her here for a day or two till we know what's happening?'

'Of course. There's someone else on the waiting list for that room but we just heard he's delayed another week as there are problems with his house sale. Do you know how long Miss McCallister has been in the lodge house?'

The doctor shook her head. 'Sorry, I can't say anything more until I've spoken to Mrs Sinclair.' She looked at her watch. 'I must be off. I'll be late for afternoon surgery.'

X

Craig loaded the plate into the dishwasher and turned to Rona. 'Why don't you have a nap, love? You look worn out. I can do whatever you need doing after lunch.' He went over to the table and kissed the top of her head. She touched his cheek. 'Thanks, darling, but I really want to go and see Miss McCallister now – to see if she's okay. And Mrs Bell, I wanted to ask her if she knows anything more about Martha.'

'Okay, but then come back and lie down for an hour or so if you can?'

'If you say so, doc.' Rona smiled and watched Craig head back into the main house. He'd been far less secretive about what he was up to these days and was seldom out at night. He must have stopped drinking, surely, but she didn't want to ask him. It was only a couple of weeks now till the baby arrived; perhaps that had made him realise he had to be more responsible.

She looked at the clock. She was also keen to continue reading Mrs Bell's husband's notes about the Victorian family who lived in the house, but if she didn't get up now, she'd fall asleep. Craig was right, perhaps she did need a rest, but only once she'd done these couple of things.

Rona headed first for Janet McCallister's room and knocked on the door. She peeked her head round the corner and saw the woman sitting in the wheelchair at the window. She had a scarf up at her neck as far as her nose. Perhaps she had always done that to try to cover her distinctive birthmark. Rona crept in; the old woman blinked. She opened her eyes wide, pulled down the scarf and her face relaxed into a smile when she saw it was Rona.

Rona spoke gently. 'Sorry, did I wake you up? I just wanted to see how you're settling in. Hope we can get some of your bits and pieces from the lodge house soon, make you feel more at home.'

The old woman nodded and loosened the paisley scarf round her neck. She was still smiling.

'The doctor says you're doing really well, so hopefully you can stay with us for a short while till, well, until we know what's happening. Is that all right?'

She nodded again.

The lack of speech was hopefully not dementia-related and was just prolonged shock. She certainly seemed to understand everything, so Rona hoped she'd start speaking soon.

'The doctor also said your name is Miss McCallister. Janet McCallister. But is there another name you prefer to be called?'

She nodded.

'Is it Jan? Or Jeannie? Sorry, I don't know any other names for Janet.' The woman continued to look at her. 'Oh, do you want to write it down? Ian said he left you a pencil and paper last night.' She rushed to the bedside and brought the notepad over.

Rona watched as the woman took the pencil and wrote, in a spidery hand, the word 'Jessie'.

'That's good. Jessie. Nice name. I always thought it was short for Jessica. Anything else?' Rona indicated the notepad.

Jessie took up the pencil in her gnarled fingers and slowly wrote down some letters. She handed the pad to Rona. The words read, 'Where is Martha?'

Chapter 36

1899

Jessie held up the knife, the blade glinting in the candlelight. Matron released her grip and Effie sprang towards Jessie. 'Give it to me, Winzie.'

Jessie handed the knife to Effie; Matron began to tiptoe backwards.

'Stay there, Bella, don't move.'

Effie strode in front of her sister and pushed the door shut. She scratched her fingernails down the wooden panel and Jessie saw Matron flinch as her sister turned the knife over and over in her hand.

'Now don't be foolish, Euphemia. Give me the knife and we shall have a little talk.' She passed the figure wielding the knife. 'Jessie Mack, come here and help me get the knife off her. She is mad, deranged. She will kill us both.'

'I am only mad when I choose to be, because I do not sleep.' Effie's voice was bolder than Jessie had ever heard. 'But now I have just learned you killed my baby, the madness, as you call it, is lifting. Everything falls into place. Those nightmares were not bad dreams, they were the truth. The baby opened her eyes, then you took her from me and killed her. Dead.'

'I was not being truthful, Euphemia. Of course I did not kill her. How could I have? I had this lovely photograph commissioned before she died, tragically of a seizure. Here, let me put it on the table. You can have it now. Look, I shall place it just here.' Matron walked towards the table and placed the crumpled photograph on the wood then spread it out with the palm of her hand. 'There, now you have the photograph, all is well. We can discuss the other matter, that of the diamond, another day. Now put the knife down.'

Effie glanced at the photograph and smiled. She went towards it, lowering the knife, and as she reached the table Matron grasped her from behind and locked both arms around her. Effie jabbed her bony elbow into her sister's stomach and held on tight to the knife in her other hand. 'Here, Jessie, take it.'

Jessie rushed to take the knife from Effie and ran to the other side of the room. Matron let one of Effie's arms go and swivelled her round with the other one. She leant in close and hissed, 'You will never get away with this. I am going to have you sent away to the madhouse where you should have gone all those years ago. It was Andrew's decision. He felt sorry for you and insisted on keeping you here.' She lifted up Effie's chin so that Effie had to look directly at her sister. 'And now you refuse to tell us where you hid the diamond. The one thing that would restore our wealth. Tell me, I beg you, dear Euphemia. Tell me at once and we will forget all this, this nonsense. We will forgive you for making our lives so vile in this place. But,' she continued, 'should you decide not to tell me, you will be sent away. It was your pig-headedness hiding it that caused our downfall. Having to convert our beautiful home into this foul poorhouse because we were destitute.'

'It was Andrew's fault too,' Effie protested. 'He and that woman and—'

'It was your fault. Yours alone.' She was bellowing now. 'Where is my diamond? The diamond you stole from me!'

There was silence in the room. No one moved. Then a low booming noise reverberated all around. It was the foghorn sounding down on the Forth. Effie was the first to react. She yanked her arm away and sped over to Jessie, grabbing the knife again. 'I will never tell you, Bella. You killed my baby. How could you? I will never forgive you. Never.'

Effie lunged at Matron, stabbing her in the stomach and then the neck.

Jessie put her hands up to her face as she watched Effie plunge the knife one more time into Matron's stomach then fling the knife down and collapse onto the floor, sobbing, beside the bloody body of her sister.

Chapter 37

1982

Rona joined Mrs Bell at her bedroom window. 'Can you tell me anything about the lodge house? When you lived in the house opposite, who lived there?'

'Sit down, young lady. It's a strain on my neck having to look up at you. Besides, you shouldn't be on your feet as much as you are. In my day, an expectant mother would be confined to the house, not displaying her vast belly for all and sundry to see.'

Rona smiled and pulled a chair over to the window.

'There was an old lady, a Miss Ramsay she was called, when we bought our house in 1934. She appeared to live alone, though we never saw much of her. But as she became old and frail, she had a companion live with her and it was this woman who presumably inherited the house once Miss Ramsay died. When we left five years ago, this companion was still living there, alone, though she must have been into her nineties. We never saw her.' Mrs Bell paused and looked over her spectacles at Rona. 'She was apparently a perfectly nice woman, but kept herself to herself. We never met her, not once. We never bumped into her. How very strange that seems. I'd no idea she had died, but then why would we have heard?' She shrugged. 'You see, that is a fault of city life. In our little suburbs we have the semblance of village life, but in fact everyone is a stranger. No one knows anything about what truly goes on behind closed doors.'

'But how do you know the companion had died?'

'Well, the Yank moved in while we were moving all our furniture and so on from our house and she said she had inherited the house from her great aunt, presumably the companion. There was no one else to ask, so we just assumed that was the truth.'

'And was it not?'

'It can't have been, Rona. The Yank's obviously been lying all these years and the great aunt must have been that poor old lady Ian and your husband rescued from the fire.'

'Who told you about the fire?'

The staff had been briefed not to say a thing about what had happened and if anyone asked about Jessie, they were just to say she was a temporary resident, staying until her family made their house wheelchair-friendly.

'Never mind who said, it's not important.'

Ian was becoming a bit of a gossip. Rona would speak to him.

Mrs Bell removed her spectacles and wiped the lenses on her cardigan. 'Where is the American?'

'That's what we'd all like to know. Especially Jessie.'

'Who's Jessie?'

'That's the name of the lady in Room 10. From the fire.'

'I see. Well then, it isn't the same woman. If I recall, her name was Miss Janet Mc-something-or-other.'

'No, that's her, but she likes to be called Jessie.'

'Can't you ask her about the Yank?'

'She refuses to speak – or can't, somehow. The doctor says it might just be the shock, so we don't want to push her.'

'Curious. And yet I recall one of my great nieces refused to speak till she was four. They called it selective mutism. Caused by anxiety, the doctors said. Milly's now a barrister so obviously her condition has gone. I am sure Jessie will get better.' Mrs Bell lifted her head and stared at Rona. 'But as for the American, can't someone go into the house and check to see if she's still in there but refusing to answer the door?'

'She must've gone, I mean otherwise she'd have no food or anything.'

'She's a cunning person. I only met her twice before I came across her in here again, but both times I mistrusted her greatly. One of those times she even made a pass at my husband, who, I have to say, lapped it up. Ridiculous. He must have been forty years older than she.'

So it wasn't just Craig and Ian she flirted with. Rona stood up. 'Thanks, Mrs Bell. And I'm going to read through your husband's papers tonight. There's always been something getting in my way.'

'He may even have included an addendum about the Yank, since she came to the house while we were moving into our bungalow.'

'I'll have a read tonight.'

'And Rona, why not get Craig to go up into the attic after dark? See if there is any sign of life? I'm sure you can see the lodge house and garden from up there.'

'Good idea.'

✕

Rona and Craig sat at the table after dinner, discussing baby names.

'I really don't like Henry, sounds like some fat king. Far too southern-sounding for my Hebridean relatives anyway.'

'Hamish?' Craig was smirking.

'Now you're talking!' They both clinked glasses of milk and smiled at each other.

'And girls' names – I really like Emma or Hannah.'

'Not sure. Didn't you have a girlfriend called Emma?'

'Yes but ...'

'No way.' Rona laughed and stretched. 'Anyway, once we've cleared the plates away, can you nip up to the attic just as Mrs Bell suggested, please?'

'I'll wait till it's darker. If Martha's in there, she'd only put a light on if it was pitch black. Maybe just before we go to bed.'

'Okay.'

Craig took the glass from Rona's hands. 'You go and sit next door, get your feet up. Look through that history stuff you're keen to read. I'll do the dishes.'

Rona was only too glad to follow orders. She wandered through to the living room, picked up Mr Bell's folder of notes, flicked through to where she had left the story and spread out the pages. It was the mid 1870s before Wardie House had been converted into a poorhouse.

Isabella Ramsay, the elder of the Ramsay sisters, had discovered that her brother had had an affair with the captain's wife and that the woman was making slander-ous accusations about him; when she was widowed he had refused to marry her and had finished their liai-son. Isabella suggested Andrew Ramsay give the woman some expensive jewellery in order to placate her. The family thought that was that, until the woman arrived in Edinburgh one day to have a meeting with the editor of The Scotsman, who ran a full-page article about the fact that she had been given a diamond by Andrew Ramsay, the owner of the illustrious jeweller Ramsays. The trou-ble was the diamond, although large and striking, was not real. Paste diamonds in the late nineteenth century were made from artificial lead glass moulded into the shape of a diamond and polished. When set into a piece of jewel-lery with a closed back setting, it was difficult to see the artificial coating underneath the stone. The mistress had been to a jewellers to have it valued, which was when she discovered the treachery. She had gone to the newspaper to publicly shame him. It worked and the public disgrace brought the family business into disrepute.

They sold on the jewellery business but Andrew and Isabella Ramsay decided that, in order to keep the house,

*they would convert it into a poorhouse and they would
become Governor and Matron. They believed their status
in the community would rise since their work was charitable and was endorsed by the local churches. They presumed that their lack of finances was temporary and soon
they could regain their splendid house for themselves, perhaps after a few years.*

*Before their demise, the Ramsay family had boasted
of a precious family diamond. This was a large, rough
South African diamond that had arrived at the port of
Leith with Ramsay's South African mother who died in
childbirth. It was cut in Amsterdam soon after her arrival
and was an extremely valuable 15.5 carat 'round' cut diamond.*

*In 1899 another scandal hit the Ramsay family. This
caused the poorhouse to shut its doors and occurred
around the same time that the Ramsay family diamond
mysteriously disappeared.*

The scandal that took place in 1899 involved—

'Rona, Mrs Bell's idea was genius.' Craig sat down on the sofa
beside her. 'There was a really faint light at the back in the kitchen.
She must be in there with a torch. Want me to go round now?'

Rona looked up at the clock. 'Why don't we both go round first
thing?' She yawned. 'Let's go to bed, I'd no idea it was so late.'

Chapter 38

1899

'You've got to go and take that dress off right now, Effie.' Jessie was fighting the urge to scream; she had to remain calm. 'Do you have any other clothes in this house?'

Effie was staring at the bloodied body of Matron, her mouth wide open. She stepped aside and beckoned for Jessie to follow her. Together they walked round the body then out and along a dim corridor.

They entered a small room with a bed and wardrobe. Effie opened the wardrobe and pulled out a plain gown. She unbuttoned her dress with trembling fingers, shuffled it off then slipped on the other. Jessie buttoned it up then Effie handed her bloodied dress to Jessie who took it and held it at arm's length. 'Come and wash your hands, Effie. We've got to go back into the kitchen now and think what to do.'

In the kitchen, they twisted their heads away as they stepped around Matron's body. Effie washed her hands at the small sink. Jessie opened a drawer and took out a couple of kitchen knives. She held each one up, measuring them, then put one back. 'Do you know when the Governor usually comes back home?'

'On one of his nights down at Leith – late.' Effie was drying her hands, which were still shaking, on a cloth. 'He'll be in a drunken stupor when he returns. He always goes straight to bed with all his clothes on.'

Jessie bent over Matron's body with the kitchen knife. She screwed her face up in disgust as she inserted the knife into one of the deepest gashes in Matron's dress where blood was flowing. You're gutting a herring, Jessie, that's all, she told herself, trying to steel herself against the horror. She turned her head away as she twisted the handle, then removed the knife, now daubed with blood.

Jessie then went out into the corridor and laid the knife on the floor just beneath the gas lamp. She lifted her smock up, wiped the handle all over and then went to the front door and looked back. Yes, it was visible from there. Surely he would pick it up.

For the first time, Jessie looked down at her own clothes. Her dress was black all over, covered in soot and coal dust. There was soot on the floor. There was no time for her to change. She ran and fetched a broom at the back door and began to sweep.

Effie was standing, immobile, gazing down at the blood that had seeped into stagnant puddles around her sister's body.

Jessie put the broom back and came to stand beside her.

'Effie, this is what we need to do.' Effie scratched her fingernails on the wooden table. 'I will go down the tunnel to Newhaven with the gutting knife. I'll get rid of it down there and I'll take your dress too. I'll think about what to do with that.'

Effie's face was pinched as she swivelled her head from side to side. 'But Winzie, they're going to blame you. If you run off, they'll blame you. They'll come and find you.'

'I'll come back. I'll come back tonight and get into bed and then I'll say I know nothing. You can go back down to the cellar or into bed here. When the Governor comes back, he's bound to pick up the knife. Then he'll get the blame.'

Effie nodded.

'Is that what you want?'

Effie nodded again. 'He laughed when she killed my baby.'

'If you're asked what happened, say you have no idea, you were down in the cellar. But then you might be asked if it was possible he could have killed his sister in a rage and you could say he was drunk.'

'Drunk. Yes, yes, he's often intoxicated. He used to hit me when I scratched his walls after he had been drinking. No one else would see, only Bella and I knew. Yes, Andrew will be inebriated.' Effie screwed up her face. 'Will everything be in order, Winzie?'

'I don't know, but it's all we can do. I'm going back down the tunnel now and I'll be back to bed before he gets home. Are you going to be all right, Effie?'

Effie nodded then looked up, her eyes narrow. 'She deserves it. They both do. They killed my baby. We loved each other you know, Paul and I. He was the most wonderful artist; he taught me so much. He had to go back to France when they found out about the baby.' She began to scratch up and down her dress. 'I often wonder what happened to him.'

There was the booming noise of a foghorn again and Jessie headed for the coal cellar. She wrapped the gutting knife in the bloodied dress and bent down as she came to the little door. 'Go now, Effie, back to the pram in the big cellar. Stay down there. And shut this door behind me.'

Jessie cowered down to go through the little door then as she clambered over the coals and into the pitch black of the tunnel, she could hear the key turning in the lock. She held out her hand with the knife wrapped in the dress, like an unlit torch, all the while wondering if the curse would ever leave her.

Chapter 39

1982

Rona and Craig shut the door to Wardie House and headed round the corner towards the lodge house. Donnie the postman was coming out of Martha's gate carrying a parcel.

'Good job I saw you. Could you take this in for Miss Sinclair please? There's no one answering her door.'

Craig reached out to take the parcel. 'No problem. I know you've not been on this round too long, Donnie, but do you know if Miss Janet McCallister's been getting post at the lodge house too?'

Donnie moved his glasses up his nose and peered at them through thick lenses. 'Yes, but not often. Why?'

'It's just that no one's seen anyone else living in the lodge house. Just Martha.' Rona smiled in encouragement.

'Oh, I saw them both. But just the once. It was really foggy, I could hardly see the end of my nose. I was on the afternoon post and was popping a letter through the box just as the door was opening. I saw Miss Sinclair beside a wheelchair with an old lady in it. As soon as she saw it was me, she pushed the wheelchair to one side, grabbed the letter from me then slammed the door in my face.'

'So that was the only time?' Rona continued.

'Yes and the next time I had something for her, Miss Sinclair opened the door to me by herself and she apologised. She was so sweet, said how her aunt was staying with her and she wasn't feeling well. She was worried she'd catch a cold in the thick fog. She was really nice about it, ran off to get me some delicious little chocolate cakes to take away with me. Brownies, I think she called them. My oh my, they were delicious. Doreen and I really enjoyed them. An American recipe, she said it was.' Donnie looked at his watch. 'Must be getting on, I've got to meet the van driver for the afternoon deliveries. He's always telling me I'm late. Bye, then.'

They walked along the path to Martha's house. Rona pulled Craig's sleeve and whispered, 'So presumably she won't answer the door. What are you going to do?'

'Let's just wait and see.'

⚜

They placed the parcel on the mat, then knocked on the door and rang the bell. As anticipated, there was no reply.

'Did you go round the back before?' Craig asked.

'Yes and you can't see a thing, all the curtains are drawn.' Rona followed Craig around the back and watched him hammer on the door. He went over to the bin in the garden and looked in. It was full of bin bags. 'Looks like she didn't put the bin out yesterday.'

'She's obviously not inside, she'd have answered. Let's go.'

'Rona, I'm positive she's in there but not answering. Where else could she have gone?'

Craig gestured for them to go round the front of the house again and bent down close to Rona. 'Go and open and shut the gate then come back here quickly,' he muttered. Once she had returned, he whispered, 'You watch the front windows, I'm going to watch the back ones.'

They both stared at the windows with their fully drawn curtains until, just as Craig predicted, there was a flicker of movement from one at the back.

Craig bounded over to hammer on the door again. 'Martha, open the door! We need to speak to you.' Rona joined him round the back. Craig hammered again on the door. 'I know you're in there, Martha. Open the door or I'll have to call the police.'

Slowly the door creaked open and Martha stood there in a towelling dressing gown, pale and without a scrap of make-up, her hair lank and unkempt. She seemed to have aged ten years in the intervening two days since the fire.

'Are you okay, Martha?' Rona whispered.

'Not really. I've been ill since the fire and everything still stinks of smoke inside and my asthma is back and ...'

'Then open the windows, for God's sake, let in the air,' shouted Craig as he forced the door wide open and pushed past her. He leant over the sink, yanked the curtains back and unlocked the window, opening it wide. Rona stood at the kitchen door. The dingy kitchen obviously had not been changed since the 1950s. Only the cooker looked relatively new. Craig unclasped another window lock and pushed the pane wide.

Rona turned her focus to Martha, who had taken a seat at the small table. Martha looked up through the mat of uncombed hair. 'Sorry. I know you'd come to see me but look at me, I couldn't answer the door like this.'

'It's all right, Martha,' Rona said, patting her shoulder. She must be really ill, Rona thought, as Martha started to snivel.

'Yes, you could have answered the door. And you could have answered the phone,' Craig yelled. 'Were you not even interested in what had happened to Janet McCallister?'

'I saw you two and Ian wheel her into Wardie House, so I knew she'd be all right.'

'That was two days ago, why the hell have you not made contact?'

Martha shook her head. 'I couldn't, I just couldn't, I didn't feel up to it.' Her eyes filled with tears.

Craig opened his mouth to speak but Rona held up her hand.

'Martha, you're obviously not well. And this place still stinks of smoke, it can't be healthy for you.'

Craig went out into the corridor. 'I'll go round and open all the windows. You need to air the house, for God's sake.'

'Martha, d'you want to come and stay with us for a night or two? Just till you get better?' Rona felt sorry for the woman before her, a shadow of her former confident self. 'I'm sure it'd help Janet's recovery too.'

'What's she been saying?'

'Nothing, that's the trouble, she won't speak. But perhaps if you came to see her, you could get some more out of her? And, in fact, could you get some of her clothes and things from her bedroom?'

Martha nodded. 'All right, I'll shove some stuff in a bag. And then I'll come to Wardie House for a couple of nights. I'll be able to sleep in clean, fresh air.' She stood up and glanced in a tiny mirror on the wall behind. 'Give me half an hour though, guys. I look 100 years old.'

Chapter 40

1899

Molly sat at the kitchen table, wringing her hands. 'How could this have happened, Jessie? How? I just don't understand why he would have killed her. And in such a horrible way.' Molly wiped her nose on the back of her sleeve. 'I mean, I know he was a drinker – his room always smelt like an inn – and he had his rages, but this!'

Jessie bit her lip and sat up straight. All morning the police had been asking them questions. The conclusion – according to two constables she overheard speaking – was that Andrew Ramsay, that philandering gentleman who had lost his business through bankruptcy then supposedly mended his ways by running a charitable institution, had stabbed his sister in the lodge house after coming home at midnight drunk and smelling of the cheap perfume from the whores down at the docks.

It was Annie Rae who had found the Governor staggering around downstairs in the main house. She had sneaked down to the kitchen to get a drink of water and had come across him, dishevelled and confused and with a bloodied knife in his hand. He had mumbled to her to go and get one of the men to fetch the police. He had told her that he had just killed Matron.

Jessie had followed all the others rushing downstairs on hearing Annie Rae shouting for help. Jessie had caught sight of Effie emerging from the cellar door and she nodded at her. Effie had given her a nod back then headed in the other direction as Jessie followed the line of inmates wanting to catch sight of the Governor on his knees in the corridor, weeping over the bloody knife in his hand, just as Annie Rae had described to them all upstairs. But the Governor was now nowhere to be seen.

While they had waited for the police, two of the men had gone to the lodge house but found it locked. No one knew where to find a key and so they all had to wait, the inmates standing around in their nightclothes, shivering, not knowing what to do. Jessie had caught Effie's eye again but they'd both kept their heads low.

When the police had eventually arrived and forced open the door to the lodge house, it was a sorry sight. There was Matron lying on the kitchen floor, drenched in her own blood. In his bedroom, was the Governor, hanging from a rope attached to a hook in the ceiling.

'What will happen to us all, d'you think, Molly?' Jessie asked the cook, who sat, her large body rigid, clasping and unclasping her hands.

'Who can say? It's all too much to take in. He must have come home drunk then took a knife and stabbed her. Stabbed his own sister! He deserved to die. He deserved to hang by the neck.' She grimaced. 'I know he had rages, we heard him often enough in the dining hall. Well, that was nothing compared to when he's been drinking, at night, when he thought there was no one to hear him. I told the policeman that. Matron had to put up with a lot and try to keep it under control, but … she didn't deserve that.'

There was a knock on the door and Effie came in, her dress from the night before all rumpled and crushed.

'Effie, come here. Are you all right?' Molly held out her arms and pulled Effie in towards her.

'Fine, Molly, thank you for your concern.' Effie stood rigid, not responding to the embrace.

'Where were you last night? Were you down in the cellar with the pram?'

Effie nodded and briefly caught Jessie's eye.

'Is there any cake left, Molly?'

'Yes, there is. Now just you sit down and I'll away and get it.' Molly bustled off into the larder.

Jessie leant over to Effie. 'Where did you go? I came to see you in the cellar when I came back in.'

'Asleep, I was asleep in my bed in the lodge house with the door locked in case he came in. It was the first time I've slept in years and even though it was only perhaps two hours, it was good. Then I heard the police trying to get in through the front door so I left by the back door and joined you all inside. Even now, I feel strangely well.' Effie yawned.

'Here you go,' said Molly, putting a large slice of Madeira cake in front of Effie. She put another plate with a slice cut in two on the table. 'Jessie, you and I can share this one. We've all had such a shock.'

✳

Jessie was stirring a large pot of broth for supper. Molly had gone to lie down; she said she had to go for a sleep, her head was about to burst. The broth had been handed in earlier by two ladies from Wardie Kirk. News had spread all round the area about the deaths and the church ladies had got together that morning to bring soup for the inmates.

'What else could we do? These poor people need some sustenance,' they had said when Molly and Jessie helped their servants bring the vast pot into the kitchen. It was strange to see two ladies all dressed in their finery, in the dingy poorhouse kitchen. Jessie stared at their hats, one with large green bows, the other with high black feathers. One of them wore dainty lilac gloves that looked so soft, Jessie had the urge to go over and touch them, feel the silky softness. One lady had a short, high-necked jacket with tiny silver buttons all down the front of her ample bosom. The other had a long fawn cloak made of something soft and thick. Molly had said afterwards it was called velvet.

Jessie put in a spoon and tasted the broth. It was so hot, it nearly burnt her tongue, but how good it was! Instead of tasting watery and of little else but onion, this was rich and fatty with meat and bulging with barley and vegetables. The inmates would not believe their luck.

Jessie struggled through to the dining hall with the pan then went to ring the bell. Soon, everyone shuffled in, looking crestfallen, even Annie Rae, whose usual smug, sly expression had gone. They were all stunned. Of course, everyone had loathed both Matron and the Governor, but for this to happen?

'What's to become of us now?' they asked, as Jessie ladled the broth into their bowls. Jessie shrugged and continued serving up.

Instead of the usual miserable expressions everyone assumed while eating, looks of elation lit up their faces as they began to sup. They hadn't had to do any work that morning and now this soup both smelled and tasted like nectar. They gobbled it down. Two of the boys came up to ask if there was any more. Jessie ladled out some for herself and some for Molly, for later, and then said, 'Yes, hand me your bowl.'

Chapter 41

1982

Betty Chalmers was in the office showing Rona the little boot-ees she was knitting for the baby. They were yellow, which would suit either a boy or a girl, she'd said. 'I couldn't let Mrs Bell be the only one knitting for the new arrival!' Carly, her new carer, stood behind her, hands on the wheelchair handles, waiting patiently. 'By the way, Rona, I was looking at that portrait you have out in the hall. I see the woman has a diamond between her gloves.'

'I always thought it might be a diamond, but Mrs Bell said it might be an opal or just a trick of the light.'

'What does she know? My husband's family was in the jewellery business. That looks to me like a large diamond, a real one, I'm sure. If, as we discussed some time ago, Rona, the portrait is from the 1870s, then that was when paste jewellery was coming into its prime as they simulated the real thing. That's why they were called diamantés.'

'Oh, of course,' said Rona, glancing at the pile of paperwork on her desk.

'But no, I'm sure that's a genuine diamond. The people in this house would have known the difference. People of standing would only have true diamonds. Well, I must be getting on. Wheel me back to my room, Carly, there's a good girl.'

Betty Chalmers had just left when Ian stormed into the office.

'Rona, sorry to bother you, but Fay just said Martha's getting Mr

Wilson's old room for a couple of days. Is that true?'

'Yes, Ian. It was my idea. Mr Wilson's far happier downstairs. Whatever Martha's done or not done with regards to Jessie, she's the one who might be able to get her to speak.'

'But look at how she kept her in the lodge house – locked in the room, unable to get out herself if there was a fire! Shocking.'

Rona sighed. 'We're going in to see her soon. We'll find out what's been going on. Give her a bit of leeway. She's been ill since the fire.'

'Ill, my foot. It's all an act. She's an actress playing whatever role she fancies.'

Rona picked up a letter from the pile on her desk. 'Ian, we'll speak later about Martha and Jessie. But I also wanted to say I've had your reference in at last.'

Ian froze. 'Is it okay?'

Rona nodded. 'What was the problem of getting it before now?'

Ian shrugged. 'Sorry, Rona, I just really wanted this job and so I had to leave the gardening one pretty swiftly. I'd had some health issues. I didn't know how they'd be.'

'All seems good on paper.' Rona looked up at the clock. 'Right, got to get along and speak to Martha in Room 9 now. Have you seen Craig lately?'

'Dining room, helping them clear away after lunch.'

'Okay.' Rona smiled. At last Craig was taking on extra chores without being asked. 'Oh, is it this afternoon you're off for a couple of days?'

'Yes. I'll be leaving in half an hour, back first thing Sunday morning.' Ian turned to go. 'By the way, I've hidden Mr Burnside's photo at the back of one of his drawers. I don't think it's a good idea he keeps looking at a picture of a dead baby.'

'Thanks. Obviously neither do I.'

Rona laid her hand on her belly. She hadn't felt the baby move for a while, at least two days, maybe more. She had begun to worry, but when she'd phoned a friend from antenatal class, she had said there was far less room for the baby to move about now and it was normal to feel less action, certainly not every day. Still, if Rona hadn't felt movement by tomorrow, she was going to see the midwife.

✕

Craig and Rona headed up the stairs to Room 9. They had discussed what to say and Craig had agreed not to be aggressive. Rona would do most of the talking. Like Ian, Craig was still furious with Martha for apparently locking the old woman in her room so she couldn't get out. But Rona said that was not to be the first thing they asked about. Rona had popped along to see Jessie earlier and she seemed content, more so now that her drawers at least contained some of her own sweaters, nighties and underwear. She was still not speaking, however. Presumably she had no idea that Martha was in the next room to hers.

Rona tapped on the door; she and Craig walked in.

Martha sat at the window, hair perfectly coiffed once more, but still looking haggard.

'How are you doing, Martha? Did you have a sleep?'

'Yes, thanks, I slept before lunch. My chest seems to be rather better.' She coughed feebly.

Rona sat on the chair beside her. 'As you know, Martha, we had to get the doctor to check Jessie is okay. She can only give out medical information to you as you are her guardian. There are many things we'd like to ask you, but most importantly, why did you not tell us you were legal guardian to a ninety-seven-year-old woman and that she lived with you at the lodge house?'

Martha took a deep breath. 'I never really thought it was relevant. I mean, I know you guys decided to open this care home for old folk and I had an old person in my care, but I still kind of thought it was my business. No one else's.' She swallowed. 'Remember that day, Rona, you were asking me if I was Canadian or American and I said there was a difference but no one in this country gets it? Well, Canadians, unlike Americans, don't care to share every detail of our lives.'

Rona shot a look at her husband. 'I see. But since we're now looking after Jessie, I feel we have a right to know who she is. Why are you her legal guardian?'

'Great aunt, she's my great aunt and I wanted a job over here so I volunteered to come take care of her. Easy as that.'

'Except it's not that easy, is it? That doesn't explain why you kept her a secret from everyone. She seems pretty well cared for, but there seems no reason why she can't speak, apart from the fact the doctor thinks she might be suffering from shock after the fire. We're hoping she'll soon be able to tell us something about herself.'

'How are you actually related?' Craig frowned.

'My granny's sister. She's Granny's sister – they used to be fish-erlassies together down at Newhaven, then my granny went to Canada, but never returned to Scotland. I used to hear all about Great Aunt Jessie from her.'

'That's amazing,' said Rona. 'And the night of the fire? What actually happened that night?'

'Yes,' Craig leant towards Martha. 'How come you got out okay but she was stuck in her room – locked inside and in a wheel-chair?'

'I'd been out that evening and got back to find the fire started. I don't know how.' She looked down at her lap. 'The fire brigade said they don't know yet how it started.'

'Why would you lock an infirm, elderly lady in her room in an empty house? That's illegal.'

'I wasn't out for long, just getting something at the late night garage. It's safer for her.'

'Safer how?' Craig yelled. 'We lock our residents' doors at night for their safety, but carers check on them regularly. You aban-doned her.'

'Look, can I see her?'

'Of course,' Rona said. 'But one of us has to be with you. We'll bring her in to you. We'll go and get her right now.'

Craig stood up and Rona followed him to the door. 'Don't be too quick,' she whispered. 'We don't want her to know Jessie's right next door.'

Craig nodded and strode along the corridor in one direction before turning back on himself.

✕

Craig wheeled Janet McCallister into Martha's room. Rona watched the old woman's face. She was still pale, but she had a little more colour in her cheeks than she had when she arrived. As usual, she had a scarf high around her neck and she raised this over her mouth with one hand. She looked at Rona, not making any eye contact with Martha at all.

'Jessie, come on in, Martha's keen to have a chat.' Rona watched as Jessie fixed her gaze on Martha, her expression unchanging.

'Hi, Jessie. I heard you were doing okay, so I stayed put as I got my asthma back after the fire.' Martha shuffled in her seat. 'They treating you well in here, then?'

The old woman nodded and continued to stare.

'Good. Then that's all fine and dandy. I'm here resting for a day or two then I'll be back in the lodge house and you can come and join me there.'

Jessie shook her head.

'You don't want to come back there with me? I'll make those soups and stews you like. And I'll do some oatmeal herring?' Martha attempted a smile but it came out as a grimace, her scarlet lipstick now clownlike on her pale face.

Craig opened his mouth to speak but Rona held up her finger. 'Jessie, is there anything you'd like to say to Martha while we're here? Would you like to write anything down?'

Jessie nodded and let the scarf fall from around her mouth to reveal her mole. It was difficult not to stare at it, it was so large. She must have gone through life with people gaping.

'Craig, can you nip next door and get the pencil and notepad in Jessie's room?' Rona kicked herself; why had she let slip where Jessie's room was?

Craig arrived back and handed the pencil and pad to Jessie. All three of them watched as Jessie picked up the pencil with a shaky hand and wrote in spidery writing. She handed the notepad to Rona and returned her gaze to Martha. It read, 'You will never find my diamond. And you will never live in the lodge house again.'

Chapter 42

1900

Jessie sat on the harbour wall at daybreak, looking out to sea, watching the water ripple into gentle waves. It was low tide so some of the boats at the southern end of the harbour were sitting in heavy silt. Within the hour, water would flood into the harbour and float all the boats.

Jessie breathed deeply. It was good to feel the salt of the sea spray on her skin and the breeze ruffle her hair. She couldn't linger; she had much to do. She had to fill the creel then lug it up onto her back and start the long day, hawking her wares round the big houses.

The previous week, on her way home from Inverleith, she had passed Laverockbank Road and diverted along the road to see Wardie House. The new owners were making many changes, presumably converting it back into the grand house it had been before it was a poorhouse. It was odd to see the gates open and the bars on the windows dismantled. She hoped it would be a happy house for the young English family who had bought it. Presumably they knew what it was before, everyone did. But only Effie and Jessie knew the whole truth.

Jessie had decided to go and ring the doorbell of the lodge house that day as she had heard that Effie now lived there by herself. Jessie had been nervous when she pulled the bell, wondering whether to take off the tall basket of fish from her back. But when the door had opened and Molly stood there, Jessie had been reassured. Molly had become Effie's housekeeper since the poorhouse closed, though she insisted on continuing to live in Granton. Just as she had done when she worked at the poorhouse, Molly refused to sleep there.

There was now a high stone wall between the main house and the lodge house to give the new inhabitants of Wardie House privacy. Jessie had told Effie she didn't want to dirty the furniture, so suggested they sit in the kitchen for tea. 'I stink of fish,' Jessie had insisted, hauling the creel off her back and dumping it in a corner of the kitchen. As she'd headed for a chair, she remembered the last time she had been in this room, a night she would never forget. Then Jessie had sat at the table while Effie told her what had happened since then.

Effie had been left Wardie Lodge House, but there was no money remaining in the estate. The money the Ramsays had hoped to recoup from running the poorhouse, to help compensate for the disastrous loss of the jewellery business, had come to nothing. The meagre funds they had from the parish and city council had been frittered away by Andrew's increasingly frequent sorties to Leith.

The sole asset left to Effie, as the remaining Ramsay family member, was the lodge house, although Jessie presumed Effie still had the diamond, the one Matron had wanted. She had plucked up courage that afternoon to tell Effie she'd given Bertha the diamond she found tucked into the baby's bootee on the shelf high up in the coal cellar to use for her passage to Canada. Effie had looked more curious than cross. 'I'd wondered what had happened to that stone. But I still have the big one. I'll show you one day.'

Effie had told Jessie over tea how Isabella had been their father's favourite and so she was given the big diamond. Effie was given nothing; her father had never stopped resenting his third child, whose birth had resulted in the death of the love of his life.

Now that Effie slept at night in her bed and didn't wander the corridors pushing a pram, she had seemed to Jessie to be better, though she was still scratching at the wooden table with her long fingernails. One remarkable difference was her hair. Instead of being pulled back into a tight plait, it was loose around her shoulders, long and straggly. While Molly had fussed about in the kitchen getting a tea tray ready, Effie had shown Jessie the rest of the house, stopping to point out her portrait which hung in the hall. 'Look, Winzie! My hair's over my shoulders now, just the way Paul liked it.' Jessie had smiled but as she looked from the painting to Effie she saw not the luscious thick chestnut hair of the eighteen year old in the portrait, but the thinning grey hair of a forty-five year old. She had seen not the clear, unblemished complexion of youth, but the red-veined, wrinkled skin of an old woman.

Effie had shown Jessie into her bedroom where her eyes had been drawn to a small inlaid jewellery box in polished wood. Beside it, on the bedside table, the photograph of Effie's baby was now in a little silver frame. She had brought it back into the kitchen and Jessie had taken it politely, noticing that it was rather crumpled under the glass, still creased from Bella's angry hand that night. Jessie had had several months to consider that photo and so, when Molly had gone off to look for some jam in the larder, she had asked, 'Why d'you think they took a photograph of the baby if they were about to give her away?'

Effie had touched the silver frame and checked Molly was not listening. 'They wanted to make it look as though she had died.'

'Why?' Jessie had screwed up her face.

'Most people of our standing have a photograph taken if the infant dies. That is why these flowers are laid on her shawl. But I heard her cry, I definitely did. I know she was alive when she was born, but Bella took her and smothered her. Andrew helped her. You heard her say that. It was the truth.'

Effie had had a crazed look in her eyes and Jessie had patted her scrawny arm but could think of nothing to say as she watched Effie place the frame in the middle of the table then rock back and forth, staring at it.

Jessie had left, promising to visit Effie the following week.

And now here Jessie sat, dangling her legs over the side of the harbour wall, above the lobster pots stacked up against the stone. She jumped down and walked along to the lamppost, remembering when she had left Bertha here all those months ago. She went up the narrow wynd towards the little cottage which she shared once more with Dorrie and her mother. Ma hadn't needed much persuasion from Dorrie to accept Jessie back into the house. She had become even more pleased when Jessie showed her the gold brooch from Effie's jewellery box. It was a gift, but her mother had insisted on pawning it immediately. She was delighted with the prospect of her daughter being friendly with a wealthy woman. 'See if you can get something else from the mad old crone.'

'Effie is not mad,' Jessie had protested. 'And she's not rich, Ma. You know all she's got is the lodge house. All the family money went on the burials.' Her mother had disagreed, insisting that once rich, was always rich.

Effie had to be chief mourner at her sister's funeral and she told Jessie that she had stood at the end of the grave smiling under her black veil, for she was so happy that her sister, her baby's murderer, was dead. If only the little one could have been given a true Christian burial, Effie had said. She had no idea what they had done with her tiny body. As for Andrew, that was a different matter. The Church normally refused to bury someone who had taken his own life as he had; he was also an unconvicted murderer. But the minister at Wardie Church had made an exception and agreed that he could be buried, not in the same plot as his sister at Comely Bank cemetery but just outside the cemetery gates, by the wall. On the other side of the wall were crossroads, which, Effie had said, was appropriate, given the old custom was to bury people who took their own life beside crossroads.

There had been several constables in Newhaven asking questions about the murder too. It had been suggested, soon after the Governor had been buried, that in fact it was not he who had murdered his sister, but an intruder. The police had noticed a couple of sooty footprints on the kitchen floor and traced them down into the coal cellar, but because the coal man had just tipped a new bag of coal in and the coal reached up to the ceiling, their investigation had been put on hold. It was presumed the coal cellar was just that; there had never been any suggestion that it led to a smugglers' tunnel. They soon gave up asking the fisherfolk about what they had been doing on the night of the murder. Besides, if he was not guilty, why would the Governor have taken his own life on that dreadful night?

That was the night that, once she had managed to clamber her way over the coal, Jessie had headed down the tunnel in the pitch black. Once out at the beach, she had run straight to the harbour, lowered herself down the slippy ladder and onto a rowing boat then rowed out into the Forth. It was foggy but she knew which direction to row. She had stopped after a few minutes, resting the oars on her legs, then leant over the side to wash the blood off the dress in the water. Then she had ripped the material into shreds with the knife and finally flung the knife far out into the deep water where it would have sunk into the sandy sea bed of the Firth of Forth.

Once back at the harbour, she had run along the harbourside towards Evelyn Peddie's house. Outside her cottage was a basket of rags, cut into strips, for the fisherlassies to tie up their fingers each morning before they started on the gutting. She had lifted the wicker lid and thrown them in. It had been funny to think that her friends, and maybe even her sister, would be wrapping bits of Effie's dress round their fingers the next day to protect them from their gutting knives.

And now, as she walked along the harbour towards her own cottage at dawn, Jessie looked down at her bare feet and thanked God she had big feet for a lassie. If the police had thought at any time it might have been a woman's sooty footsteps, perhaps the blame would have shifted to her, but that had never even been considered.

Effie had been assessed by the doctor as sane enough to inherit. Molly had tidied her up before the doctor's visit and insisted on cutting her nails, though she had let them grow since. She had put up Effie's hair too and dressed her in her finest gown. Molly had whispered to Jessie at the door that she was still 'no' quite right', but could at least attempt a veneer of normality now she was sleeping again.

Jessie looked up at the squawking gulls above, then pushed open the cottage door. Expecting there to be silence, she was surprised to hear voices. Now that she was living back home, Dorrie usually got up a little later, teasing Jessie that if she wanted to be best maid at her wedding the following month, she had to be the one to get up first and make the fire.

Jessie walked into the main room and noticed the bed Dorrie and she shared was empty. She looked towards the fire and saw a sailor sitting on the stool, warming his hands while Dorrie filled a kettle of water.

'At last, Jessie. I wondered where you'd got to. This man's come to see you.'

The sailor stood up and delved into the pockets of his navy-blue trousers. 'I've just come off the ship from Halifax. My cousin said to bring this to you.'

Jessie took the letter and opened it. She skimmed down to the bottom. She smiled. 'It's from Bertha, Dorrie! Look at her terrible handwriting!'

Jessie sat down and read it out aloud.

> *Dear Jessie,*
>   *I hope this finds you well. I have some news. My baby boy was born on 16 August 1899 and he is bonny and healthy. I am a mother, Jessie. Can you believe it?*

'Bertha's got a wee boy, Dorrie, isn't that grand?' Jessie said, laughing.

*His name is Peter Mack Smith. The Mack is after you
and the Smith is my husband's name. I met Peter Smith
on the ship and we married when we landed in Canada.
I am happy to be safely here and to have a husband and a
bairn. And all because of you.*

*Jessie, I don't know why, but I was given back the
bootee on board ship by the captain who was an angry
man. He was always very mean to me. He flung it at me
one day and called me a terrible name I will not write
down. I have no idea why he would give me back a precious thing like that, but he did and I thought you should
have it back. Thank you, Jessie Mack.*

From your good friend,
*　Bertha*

'There's this wee thing too,' the sailor said, delving once more
into his pockets. He handed Jessie a small cloth bag with a drawstring which Jessie untied. Thrusting in her hand, Jessie pulled
out a little baby's bootee. She poked her fingers inside and gasped.
She'd be heading up to Wardie Lodge House as soon as possible
with a gift for Effie.

Chapter 43

1982

'So did you get a video?'

'No, sorry, darling, the video shop was shut.'

'How come?'

Craig shrugged. 'Shut on a Monday night.'

Rona lifted her feet from the coffee table and stretched over to pick up a newspaper. 'Oh well, I'll read the paper instead. Mrs Bell gave me her copy of *The Scotsman*.'

Rona flicked through several headlines until she came to one which said, 'Cat predicts deaths in nursing home.' She read the story about an old folks' home in Lerwick where the resident cat had the habit of going to lie on a resident's bed the night before they died. It described how the tabby, Vaila, would enter the room of a patient, stretch out on the bed beside the elderly person and go to sleep. Either that night or the following morning, the person died. One of the night nurses said she had taken to following Vaila up the stairs and watching the cat stop at the top as if assessing which direction to take. Vaila would slink along to a door, push her way in with her nose and settle down on the bed. Over a couple of years, Nurse Johnson said, the cat had predicted twenty-three deaths. Though there were two other cats in the home, neither of those had ever displayed a similar ability. 'We are now wondering whether to alert the families when Vaila goes to sleep on a patient's bed,' she said.

Rona shivered and flicked onto the next page. There was a
photo of a long kitchen knife which had been plunged into the
neck of a woman lying in a hospital bed in Toronto by the patient
in the next bed. She flung the paper onto the table.

'Nothing but horrible news. Look at that knife.' She pointed at
the newspaper. 'And thank God we never got a cat.'

Rona gasped.

'What is it?' Craig rushed over.

She smiled as she took his hand and laid it on her belly. 'The
baby obviously loves horror stories. It's just done a couple of massive kicks. It's so good to feel it move again. First time in ages.' She
reached up and gave Craig a kiss.

Rona sat back, then frowned. 'Craig, can you nip upstairs and
check on Martha's room, please? I don't trust her. I know she's not
well but ...'

'Don't be daft. What, you think she's going to murder someone
with a kitchen knife?'

'Please, just check?'

Craig sighed and headed for the door.

✳

Rona was sitting up in bed reading Mr Bell's history file when
Craig came back in. 'Wait till you find out what happened in
Wardie House in 1899.'

Craig came to sit beside her on the bed.

'Everything all right next door?'

'Yes, I spoke to Fay. All's quiet. She's done the medicine trolley,
lights out any minute.'

'But did you check Martha's room?'

'I can't just wander into her room without an excuse. Fay said
everyone was in bed and ready for sleep. Now, what were you
going to tell me?'

'Remember the house was converted into a poorhouse in the

1870s? Well, in 1899 the matron was killed by her brother who was the governor. They were the Ramsays who used to live in Wardie House. And the younger sister inherited the lodge house when the main house had to be sold again.'

'This place has had a bit of a dodgy history, hasn't it? Is that why you reckon some of our residents could be crazed madmen and women intent on murder?'

'Those newspaper articles didn't help. And I was remembering when Martha tried to persuade me to get a cat; she reckoned it would be good for the residents. Actually, maybe it was a dog.' Rona pushed the pillow up her back, wiggling into it to try to find a comfortable position. 'The sooner we get rid of her the better. Also, I've been thinking about Jessie. How can we keep her here? A few days are okay, but with no one paying her fees it could become tricky. We've still got that loan to pay off. We're not a charity. Sorry, that sounds mean. I'd love her to stay, but ...'

'You think too much. You should be having calm, gentle thoughts that are good for our baby.' Craig pulled back the duvet and placed his hand on Rona's belly.

'Craig, just one final thing.' Rona was frowning.

'What are you worrying about now?'

'It's something I'm not worried about any more.'

'What's that?'

'You.'

'Me?' Craig looked uncomfortable.

'You're back to how you were before we moved in here. Not all edgy and ... selfish.' Rona studied Craig's face carefully. 'You're not drinking at all now, are you?'

Craig took a breath. 'Been going to AA once a week for some time now.'

'What? You should have told me.'

'I didn't want to tell you in case I couldn't keep it up. I've let you down before. It's been a struggle, with the worries of the new business and all the money we've spent, but, well, I've done it. And

Ian's been brilliant.'

'What's Ian got to do with it?'

'He's been my AA sponsor for the past six weeks. He helps me along. He did so well himself in recovery.'

'Why on earth did I not know this?'

Craig shrugged. 'No need, darling. He's been there when I needed to talk. He's been brilliant to have around.'

Rona leant back against the pillow. 'Now that kind of makes sense. The alcoholism must've been the health issues he referred to when there were problems with his references.'

Craig stroked his wife's cheek. 'Main thing is, Rona, I'm doing fine. I'm determined to keep on track. This baby will have two responsible parents, don't worry.'

Part 4

Chapter 44

1978

Dear Miss Mack,

I am writing from Saskatoon, Canada. My family used to live in Halifax then moved out here to the Prairies where I was born.

I was given your address by my grandmother, Bertha Smith, who sadly passed away last year in her home in downtown Halifax. The reason I am writing is that I think you knew her well when you were young. Her son, Peter, was my father and though he too has passed away, I have heard stories about Bertha from my mother, Meg Smith.

I don't know if you kept up with Bertha at all, but from my memory (we didn't see them often – Halifax to Saskatoon is a five-day road trip) she was a sweet, kind old lady who cared very much for her family. She only had the one son, Peter, and he married my mother late – he was forty, she only twenty-five – but they were happy. He was a wheat farmer and was doing really well till his heart attack last year. Though Dad never spoke much about his mother, I got some stories from Mum, how you two lived in a place near Edinburgh called Newhaven and how you used to have to share a bed and have fun in that big house you both lived in. Mum wasn't sure why you were there. She thought you might have been servant girls in a wealthy family's house.

There is a classic story she told often about the family's diamond, and it was the smuggled diamond which helped Grandma Bertha get to Canada in the first place, but then the diamond was returned to Scotland. Mum said Grandma Bertha told her about that trip by sea, how Grandma felt so nervous, then she met my grandfather who was working his passage out there to stay with relatives from Scotland. She didn't even know where Canada was, but for some reason just wanted to get away and go somewhere new.

It would be wonderful to meet up with you. I presume you are at the lodge house still? If you are living by yourself, I hope you don't think it too brash if I propose something. We North Americans are a bit less formal than the Brits! I am trained as a chef but also did some nursing when I left high school. I've done lots of other things, including marry an unsuitable American, but that is over now. I wondered if you might need someone to take care of you now you are in your nineties? Sorry if that sounds rather forward. But I am keen to visit Scotland and would love to have some kind of job. Would you consider taking me on? I am free, job-wise, from January.

I look forward to hearing from you.

Yours sincerely,

Martha Sinclair

P.S. I make great stews and soups – and cakes are my speciality so I could take real good care of you!

※

Dear Mrs Sinclair,

How wonderful to think about Bertha after all these years. I was so sorry we did not keep in touch. But I have fond memories. I had heard, however, some news from someone who used to be with us in the big house you are talking about. She had met your grandmother about twenty years ago and I heard the sad news about your father going to prison. I had no idea Peter had a daughter, all of which makes it a delightful surprise that something good can come out of a tragedy that must have been so difficult to cope with.

The diamond story was in fact true. Isn't it a lovely tale? If it had not been for the diamond, your grandmother would never have been able to set sail across the Atlantic. I have many more stories I can share with you. I must admit, I do get a little lonely as my only relative, my sister Dorrie, died ten years ago and her family live in Northern Ireland which is impossible to visit these days because of The Troubles.

I am so delighted you are willing to make this long trip not only to see me but also to offer your services. To have some regular company would be good.

At the moment, I have a woman, Nora, who cleans and helps me around the house every couple of days, but this house, though not large, is a little too much for me. I am confined to a wheelchair for much of the day, though the doctor keeps telling me I must try to use my legs more. If not, I will lose the use of them completely. Perhaps you could help me to continue walking, round my small garden. Nora, sadly, has no time for that.

I find cooking a chore nowadays. I would, therefore,

relish the prospect of having someone stay with me for a while who can both cook and nurse. Shall we see how the arrangement works? Upon your arrival, we can discuss terms.

I look forward to hearing when in January you might arrive. I shall then give Nora notice that I shall not require her any more. She has been struggling to fit me in with her other commitments as grandmother of three little ones under four with a working mother, so I am sure that will suit her well.

Yours sincerely,

Jessie (Janet) McCallister

Chapter 45

1982

'How come Martha's still in Room 9, Rona?' Ian asked. 'I thought she was only here for a night while she got better?'

'It's all become a bit complicated. Martha will be leaving today or tomorrow, the lodge house is aired now and she looks a bit better ...'

'Sorry if this sounds out of place, but do you believe she really was ill?'

'She did look terrible when she came in. She looks better now, which is why she'll be going home.'

Rona wriggled in her chair. The baby was pressing down and she couldn't get comfortable.

'You all right?'

'Yes. The baby started kicking with a vengeance last night. I'd just been reading some horrific things in the paper – he or she's obviously sensitive.' Rona smiled and stroked her belly. 'Anyway. Jessie doesn't want Martha to stay in the lodge house any more. She's still not speaking much, but when she's alone with me, she'll say a little. She might speak to you too and ...' Rona frowned. 'Why are you looking like that?'

'Did you say Jessie? I thought the new lady was called Janet McCallister?'

'That's her real name, but she likes to be called Jessie. Why?'

Ian sank into the chair beside her.

'Remember I went to that family party at the weekend? I wanted to go for Mum as, even though her dementia's bad, I could tell her about it after, maybe spark something. It was her aunt and uncle's golden wedding. They all lived in Northern Ireland so came over to have a party here for long-lost relatives. Because of the situation in Ireland, Mum's never been over there.'

Rona glanced at the clock.

'Sorry, there is a point to this. When I told them I worked in a care home called Wardie House near Edinburgh, they said I should speak to my cousin John. Which I did. Turns out, his mum was someone called Dorrie who died about fifteen years ago. She was Jessie's sister.'

'Hang on, your cousin is Jessie's nephew ... so Jessie is your aunt?' Rona shook her head. 'I know you're from Newhaven, but it doesn't make sense – she's too old.'

'No, John is my second cousin, my mum's cousin. So Jessie's my second cousin once removed or forty-second cousin or something. Anyway, we're kind-of related. It must be her, surely. But ...'

'What?'

'This sounds terrible, but none of them mentioned the mole. I mean, you'd think they'd have known. It's so distinctive.'

'Maybe things like that weren't talked about. My great uncle had a hump back and we youngsters just accepted it as normal. He was just Uncle Murdo. It was only other people who would stare sometimes, which we thought was odd.'

'Suppose so. Of course, it isn't what defines her.'

Rona's shoulders stooped and she bent down a little. She couldn't find a comfortable position. 'Why don't you go up and see her? Ask all about these people?'

'Okay. I will. Wouldn't it be amazing if it was true?' Ian got up to go. 'Got to help Mr Burnside with his shaving then I'll see Janet. I mean, Jessie.'

Rona nodded.

'You sure you're all right, Rona? You're looking a bit pale.'

'Baby's just pressing down a bit. I'll be fine.'

※

Rona flicked on the lights in the cellar and walked down the steps, holding on to the handrail. They had had their pram delivered and put down here for safe keeping and she wanted to check its length. Her mum's friends in Stornoway were all busy knitting, one in particular making a pram blanket. She insisted that prams nowadays were far shorter than the huge prams of old. Her mum was horrified when Rona told her that she and Craig had ordered the pram and cot in Mothercare and already had them delivered. 'It's bad luck,' she had said on the phone.

'We won't have time to go shopping when the baby's here,' Rona had replied.

'I'll be there to help you. Craig can go to Mothercare and buy it then. I tell you, it's bad luck to buy things for a baby before it arrives.'

Rona's mother didn't seem to realise that running a care home was not a nine-to-five job and that, even when the baby was here, they would both have to continue to work.

Rona walked over to the new pram covered with plastic sheets, wondering about the old-fashioned superstitions. What nonsense. The old traditions were just as daft. Like the Scottish tradition of Showing the Gifts. A bride had to invite all those who gave wedding presents round to her house, where they were entertained with tea and home-baking while rummaging nosily through the gifts. Rona's refusal to have a Gift Showing had not pleased her mother, who said that apart from the wedding it was to be the highlight of her Stornoway friends' social calendar. 'A nice thing for only us women to do. No men to bother us.'

Rona bent over to lift up the plastic sheets from the pram when she felt a sharp pain. She held on to the handle then let out a long breath. That was better. She began to lift off the plastic sheets, placing them on the stone floor beside her. She frowned as she looked at the pram handles. These didn't look like the ones they had seen in the shop. She lifted the last sheet off and gasped. It wasn't her pram, it was the old one, ancient and worn. Where was their brand new pram? And why was this one down here? The pram hood was up. Rona unclipped the hinges to push it down. She peered inside. On top of the little pillow that one of the nurses had given Mr Burnside was a photo. She stared in disbelief. It was the photo of Mr Burnside as a child with the dead baby.

Chapter 46

1979

'Martha, please can we try to walk one more time round the garden? It's so stuffy inside, I need some fresh air.'

'Jessie, I told you, you'll get sunstroke, it's too warm. Geez, if I knew Scotland was going to be as hot as Mexico, I'd have thought twice about coming.'

'I'd like to sit at the door then, please, and get some fresh air. I'm used to being outside, Martha. It's stifling in here.'

'I'll wheel you to the door, but no farther. It's not good for your chest.'

'My chest is perfectly fine, you know that.'

'Good,' said Martha, wheeling Jessie towards the back door. 'Now, have you had any more time to remember where that diamond might be buried?'

'I was sure it was over there in the far corner, but you tried that the last time, didn't you?'

'Yeah. I'm getting muscly arms with all that digging.'

'But you know you can't dig any more. The neighbours might see and wonder what on earth you are doing, when the garden is so unkempt.'

'Then I'll dig at night. They won't see or hear a thing.'

'I really would like you to employ a gardener for me. Please?'

'No, Jessie. It's something I like to do for you. You pay me well, so it's the least I can do. And thinking of neighbours, there are none that can see into the garden. I reckon only that small attic window in Wardie House overlooks.' She clicked on the wheelchair brakes. 'But just to be on the safe side, I'll dig in the dark.'

Martha spread out the tartan travelling rug over Jessie's knees. 'Remember we decided how nice it'd be to find that diamond in the jewellery box you and Effie buried for safekeeping years ago? Make you a wealthy woman.'

'Yes, of course I do. It's where I buried it that's the problem. My memory these days.' Jessie shook her head. 'It might even have been left somewhere in the big house. I just can't recall ...'

Martha smiled at Jessie. 'Have you managed to think of the name of your lawyer yet? Remember we thought it would be a good idea to give me power of attorney, in case you aren't able to get to the lawyer's office to sign stuff?'

'You can wheel me there, surely. Or actually, I'm sure they can come here to us, too?'

'Let's see about that. I had a look through the Yellow Pages. I know you said it was a Mac-something name, but there are about fifty frickin' Macs in there.'

'Martha, I wish you wouldn't swear. I keep telling you.'

'Listen to you. You'd think you were Euphemia Ramsay, not poor, common Jessie Mack from down the harbour at Newhaven.'

Martha sat down on the step beneath Jessie and together they looked out onto the grass, yellowed with many days of sun and drought.

'I remember one summer being out here with your grandmother. Though Bertha was meant to be inside sewing some sacks or shirts, Molly the cook asked her to help me in the garden with the rhubarb. She was terribly strong, your grandmother, so Molly said we could pull the rhubarb together. It was about this time of year and the rhubarb wasn't pink any more, it was greeny red. So Bertha pulled up the stalks with her powerful arms and handed them to me and I'd chop off the leaves and put the stalks in a basket for Molly to stew. It was meant to be good for us, but she was only allowed to put in a tiny amount of sugar, so it tasted horrible, so bitter.'

'There's some rhubarb left over there. I'll make a pie for dinner,' Martha said, yawning.

Jessie smiled. 'Anyway, this time, Billy Muir had stolen a little bowl of sugar from the Governor's tea tray when he was clearing the tea from his room. He came into the garden with it and the three of us sat down, over there near the rhubarb patch, cross-legged in a circle around this bowl. I chopped the dirty ends off three stalks of rhubarb and we dipped our stalks into the sugar bowl, one after the other. I can still taste the crunch of the sweet white sugar and the crispness of the sour rhubarb.' She shook her head. 'It was just wonderful. Especially since we were never caught.'

'I'm sure I remember Dad telling me that story whenever we had rhubarb.'

'I thought you said you and your mother never saw your father after he was put in prison? You were only three at the time, surely you can't have remembered?'

Martha stood up and went inside, shouting back to Jessie, 'He must've told Mum then. I'm going to put the kettle on for tea.'

Chapter 47

1982

Rona jumped back. The sight of the baby in that photo was horrific now she knew it was dead. But then another sharp pain made her double over. Pant – that's what she'd learnt to do in the antenatal classes when in pain. She puffed rhythmically then tried to stand up straight, easing the back of her hand against the base of her spine. Her lower back had been sore for a couple of days now; it must be that new chair in the office. Rona had asked Craig to order a comfortable one and he got an ergodynamic one that was unsuited to her body shape. She kept telling him that, though she wasn't very tall, she had a long back.

Rona grabbed the plastic sheets from the ground and flung them over the old pram, then hobbled over to the stairs. As she climbed the steps, holding on to the rail, she felt a little better. Good, nothing to worry about. Apart from trying to find where her new pram was. Where on earth could …? Oh no – another sharp pain, like really bad stomach cramps, but lower down.

It can't possibly be the baby, Rona thought, there's still two weeks to go. Craig was out at the cash and carry buying industrial quantities of tea, sugar and coffee for Wardie House. Rona looked at her watch. He'd only left about half an hour ago, he'd be at least another hour. She shut the door to the cellar and looked up at the portrait. The lady's expression was blank. Rona walked backwards across the corridor, checking that the eyes followed her. They did, and from the other side of the hall something seemed to flicker into life in the lady's face. It was oddly comforting to think she was being watched.

'Rona, are you all right?' Mrs Bell hobbled across the hall. 'Why are you holding your belly? Is the baby on its way?'

'Ow, ow.' Rona leant over and breathed out long and hard. 'Can you ask Fay to come, please?'

Mrs Bell stomped back across the hall, her stick thumping on the wooden boards. Rona went into the annexe and slumped down onto a chair at the kitchen table.

'Are you all right?' Fay rushed in and knelt down beside her, taking her hand. 'Is Craig around? If not, we'll drive you to Simpson's.'

'It's early though, Fay. Surely it can't be the baby already? I'm only thirty-eight weeks.' Rona's face pinched up in pain. 'Ow, ow.'

'Wait.' Fay ran out of the annexe and came back with one of the carers, the new girl, Tracey, from the ground floor. 'Sit with her while I go and try to get hold of Craig. If we can't, someone'll have to take her to hospital.'

'I'll drive her. I've got my car outside,' said Tracey. 'I passed my test a fortnight ago. I'd love to go fast like an ambulance through town.'

Rona writhed up in the chair and cried in agony as the next contraction came.

Tracey's eyes grew wide. 'Maybe it's best for Fay to drive you, Rona.'

⋊

'Everyone's asking for you at Wardie House. I've just phoned Fay and told her to pass on the good news.' Craig bent down and stroked his daughter's downy head. 'She's so beautiful. You did really well.'

'No I didn't. I was yelling for pain relief and then when you arrived I shouted at you like some mad old witch and …' Rona beamed. 'She is gorgeous, isn't she? Can't wait for Mum to see her.'

'She's got her bag packed, ready to come down the minute we say.'

'No point till we know when we can get home. You don't want her hanging around Wardie House.'

'So. Names. Did we decide for sure on Hannah?'

'I don't know, I like Joanna too. And what about a middle name?'

'We hadn't anticipated her arriving early, had we? No idea.' Craig kissed the top of Rona's head then glanced up at the clock. 'I'd better go, leave you to try and sleep. Do they wheel away her little cot or does she stay with you?'

'I don't know. I'd like her to stay so I can gaze at her all night.'

'Try to get some sleep. If they offer to take her into the nursery, then let them.'

Rona nodded. 'Oh, Craig, I've just remembered something really important. Someone's taken our brand new pram from the cellar and put that horrible old one in its place. Can you find out where it is, please?'

'Odd. I suppose it could've been Mr Burnside, but I don't see how he could have lifted the new one up those stairs. Don't worry though, love, I'll sort everything out for you.'

Chapter 48

1980

'Please can we go for a walk outside, Martha? It's my birthday and you promised we could do something nice.' Jessie pulled back a corner of the heavy curtain. 'Look, the sun's out.'

Martha yanked the curtain shut and stood in front of the wheelchair. 'We could maybe go round the block. You could see the new wrought iron gates on Wardie House. They're trying to convert it into a hotel, but how the hell that'd work beats me.' She shoved Jessie's chair towards the door. 'And by the way, you've got something nice for your birthday. Remember? I went down to that fishmonger and got herring fillets for your tea. Not that you deserve it.'

Martha threw a scarf at Jessie. 'Wrap this round you, there's a cold wind out there. 'Come on, hurry up if you want to catch a glimpse of this frickin' Scottish sun.'

Martha bumped Jessie's wheelchair down the steps, the old woman wincing with each thump, and headed along the path to their gate. 'Jessie, don't think we'll get you out much more. It's a nightmare getting the wheelchair up and down the steps.'

'What about one of those ramps you see in some places?'

'Our steps are too wide. Wouldn't work.'

'Could we just ask Rory the handyman when he comes next?'

'Nothing more for him to do now he's installed that shower for me in the bathroom. No, I reckon you'll just have to get used to being inside. Make the most of this walk, Jessie Mack.'

They walked round the corner to Wardie House and stopped at the gate. Jessie lowered the scarf at her neck and stretched forward to peer in. 'Oh, Martha, I remember the first day I arrived at Wardie House. I was only fourteen and had left Newhaven as a fisherlassie to come and work here. I was really nervous and the cook, Molly, was cross at first but she was fine once I got to know her. And then I met your grandmother and we shared a bed, well, a mattress in fact. We didn't even have a proper bed.'

'Yeah, you've told me all that before.'

'Bertha was a big girl so it was really nice to snuggle in beside her, she was always so warm. We only had one thin blanket between us. Sometimes when I move in bed at night, I feel she's there. Then sometimes I think it's Dorrie as she and I shared a bed for the first fourteen years of my life. I feel I'm sleeping with ghosts, but then I get sad and wake up. I missed Bertha, you know, when she left for Canada, but it wasn't long before the poorhouse was shut and —'

'Let's get you home now. Seen enough?'

'Please can you wheel me to the top of the road along there? So I can see the sea?'

'We might as well, I've just seen Mrs Nosey Parker Bell from over the road come out her front door. She'll be over here in a flash if she sees us out here.'

Martha released the brake and shoved the wheelchair along towards Laverockbank Road. She stopped and flicked the brake on at the top of the hill. Jessie sat up and shook her head. 'Isn't it beautiful, Martha? Look at the sea.' Jessie breathed in deeply. 'I can almost smell its salty tang.' She pointed down to the high stone wall running along the shoreline. 'You see that wall? It's just like the one between our lodge house and Wardie House. It was built in the early 1900s. It runs all the way from Newhaven harbour to the Old Chain Pier, then beyond.' Jessie gestured in the direction of Granton. 'It meant that all the gorse bushes – whin, we used to call them – were ripped out and those tunnels blocked off.' She turned to Martha who was yawning. 'I've told you about the smugglers' tunnels, haven't I?'

'Yeah.'

'Oh, listen to the herring gulls! They were the sound I grew up to. We worked hard in those days, you know, we —'

'Yeah, you've told me that before too. Right, let's get you back home.'

'Hello, Miss McCallister, how nice to see you out and about. Are you feeling any better?' A middle-aged woman with a purple coat and matching hat appeared behind them.

'I'm fine, just fine. How lovely to see you too.' Jessie turned round in her chair. 'Have you met Martha? She's my Canadian carer, granddaughter of a good friend of mine from years ago. Martha, this is Mrs Benson. You used to be my elder, didn't you?'

'I still am, but I've not managed to find you in. Whenever I call at Wardie Lodge House with your communion card, no one answers the door. You opened it to me once, the first time I met you, Martha, and you said Miss McCallister wasn't well. I know the minister's tried to visit a couple of times too, but no answer.'

'That doorbell's not reliable, I'm real sorry about that.'

'Mrs Bell opposite said she's not seen you out in your wheelchair for weeks. We all wondered if you'd been ill, but there had been no sign of Doctor Bruce's car outside, Mrs Bell said.'

Martha released the brake. 'Anyway, we must get home, she's still not great and I don't want her catching a chill from that cold wind.'

Jessie stretched out her hand to shake Mrs Benson's, but Martha strode off up the hill and Jessie's arm was left dangling by her side.

X

'That's tasty soup, Martha. You really can cook, can't you? Where did you say you learned?'

'Oh, here and there, you know.'

'But I thought you'd trained as an actual chef? You said that in that first letter you sent me.'

Martha shook her head. 'Don't think so, Jessie – your memory must be playing up again.' She lifted the dishes into the sink then sat down beside the wheelchair.

'Mr MacIntyre's arriving at 2 p.m., and all you have to do is sign the papers. It's all going to be just as we discussed earlier, d'you remember?'

'Well, yes, if that's what my lawyer advises. Why could Mr McLean not come himself?'

'I told you, he's on sick leave, could be off a while. But Mr MacIntyre is his assistant and he agrees with me that this is the best way forward. He said it was no problem for him to come down here with the papers. You know it makes sense; giving me power of attorney means I can go to the bank for you and there's far less for you to worry about.'

'Yes, I do see that. And then you just need me to sign cheques and things and you can cash them for me?'

'I'm hoping we can sort out something similar with the bank once this has all been set up with the lawyer, so I can sign your cheques too.'

'I suppose that makes sense.'

Jessie stared at Martha. 'Do you mind me asking if you dye your hair, Martha? It's so black and even though you're only just over forty, a lot of women begin to get grey.'

'I will always be black-haired. No intention of giving in to grey at any stage.'

'What colour of hair did your father have? Your grandmother's hair was a sort of fair, gingery colour.'

Martha smirked. 'Gingery too, but then he had to shave his head. Great big round face like a balloon and that shiny bald head.'

Jessie frowned. 'Why did he have to shave his hair off?'

Martha shrugged. 'What happens to convicts.'

'So was he allowed to send you and your mother photos from prison?'

Martha stood up and headed for the sink with the water glasses. 'Suppose so. Yeah, that's what I must be remembering.'

✳

Jessie was in the sitting room staring at the shut curtains. It was gloomy inside but she could not move the wheelchair near enough to the curtains to open them. She looked around and sighed. There seemed to be nothing of Effie's anywhere. Where was the pretty pearl-encrusted pill box, the silver magnifying glass and the ornate picture frame which Jessie had filled with that lovely photograph of Dorrie's grandchildren? She leant back into her chair and shut her eyes. She had felt rather confused during the lawyer's meeting and though Martha had been sweet and charming to young Mr MacIntyre, the minute the garden gate had shut behind him, she'd shouted at Jessie. She had accused Jessie of trying to interrupt the meeting. Martha had wheeled her back into the room, pulled the curtains shut and Jessie had not seen her since. Jessie took a deep breath. Then she opened her eyes wide. That smell was unmistakable. She wrinkled her nose up and smiled, for from the kitchen came the most wonderful aroma.

Jessie shut her eyes again and was transported back to when she was a child, coming home after an exhausting day down at the harbour mending the nets and gutting the herring. She had just unwrapped the cloths on her fingers; her hands ached and she stretched each finger out as she had seen Mrs Smart the organist do at church before she played a hymn. At the door of her cottage, Jessie could smell it, wafting over the threshold – herring, coated in oatmeal and frying in the pan. She could remember her mother's voice as a greeting, shouting at her to wash her filthy hands and feet. She and Dorrie would then sit down on the only two chairs and take the plate of herring and potatoes on their laps and eat slowly, savouring every moment. The sweet taste of the herring and the golden crust of oatmeal ...

The door swung open and Martha strode towards the wheel-chair. 'Right, let's get you into the kitchen. Time for tea.'

Martha placed two herring fillets, burnished and crunchy, on the plate beside some steaming new potatoes in their jackets. She stuck her knife into the pack of butter on the table and dolloped a pat over the potatoes. Jessie watched the butter melt and drip down the side of a potato until she could wait no more. She was salivating. She picked up her fork and knife and leant over the table.

'Not so fast, old lady.' Martha swiped the plate away and placed it at the far end.

'I think you've been lying to me, Jessie Mack. I think you know perfectly well where that diamond is. Though why in God's name you and the crazy old bitch buried it, I have no idea. I think your memory's not as bad as you make out. So before you get your herring, I want you to try to remember where you put it.'

Martha bent over Jessie, who was staring at the plate of herring out of reach. She was silent for a moment then shook her head. 'I cannot recall, Martha. I'm so sorry. I just can't remember where we put it.'

'That's a pity,' said Martha, lifting the plate and walking slowly to the bin in the corner. She raised the lid and held the plate over it. She looked at Jessie again, tilting her head. 'Sure?'

Jessie nodded and bent down her head so that Martha could not see the tears fill her eyes and stream down her cheeks.

Chapter 49

1982

The door to Wardie House swung open and Craig walked in with the bags. Rona followed, Hannah in her arms. They looked over to the other side of the hall where the staff were lined up, Mrs Bell standing alongside, bent over her stick.

'Welcome home, Rona,' said Mrs Bell as the staff rushed over to have a peek at the baby.

'Oh, look at her! Isn't she a pretty little thing?'

'Adorable.'

'Look at her tiny little fingers.'

'We're going to get her settled in now,' said Craig, shuffling Rona over towards the annexe door. 'I'll come and see you later. I'm off to get Rona's mum from the station.'

'Rona, I have a little gift for you.' Mrs Bell handed over a little package, all wrapped up in pink paper. 'I hope they fit. I made them really tiny.'

'Thank you so much, Mrs Bell,' Rona said. 'They'll be a perfect fit.'

Craig manoeuvred them into the annexe, shut the door and grinned. 'Now's the time to ensure we always keep that door locked. We don't want the residents wandering in to bother you when you're in the middle of feeding. Is she still asleep?'

'Yes. I'll go and put her in the cot. Or maybe in her pram.'

Rona looked around.

'It's through here, hang on.' Craig wheeled the pram in from the bedroom. 'I made it up with those blankets from Mothercare. Does it look okay?'

Rona looked inside. 'Wonderful.' She tucked Hannah in and folded the blanket tight around her. 'I still think it's hilarious that Tracey lugged this all the way upstairs on Mr Burnside's instructions. He was so insistent that he should be allowed to use his pram.'

'Yes, after we'd put his pram down there in the corner of the cellar because he barged into Betty Chalmers with it.'

'Poor Tracey.'

'She was so apologetic when she realised she had given Mr Burnside our new pram. She's not the brightest, I mean she even covered the old pram with the new plastic coverings.' Craig grinned then looked at his watch. 'I'd better get going up to Waverley. Your mum's train is due in twenty minutes.' Craig kissed Rona on the forehead and ran out the door.

✕

Rona scrumpled the wrapping paper and lifted up the dainty little bootees. They were very sweet, but she did wonder if they were just too tiny. They were more like something you would find on dolls; she'd try them on the baby later. She went to the sink to fill the kettle then heard a loud cough at the door.

'Hi, hope you don't mind me popping in? Just wanted to see the baby.'

Rona sighed. She wasn't ready for visitors and certainly not her. 'Was the door open, Martha?'

'Yeah, but don't worry, I'm not staying, just wanted to see her.' Rona reluctantly led Martha through to the bedroom where Hannah was sleeping soundly. Martha stared at the newborn then said, 'Yeah, cute I suppose, but I think all babies look the same.' She turned back to Rona. 'How're you feeling?'

'Fine. Look, I've got lots to do, sorry.'

'No worries. And thanks for having us to stay for another couple of days. Those cleaning guys said they couldn't deep-clean the house properly without those really strong chemicals. Dangerous not just for me with my asthma but for Jessie at her age too. The smoke damage was worse than we thought at first.'

'Martha, I think the sooner you get back to the lodge house the better. Sorry to sound rude.'

'Oh, well, all right then. I can't even offer to bake you a cake as a welcome home. Cook won't allow me into the main kitchen, will she?'

Rona shook her head.

'You okay, Rona? You look a bit tearful. I've heard about the baby blues. Want to speak about it?'

'No, I do not,' Rona shouted. She heard a whimper from the bedroom. 'Can you just leave? My mum'll be here soon.'

Martha tiptoed over to the door then pulled it shut behind her while Rona sat down on the sofa and let out a sob. The cry from the bedroom increased to a wail. Rona wiped her tears and went to pick up her baby. She was so tired, all she wanted to do was get into that comfortable warm bed. At least when her mum was here, she could sleep and sleep and sleep.

Chapter 50

1981

'Martha,' Jessie whispered, 'What does the letter say?' She swallowed. Her voice was so faint these days, her throat always tender, sometimes sore.

'Nothing to bother you about,' Martha snarled. She put the volume of the television up to high and wheeled Jessie in front of it.

'But there's nothing I want to see on television, Martha,' she croaked. 'Can't I look outside? Can you at least open the curtains? Please?'

Martha ignored Jessie, who was straining round to see her, then took up the letter again, scanning the words, before crumpling up the paper and throwing it in the bin. 'I've got to get to the bank before it closes. Your bank opening hours are crazy – four o'clock closing is madness. Back home they open till six. Do we need any more than fifty pounds?'

Martha was writing a cheque out to 'M. Sinclair' and had written the date. Jessie watched, helpless, as Martha wrote 'One Hundred Pounds Only' and signed the cheque. She saw Martha head for the door, turning to lock it carefully behind her.

Jessie sat, her head bowed low, and wiped the tear that was trickling down her cheek. How had she come to this? A sad old woman sitting in a wheelchair, a prisoner in her own home, the house left to her by Effie in her will. She was left the lodge house and the diamond, though no one else knew about the diamond. Martha might end up getting everything else of hers, but she would never get the diamond. Of that, Jessie was sure. Effie had said it was valued in 1935 at £25,000. By now, it would be worth a great deal more. When Jessie had asked Effie on one of her lucid days why it was so valuable, Effie had said that before the world-famous Cullinan diamond was discovered in 1905, the Ramsay family gem was one of the largest to come out of South Africa. The diamond merchant near Pretoria had given it to her father as a dowry when he married the South African's daughter. Then, when she died giving birth to Effie, her father was so distraught, he kept the diamond in trust for his favourite daughter: Isabella.

As a child, Effie had been heartbroken that her sister was their father's favourite. Well, Jessie had told her, she had managed to get the diamond back for herself and hide it from her sister and brother, so at least there was some sort of retribution.

Jessie stretched her hand down the side of the wheelchair. She had tried to do this before and not succeeded, but this time she was sure she could manage. She pulled her neck back as she extended her hand round the back and tried to find the brake. She reached out as far as she could then brought up the left side of her body to help her arm stretch. And then, all of a sudden, the wheelchair overbalanced and she tipped out. Jessie fell onto the floor in a tangle of limbs. She pushed away a wheel that was on top of her leg and lay there, thinking what to do.

Using her elbows, Jessie heaved herself across to the fire, stopping every inch to take a breath. Her legs might be useless but her arms were less weak, and she was determined to do this. She had gutted fish as a child, carried great pans of soup as a teenager and then worked with her hands when she was in service. Slowly, she crossed the floor to the place she wanted to be and then lay there, panting. Then she lifted her hand up and rustled in the bin. She pulled out the letter and spread it flat on the carpet under her. She began to read.

Dear Miss McCallister,

The estate of my client Mrs Bertha Smith has been completed and I write to inform you that you are sole beneficiary. Mrs Smith left enough money to cover her funeral in December last year and a small sum which had been previously allocated to her son Peter but he was executed in 1976 at the Ottawa State Penitentiary, therefore excluded from the will entirely. I am not sure if you were aware that his crime was so heinous there was never any question he would be executed.

Since he had neither spouse nor issue, the monies are to be sent to you. You might wish to alert your bank that a cheque will arrive from our bank, the Halifax Banking Company, payable to yourself, and that this will be in Canadian dollars. They should waive attendant charges for international monies because it is from a will, but it is best to give them advance notice. The cheque will be sent to you at this address in the coming fortnight.

Jessie felt a tear trickle down her face as she thought of Bertha. She'd not heard from her since that time, years before, when she'd returned the bootee and inside it the diamond that had paid for Bertha's passage to Canada. Jessie had returned it to Effie along with the little bootee, one of the pair Effie had knitted for her baby.

Mrs Smith's illness in the last two decades of her life meant that she was unable to travel but I want you to know that, on my last visit to her in the care home, she spoke first with great sorrow about her son and his evil crime of murder and how it was fitting that he should be punished. But then she talked about you and what a loyal and devoted friend you had been and how you risked everything for her. The cheque is for 2,000 Canadian dollars which might appear a relatively small

amount, however, it was all she had and she instructed
me to tell you that you were a good person and meant
everything to her.
  Yours sincerely,

      Ronald Mackintosh
      Solicitor
      Mackintosh and Mackay, Halifax

Chapter 51

1982

Rona pulled Mrs Bell's little woollen bootees onto Hannah's tiny feet and laid her in the pram. They just fitted and Rona was keen to show Mrs Bell. Her mum, Morna, had arrived before lunch, so Rona was able to go to bed where she had slept for two hours. She felt much better now and wanted to go and show her baby off round Wardie House. Hannah was fed and changed and looked as 'cute as a button' as Morna kept saying.

'I'm just going to make a stab at the ironing then I'll start getting tea ready,' she told Rona as she headed for the door.

Rona pushed the pram out into the hall and looked up at the portrait. The dark eyes followed her as she walked. Perhaps the woman in the painting had had a small baby too. She moved closer to the painting and noticed once more that she held something between her fawn gloves. Was it, as Betty Chalmers suggested, the tip of a large diamond?

Rona was staring at it when Betty Chalmers came towards her, her hands resting on the wheelchair sides as Tracey pushed her across the hall.

'Ah, Rona, I was just saying how very much I wanted to see the baby.' She peered into the pram. 'Beautiful, so sweet.' Betty snapped open her handbag. 'Get out my purse, child, will you?' Tracey unclasped the purse and handed it to Betty who pulled out a five pound note and tucked it into the pram, under the mattress.

'That's for luck, Rona. Now, I must be on my way. That nice young chiropodist is coming to cut my toenails.'

Rona smiled and continued along the corridor to the lift. She went upstairs to Mrs Bell's room. On the way, two more ladies insisted on putting money in the pram. Her mum had told her about the custom that when the baby went outside for its first walk in the pram, women gave money as a gift by slipping it under the pram covers. Inside Wardie House, it seemed rather odd. She knocked on the door to Room 12 and waited. 'Yes, come in!' said a voice.

Rona wheeled in the pram.

'Oh Rona, how good to see you and the baby.' At the window sat Mrs Bell and beside her, in the place where the other chair should have been, was Jessie in her wheelchair.

'Hello, Jessie. Good to see you've got a bit of company. How are you?'

'Better, thank you.' The voice was croaky but she was smiling. Jessie and Mrs Bell both peered inside the pram, cooing and saying how pretty Hannah was.

'Jessie's been telling me what life has been like in the lodge house for the past three years. She's been pretty much confined to the house, poor thing. Haven't you, Jessie?'

'Yes, yes I have.' Her voice was soft and hoarse.

'It's so good to hear you speak, Jessie,' Rona said. 'We thought you'd never speak again.'

'My throat's always been a problem, but I got hoarser and hoarser over the past two years and now can only speak in a whisper. The smoke in the fire obviously made it worse. You'll have to shout too, I'm a little deaf.'

'Oh, we're all deaf in here, Jessie, don't you worry about that,' bellowed Mrs Bell.

There was a knock at the door and Craig appeared. 'Here you are, Rona. Morna's desperate to get her hands on her grandchild again. Can I wheel her back down?'

Rona smiled. 'I'll be down in two ticks.'

'Craig is like a new man these days, Rona.' Mrs Bell said as Craig pulled the door to. 'He used to be rather, well, fickle, but now he's reliable.'

'He's a good man,' Rona said, smiling. She asked Jessie about how she was feeling and if there was anything she needed, before turning the conversation to Martha. 'You know she's still in the room next door to you? But she'll be leaving us tomorrow. I remember you wrote that you didn't want her back in the lodge house. Is there a particular reason?'

'Because the Yank is a conniving, scheming woman who is after Jessie's money,' said Mrs Bell. 'I've just been saying that, haven't I, Jessie?'

Jessie leant forward in her chair to whisper, 'I'm afraid she is not as she seems. I've been scared to say anything and am just so relieved to be out of that house and away from her. Though I shall be glad when she leaves Wardie House for good. I explained all about it to Ian, who can perhaps fill you in on the details.' She swallowed. 'I'm tired now and my throat, though eased a bit, is still causing me problems. May I go back to my room, please?'

'Of course, Jessie, you can have a nice rest before the tea trolley comes around.'

'I'd like to put something in the baby's pram. A gift. I'll fetch it from my room.'

Rona wheeled her away, thanking Mrs Bell again for the boot-ees. She set the wheelchair by the window then went back for the pram, shutting Mrs Bell's door as she did. 'Jessie, if we can rear-range some of the bedrooms and pull a few strings, would you like to stay on with us, in Wardie House?'

Jessie smiled and nodded. 'That would be wonderful, thank you very much.'

'There'll be some administrative things to work out first, though.' How could Rona subtly ask about money for the fees? 'Um, do you happen to know if you have much in the way of funds in the bank?'

The old woman screwed up her eyes tight. 'That's the thing. I don't know. Martha has been in charge of my accounts for two years now. I've no idea if there is anything left, even the money left to me by Bertha. She won't answer me when I ask her and all the bank statements in the post she takes away before I can see them.' Jessie sighed.

'Don't worry about it for now, we'll sort something out.'

'I do still have something of value.' Jessie nodded. 'Can you wait a minute, please? I've just thought of something.'

Jessie reached her hand down and pulled a drawer open. It was her underwear drawer; inside were two neat piles of socks. Jessie stretched in and pulled out an ancient-looking pair of woollen bootees from underneath. Help, thought Rona, she was obviously about to be given some old, grey bootees for the baby. She suppressed a smirk.

'I'm going to get something from the bathroom, if you could give me a hand in please?'

Rona wheeled her in. 'Can you manage?' Perhaps she wasn't getting the bootees after all.

'Yes, everything's to hand.'

Jessie shut herself in the toilet and soon knocked on the door for Rona to wheel her out, which she did, parking her beside the pram. There was no sign of the grey bootees. Instead, Jessie held up a pair of brand new baby's knitted bootees, in a beautiful pink. 'I asked Tracey to go and buy a little something for the baby yesterday,' she said, tucking them in under the blanket. 'I hope they'll bring luck.'

Chapter 52

1982

'So, Jessie, I'm going out into the garden this evening. It's foggy again and I am determined to find that diamond one way or the other. I know you're making it up and that you do actually remember where you and Mad Effie buried the box. I'm going to keep digging till you tell me where it is.'

'Please don't call her that. She wasn't mad, she was troubled. And, no, I still don't remember where we hid it.' She looked up at Martha whose expression was hard, focused. 'Sorry,' Jessie whispered. She mustn't anger Martha, she must be cautious about what she said. It was now obvious that all she was after was the diamond and she would not let anything or anybody get in her way. Martha had told Jessie how she had met the new people next door and how they were setting up a care home for the elderly. Jessie had asked Martha if she could move in there. Was there enough money in her bank account? She'd been told that, at ninety-seven, the only move she'd be making was being carried out of the lodge house in a wooden box.

The only good thing about Martha was that she could cook. Jessie was well fed with wholesome stews and soups. One time Martha had even produced a soup from bones from the fishmonger, and as Jessie took a mouthful of fishy stock, nostalgia for her childhood swept over her. She had sat in silence, her eyes shut, as she remembered the taste of her youth. Martha also produced some delicious baking. Canadians were good at desserts and cakes, Martha had told her, which came from their Scottish heritage.

After Jessie had read the letter from the lawyer, she'd put it back in the bin so Martha would never know she'd read it and that she now knew that Martha wasn't Bertha's granddaughter. There was no way Jessie could possibly ask Martha who she really was if not her old friend's granddaughter. Martha now looked after Jessie's entire life. Every single aspect of it she controlled, apart from the one thing Martha wanted, that one special object, hidden in a place Martha would never think to look.

That day of the fall was awful. Martha had returned from the bank to find Jessie lying on the floor and instead of asking if she was all right, Martha had approached slowly, in silence. Martha probably hoped she was dead.

'I'll be going out any minute. It's pretty foggy,' Martha had said to Jessie about nine o'clock. 'You can watch the news then I'll get you into bed.' She switched on the television. 'Any final ideas about where the box is?'

Jessie shook her head and as Martha slammed the door shut, Jessie tilted her head towards the window. Even through the heavy curtains, Jessie could hear it: the boom of the foghorn on the Forth, the noise she now always associated with that shocking night in 1899 when she had handed the gutting knife to Effie. And then, years later, Effie had shown her gratitude by leaving Jessie both the lodge house and the beautiful diamond.

Jessie strained her neck back a little as she heard another noise. A squeaking noise, like wheels. She pictured Martha out there in the garden, the garden she used to be in so often as a teenager when she had to pick the meagre vegetables for Molly's broth. Martha with the old, squeaky wheelbarrow that needed oiling, and the spade, digging and digging. In vain. She would find nothing. Only when Jessie could escape from here could she tell someone where it was. But who would she tell?

Jessie turned round towards the television and watched as Jan

Leeming stared at her from the screen. She missed Richard Baker, but she was happy the new newsreader was a woman. She sniffed then patted around in her pocket for her handkerchief. There was none, hers must have fallen out of her pocket. She looked around and it was then she noticed Martha's handbag, within reach. Jessie could still hear the squeaky wheelbarrow being moved round outside, and Martha digging.

Jessie grabbed Martha's bag and looked inside. Trying to remember exactly where everything was, she took out things one by one. There was a purse, filled with five and ten pound notes, from Jessie's account. There was a mirror, comb, lipstick, tissues, nail file. She unzipped one section and delved in, her arthritic fingers making the task laborious. She brought out a small, dark-coloured booklet and turned it over. It was a passport, a Canadian passport. She flicked to the end and stared at Martha's picture. Her hair was much lighter and longer but this was definitely her. Martha Jean Sinclair, it read. And she was born in 1939, as she had thought. Nothing unusual there. She was about to place it back in when something fluttered out and onto Jessie's lap. It was a small stiff envelope with 'Gate Pay' and '$100' stamped on it. She lifted the corner and looked inside. There was nothing inside, but on the flap, in Martha's handwriting, were the words, '100 dollars! Sure wasn't worth two years inside!'

Jessie's eyes widened and, with shaky hands, she put everything carefully back in the bag. She lowered the bag back down onto the floor and turned back to the television where Jan Leeming was talking about the impact of the Falklands War on the economy. But Jessie was not listening. She had remembered seeing an American movie years earlier about prisoners released from prison and given some parole money called Gate Pay. Jessie's hands were trembling; the person who had lived in her house for the past five years was an ex-convict. Was she a murderer like Bertha's son?

Chapter 53

1982

'Mum, if you don't mind watching Hannah through here for a bit, I thought I'd start looking out some bits and pieces for the Wardie House fair? It's a couple of weeks away, but I'd like to start now, while you're here.'

'No problem, my love.' Morna scooped Hannah out of Rona's arms.

Rona headed for the bedroom, pulled out some cardboard boxes and began to make piles of old books and knick-knacks for the fair. It had been Ian's idea to have a sale of work for any locals from north Edinburgh and also relatives of the residents. Their cook was going to provide sandwiches and a cream tea, and Rona had hired a pianist, so they felt they could charge a nominal fee for entry.

Rona came to something solid at the bottom of a box and lifted it out with two hands. This was the jewellery box she'd found in the wardrobes down in the cellar when they first moved in. She tried to open the lid then remembered it was locked. Now she had more time to look at it, she saw it was beautiful – a dark inlaid wood, possibly mahogany or walnut. She'd read somewhere that Victorians used those woods a lot. There were brass mounts around each corner; it really was lovely. Rona stuck a paper knife in and tried to lever it open but didn't want to break it. Perhaps someone would buy it without a key. Or perhaps someone had a key that fitted everything. She put it in the pile of fair items then took them all through the annexe and into the hall.

Rona had just put the fair things in a corner when Mr Burnside came along the corridor, each arm leaning on a stick. He was becoming increasingly unsteady on his feet. He looked bereft without his pram, but the staff had decided it was becoming unsafe for the other residents as he kept bashing into them and elderly people bruised so easily. He had bumped into Betty Chalmers' wheelchair again and she'd become angry, insisting he was trying to force her out of the way in the corridor. She sounded like a little girl in the school playground. 'He rammed me, Rona, like a bull-dozer! Tell him off!'

'That's a nice box, Rona,' Mr Burnside said, spotting the jewellery box on the top of the pile of books.

'I know, isn't it lovely? But the thing is, there's no key, so I'm not sure anyone will want to buy it. It's for the fair.'

Mr Burnside lifted up the box, inspecting the tiny keyhole. 'Rona, there's a key in the pram. I think it'll fit.'

'What pram?'

'My pram. Underneath the blanket where Morag lay, there's this big hole, it's called a footwell. When she gets bigger, her feet will go in there. That's where the key is.'

'Are you sure?'

He nodded.

'Okay, I'm going to see if I can find it but I need someone to guard this pile of things till Craig can move them all down to the cellar for storage. Can you do that, please?'

Mr Burnside stood up straight, pushing his shoulders back like a soldier while Rona hurried down the cellar steps.

Rona walked over to the pram, remembering the last time she was down here, just before she went into labour. She looked inside the pram and saw the photo was still there. She lifted it up then took up the blanket, then the mattress which was covering the footwell. She looked in but could see nothing. She felt all around

and came across something on one of the sides. There was something stuck with glue to the side. She bent over to look. There,
encased in ancient-looking, crusty glue, was a tiny key. She tried
to release it but could not, so she dashed to the foot of the stairs
where Craig kept his tools and picked out a thin screwdriver.
Rona chipped away the glue, scattering fragments over the footwell. She blew these away and lifted out the tiny key. She replaced
everything, even the photo of the dead baby, then went back
upstairs and straight over to Mr Burnside, who was perched on a
seat by the door.

'Sorry, Rona, I needed to sit down, but I'm still guarding your
things.'

'Thank you so much.'

Rona bent over and inserted the key in the lock.

'Hey, Rona, how's the baby doing?' It was Martha, emerging
from the other side of the hall. She had her colour back and was
once again made-up and well groomed.

'She's grand.'

Martha looked down to see what Rona was doing, then gasped.
'What's that box? Is it an old jewellery box?'

'Yes, it's for the Wardie House fair. Victorian, we reckon.'

'Geez.' Martha was staring at it. 'Where'd you find it?'

'With some old things, in the cellar.'

'Is that the key to open it?'

'Yes, I'm about to try. I think it should fit.' Rona turned the
key and lifted the lid. Inside were faded satin, cushioned drawers
which presumably would have taken individual pieces of jewellery.

Rona opened a drawer. It was empty. Then a second, also empty.
She was about to open another when Martha snapped, 'Can I buy
it?'

Rona closed the box. 'Well, we've not had the fair yet, Martha.'

'But if I give you money for it now then it's kind of the same,
isn't it?' Martha pulled the box towards her. 'How much do you
want for it? Ten pounds? Twenty?'

Was it worth that much? 'I suppose it is maybe quite valuable, it's an antique after all. Well, okay, I'll give it to you for, let's say twenty pounds?'

Martha held tight onto the box.

'Ha, no money, no box.' Rona reached out her hands. 'Twenty pounds first. Isn't that right, Mr Burnside?' She looked over at the old man whose chin had drooped onto his chest. He was sound asleep.

'Wait right there, I'll get my purse.' Martha sped away, bumping into Ian as she ran along the corridor.

He strode over to Rona. 'What's she up to? Why's she still here? I thought she'd gone?'

'She's meant to leave tomorrow, but I've no idea where she's going to go. Jessie doesn't want her in the lodge house.'

'Good reason too. I didn't want to bother you with the baby and everything, but Rona, have you got ten minutes so I can tell you what Jessie's been telling me?'

'Yes, let me get that money from Martha for the box, then I'll come into the office.'

Chapter 54

1982

'Who was that at the door, Martha?' Jessie's voice was hoarse as usual.

'The nosy new neighbour. I had to give her a glass of water. She was sick all over the garden. Disgusting.'

'The poor thing. It's horrible being sick,' Jessie croaked. Her voice kept giving way these days.

Martha wheeled Jessie into the lounge in front of the television. 'I don't want to watch television. Can't you read to me, Martha? Please?' She leant towards Martha to whisper. 'Effie had lots of books. Her sister Isabella was a great reader.'

'I've never asked you what actually happened to the sister. And the brother? I read all about it but it just doesn't sound feasible.'

'What d'you mean, you read about it? It was eighty-three years ago.'

'You can still read about stuff that happened in the olden days. It's called research.'

'What did you find out?' Jessie mumbled.

Martha sat down beside the bookshelf and started to rifle through the old books. 'I found out that Andrew Ramsay, the governor of the poorhouse, murdered his sister Isabella in a drunken rage one night. Then he hanged himself. That was that.'

Jessie nodded.

'Unless you know anything different?' Martha smirked. 'Murder has always fascinated me.'

Jessie swallowed. 'Why should I know differently?'

'You were living at Wardie House at that time. I remember you boring me with one of your many stories from the olden days about the smugglers' tunnels and how you used to nip out to Newhaven, but the tunnel also connected the houses. You could've been at the house where the murder took place – then made a getaway?'

Martha was enjoying the look of panic on Jessie's face.

'Where was Effie on the night of the murder, for example? What if she'd killed her sister in a jealous fit?'

Jessie shook her head.

'What if you helped Effie kill her? Or what if you killed her? You with your curse.' Martha pointed a finger at Jessie's mole. 'What was it they called you? Winzie? Then Effie could get this house and the diamond and —'

'No!' Jessie croaked. She stared at her hands as she clenched them on her lap.

'Oh, think I've touched a nerve here, haven't I? Winzie. Cursed. Does that mean you're damned to hell, since you helped commit a murder?' Martha raised one eyebrow.

Jessie pulled at the scarf round her neck.

'It'd be difficult, but not impossible to reopen the case.' Martha cleared her throat. 'One of the witnesses, ladies and gentlemen, is still alive at ninety-seven. She denies all knowledge but in fact, what do you know, she helped the murderer. How did she help her? I know! She provided the killer with the murder weapon and then afterwards disposed of it. Oh, this story has legs.'

Jessie was staring at the curtains, body rigid, hands clasped tight on her lap.

'Ha, look at you. I'm just joking, you silly old bitch.'

Jessie unclenched her hands.

Martha continued, 'But who knows what happens in the mind of a murderer? Well, I've met some in my time and believe me, they are never as straightforward as they seem.'

The silence was thick between them. Martha continued rifling through the books on the shelf then picked one out. Its title was *Daily Light*. She opened it to the first page. 'Look, here's a nice inscription: "For my beloved Euphemia, with fondest love from your sister, Isabella, 25th December 1870."'

Martha thrust the page in front of Jessie, who drew her scarf up around her throat.

'Isabella gives her sister a lovely book.' Martha leant in close to Jessie. 'And then, as thanks, the sister kills her.'

Chapter 55

1982

A dark shadow slid along the corridor, keeping close to the wall. The figure climbed the stairs, patting the rail with each step then moved silently towards the top and turned right. She looked at the numbers on each door until she found the right one. A cat darted along the corridor, stopped beside the woman to arch its back in an exaggerated pose and then slunk off down the stairs. The woman turned the handle, but it was locked. She reached up for the key dangling on a hook, inserted it into the lock and pushed the door open.

There was a gentle snoring coming from the bed and in the dark the figure came closer. A hand was raised. In it was a knife. Suddenly the boom of a foghorn sounded outside …

'Rona, wake up, love, she's crying, can you not hear her? Hannah needs a feed.'

Rona sat bolt upright in bed. 'Oh, thank God. I had a horrible dream, a nightmare.' She shook her head. 'Can you do me a big favour and go upstairs and check Martha and Jessie's rooms, please?'

Craig was out of bed and hovering over the cot. 'I'll bring her to you, love, stay put.'

Rona unbuttoned her nightie and reached out for her daughter. She smiled when she saw the tiny bundle. 'Please, darling, just humour me. It's just, my dream was so horrible, I need you to check everything's okay upstairs. It'll take you five minutes.'

Craig sighed and slipped his feet into his slippers. He pulled the dressing gown from the hook on the bathroom wall, plodded over to the bedroom door and slipped out. He walked across the hall, along the corridor then up the stairs, turning right at the top. He searched the numbers and stopped at Room 9. He didn't feel comfortable entering Martha's room, so he went next door to Jessie's room first. He found the key hanging on its hook and put it in the lock. He pushed the door open and headed for the curtains, pulling one open a fraction; there was enough moonlight to see by.

Craig saw the empty wheelchair and then, once his eyes adjusted to the light, he saw a body in the bed. He moved closer and listened. He could hear a gentle snoring. He bent down over Jessie and laid a hand near her mouth. There was a warm puff of breath. He went over to the curtain, pulled it to, then padded out of the room.

He went next door to Martha's room and looked up to see an empty key hook. Craig tried the handle but it was locked. He frowned and headed along the corridor to the nurses' station. Neil, an agency nurse, was on his first night shift at Wardie House. He was asleep in the armchair.

'Very sorry to wake you up, Neil,' said Craig, drily, tapping his shoulder. 'D'you have the spare key for Room 9 please? I've got to check on something for my wife.'

Neil sat up and rubbed his eyes. He looked at his watch. It was two in the morning. 'Sorry, Craig, I did my last check about half eleven, everything was fine. I had a quick chat with Mrs Sinclair in the corridor but then she went back to her room.'

'What was she doing?'

'She said she used to take Miss McCallister a cup of cocoa last thing at night so she'd been to her room to check if she was still awake and waiting for her drink.'

'At eleven thirty?'

Neil bit his lip. 'You're right. It's a bit late, isn't it?'

'No problem, Neil. Can I have the spare key please?'

Neil opened a drawer and stretched towards a little tray with keys. He looked at a couple of tags then handed the Room 9 key to Craig.

'Thanks. Who's on with you again?'

'Another man, Ian, I think he's called?'

'Okay, I'll go and get him from the carers' lounge.'

Craig went along the corridor to the carers' lounge. It was empty but Craig could see a light along the corridor so headed for the bathroom. Ian was on his knees, fiddling with the bath hoist switch. 'Just trying to sort this switch out. The day carers will need it first thing.' He stood up. 'Is there a problem, Craig?'

'Can you come with me? I'm a bit suspicious that Martha's up to something and would prefer if you came with me to her room. That okay?'

'Sure.'

'Rona told me tonight what Jessie had told you. That's why I thought we should go together.'

At the door to Room 9, Craig put the key in the lock and turned it. Craig and Ian went into the room and switched on the light. They looked at the bed, which was empty; a jewellery box sat upon the eiderdown, lid open. Craig looked inside. 'Nothing in here. God knows where she's gone. Will we nip over to the lodge house, see if she's there?'

They hurried downstairs. 'Hold on, Ian. I'll just pull my jeans on.'

Two minutes later, Craig came back out of the annexe. He'd explained to Rona that Jessie was fine but they were off to check on Martha. Rona wasn't happy but Craig tried to reassure her by saying he'd be back before she'd finished the feed.

The two men strode round the corner and through the gate to the lodge house. It was pitch black but, on Craig's suggestion, they went round the back to the kitchen. 'The cleaners have left all the windows on the latch to release the chemical smells. This one'll be easy to get in by.' They pulled the window wide open. 'You're thinner than me, Ian. Can you get in and open the door?'

Ian reached up and leant both elbows on the sill, then pulled his body up and in through the window. Soon the back door opened and the kitchen light went on. Craig joined him inside. They looked in every room and each was empty. Craig gestured for Ian to follow and together they went along the corridor to the bedroom at the back, the only one whose door was closed. Craig turned the handle, flicked on the switch and they both looked around. Nothing seemed disturbed in the room apart from the top drawer of the bedside table which was pulled out. They both went towards it and peered in.

'There are some bank statements and things.' Craig raked around in the drawer. 'Think she's taken Jessie's bank details with her?'

'Could be.'

'No sign, then. Reckon she's done a runner? Buggered off back to Canada?'

'She was in her bed at midnight when I did the rounds,' said Ian, 'so she can't have gone far. We're going to have to wake Jessie and ask her what Martha was doing in her room tonight.'

They walked back round to Wardie House and headed upstairs. They unlocked Jessie's room and put on the bedside light. Jessie awoke and stared at both men.

'It's all right, Jessie. We're really sorry to wake you up, but there's something we need to tell you.'

The old woman blinked and reached for the tumbler of water by her bed. 'Sorry,' she whispered, 'I'm a little hoarse again. Is it Martha?'

'Yes. She seems to have gone.'

'Good. I'm glad.'

'Jessie, remember those things you told me about the diamond? Is everything all right? You didn't say where it was, but Martha's gone. All we found on her bed was the jewellery box she bought today.'

Jessie smiled. 'Ah, the jewellery box. Good. She's found it at last. She won't get far.'

'Was there a diamond hidden in there?'

'Yes, but it was paste. It's been there for years. I remembered about it when Rona told me she'd found the box. Effie abandoned lots of things down in the cellar. I now remember she kept the key in the big pram.' She smiled. 'Effie's father gave her mother's precious diamond to her sister Isabella. Effie had nothing but the paste diamond Andrew had given to his mistress to try to pay her off.' Jessie took another sip of water. 'That ended up in the jewellery box after it was used as Bertha's passage to Canada. By the time the ship's captain discovered it was paste, they were halfway across the Atlantic.'

'So what you told me, Jessie, about the big diamond – there's no such thing as the real one now? Only the paste one?'

Jessie shook her head. 'I wasn't going to let that convict near Effie's real one, Ian. For the past four years, I've been trying to keep it from her. And I succeeded. I knew she wouldn't look in my sock drawer. Who would want to rifle through an old woman's underwear?' Jessie frowned. 'She was evil. I believe she started that fire to try to kill me for refusing to tell her. You know she's been in prison?'

'God, no.'

'She must have met Bertha's son, the murderer, before she committed her own crime. I wonder now if they had an affair, even though he was so much older than her. Anyway, at some time, she heard about the diamond and set out to find it.' She shook her head. 'She was a really bad person, a Lady Macbeth.'

Craig and Ian drew nearer; Jessie was now whispering. 'She came into my room earlier tonight. I heard her unlock the door and come towards the bed. If that new nurse hadn't disturbed her, I think she would have killed me. She hid something quickly behind her back when he came in. I think she'd been down to the kitchen for a knife. She mumbled something about checking up on me to see if I needed cocoa. I'm positive I saw a sheen of metal at her back, like a blade.'

Jessie gestured to Craig to come closer.

'Craig, go downstairs and look in your daughter's pram.' Jessie began to slip down the pillows onto her back. 'And now, if you don't mind, I want to get back to sleep. I was having wonderful dreams about sleeping with ghosts. Nice ghosts.'

She turned over and Ian switched off the light as he and Craig went out into the dark corridor.

'Craig, I know it's the middle of the night, but since there's nothing more we can do just now could you come with me to the bathroom for a minute to check on the bath hoist? I've nearly fixed the switch but another pair of hands would help.'

'No problem.'

Chapter 56

1982

Rona opened her eyes and stared into the darkness. She'd just heard a click. What could it be? She didn't want to put on her bed-side light. She'd put Hannah back into her cot just a short while ago and didn't want to wake her up. Rona must have gone to sleep immediately after feeding; she was so sleep deprived, she fell asleep very easily now. She sat up in bed and let her eyes adjust to the dark. Rona listened. Usually she could hear a gentle snuffling or the soft whistling noise of the baby's regular breathing. There was no sound at all. She flung back the covers and strode over to the cot. She peered inside then put in a hand, tentatively. The sheet was cold; the cot was empty.

Rona ran to put on the light switch. Was she going mad? She had put the baby in here, what, fifteen minutes ago? Hannah had fallen asleep mid feed so Rona had wrapped her up, all snug and warm, in the soft white cot blanket. Rona's whole body tensed as she stared again into the empty cot.

Her mum must have taken her. Rona ran through to the tiny guest room and flicked on the light. 'Mum, Hannah's gone. Where is she?'

Morna screwed up her eyes. 'What? What time is it?'

'The cot's empty, where could she be?' Rona grabbed her mother's dressing gown from the hook on the door. 'Craig went off to Martha's house. I've got to go and find him.'

'He must've come back and taken her off. Maybe Hannah was girny and Craig took her for a walk.'

'I'd have heard her.' Rona felt sick.

'Maybe not, *a ghràidh.*' Morna jumped out of bed and helped her daughter tie up the dressing gown. 'Is the pram still there?'

They both rushed into the living room and looked towards the door where the pram usually sat. There was nothing there.

Rona gasped. 'That was what I heard – it was the click of the pram brake.' She ran towards the door.

'Rona, wait, I'll come with you.'

Rona turned back to Morna, panic in her eyes. 'No, you wait here, Mum, in case Craig gets back.' Rona ran out in her bare feet into the hall and stopped as she saw movement along the corridor. It was the lift door shutting. Perhaps it was Craig taking the pram upstairs – but why would he do that? She couldn't wait for the lift to come back down so she sprinted towards the kitchen door and the back staircase, running up the steps two at a time. She was breathless at the top; she paused to stoop over the banister. Her heart was palpitating so hard her chest was about to burst.

⋇

Jessie hadn't yet fallen asleep so she opened her eyes and listened. It was pitch black but she was sure there was a noise, a sound that was familiar and yet it was one she had not heard for years. Was it wheels? She must be dreaming. It was just like the sound of Effie pushing the pram, which was many years ago.

The main bedroom light snapped on. Jessie squinted. There, on her bedside rug, stood a pram, the shiny black handles towards her bed. Jessie pushed herself up onto her elbows and turned her gaze towards the door where a figure dressed in black was twisting the key. As Jessie's eyes widened, she saw the figure turn around and tilt her head to one side.

'Good morning, Jessie Mack. We have business to discuss.'

Martha was smirking as she walked towards the pram.

There were light, snuffling sounds as if the baby was sleeping peacefully. Thank God for that. 'Martha,' Jessie croaked. 'What are you doing with the baby? Rona will be sick with worry when she realises she's gone.'

'Yeah, well, she'll get her baby back when I've been given what I came for.'

'What's that, Martha? I thought you'd taken the diamond – the one in the box?'

Martha sauntered towards the bed and sat down on the end, on top of Jessie's feet. Jessie tried to pull them away, but could not, Martha's weight was holding them firm. Martha reached into her pocket and thrust something at Jessie's face. She caught sight of a silver hallmark glinting in the light. It was a small magnifying glass, the one that had gone missing from Effie's things. Jessie looked at the pram, then back at Martha, who was now tossing the magnifying glass between her hands.

'Jessie, Jessie, you've been lying to me all those years, haven't you? First of all, you knew the diamond in the box was a fake. I've done enough research into diamonds since I've been here to know what to look for in a paste diamond.' She reached into her pocket, took out something, then released her fist and lifted her palm up to the light. She raised the magnifying glass and looked at the stone closely. 'Only close up can you tell it's not real. You can see the coating coming away underneath. This is lead glass, nothing like a diamond. It's worthless.' She shoved it back in her pocket with the glass. 'Which takes me on to my next point.'

There was a rap on the door, first a gentle tap, then a loud knock. 'Jessie, are you in there? Is the baby with you?' The voice was urgent.

'We seem to have visitors. Even more reason for you to hurry up and tell me where the real diamond is.'

'But that's all I ever had, Martha. That one in the box.' Jessie's voice sounded hoarse but she took a sip of water then yelled as loudly as she could, 'She's safe, Rona, she's—'

'Rona can't hear a thing, Jessie. The door's locked and your voice is a whisper. That diamond Effie left you – the one in her will, remember? The real one that she had valued at £25,000 in 1935? Worth a hell of a lot more now. I've done my research and a rare D colour stone like hers, it'd sell for well over £600,000.' Martha smirked. 'That'd set me up just swell.'

'How do you …?'

'How do I know about that?'

The frantic knocking at the door stopped and there was the sound of footsteps disappearing fast along the corridor.

'You seem to forget I had access to everything as your power of attorney, so it wasn't difficult to persuade that dim new lawyer to tell me what Effie left you in her will. Then,' Martha smirked, 'I made good friends with that jeweller in Goldenacre to find out more about the diamond and what it's worth.'

Jessie tried to shift up the bed but her feet were still trapped.

'Here's what we're going to do, Jessie. You are going to tell me where the real diamond is and …'

The baby began to whimper.

'And if not, it won't only be you dying in a horrible fire, but so will the kid.' Martha delved in her back pocket and brought out a shiny lighter. She flicked it on and a tall flame shot up. Her lips curled into a menacing sneer then she walked over towards the curtains. She lifted one heavy drape in her hand and yanked it open. Outside the fog hung thick in the air; the atmosphere in the room was heavy, stifling.

Jessie shifted up the pillow and tucked both hands at her back as if relieving pain. 'Please let the baby go, Martha. I don't mind dying, I'm old, but this wee mite, she's—'

'She's beginning to annoy me, that's what she's doing.'

Hannah was now crying loudly. Martha peered in the pram and shook her head. 'See, I never get the attraction of babies. What's the big deal? Look at her, all red-faced and squirming.'

'Please let Rona come and take her away. I'll tell you where it is, I promise, but the baby needs her mother.'

The door flew open and Rona rushed in. She ran towards the pram and scooped up the baby, clasping her to her chest. 'Sweetheart, are you all right? There, there, everything's fine. Mummy's here.'

Martha slipped behind Rona, removed the spare key from the outside of the door and locked it from the inside. She rammed both keys in her pocket.

'Rona, welcome to the party. Now shut the frickin' brat up!'

Rona spun round. 'I have no idea what you're doing in here or with my baby, Martha, but I'm going to take her back downstairs with me. Unlock the door. Now.' Rona's heart was pounding, her hands shaking as she clutched Hannah tight.

'No problem, Rona, I just need to ask Jessie a very simple question one more time. If she won't answer, sad to say, we're all in this together.' Martha brought out her lighter and flicked it then adjusted the flame to high. She headed for the window and held it near one curtain, her eyes glinting.

Rona felt a cold rush of terror. She bent down to kiss Hannah's downy head, while keeping Martha in her gaze.

Jessie glugged some water then spoke in a hoarse voice. 'It's here, in the room, Martha. It's there, in the pram, I put it in there for safe keeping.' She nodded at the pram. 'Look for yourself, then please, just leave. Go. Go back to Canada. We'll not bother you. Just take it and go.'

Jessie placed both hands behind her pillow as Martha flung a blanket and a little pink teddy bear then the mattress onto the floor. She scoured around inside, tracing her hand all over. There was nothing there. 'Where, Jessie?'

Rona stepped forward, turning her body so the baby was at the other side from Martha. 'Jessie, you slipped those little bootees into the pram yesterday, was it in one of those?'

Jessie nodded and she and Rona looked at Martha who was

rolling her thumb along the lighter.

Martha raised an eyebrow. 'Where are they now, Rona?'

'In our bedroom, in the baby's drawer. Can I go and get them?'

'Sure.' Martha pocketed the lighter and stretched out both her hands. 'But just to make sure you come back up here with them, give the kid to me. Now!'

There was a sudden noise and they all flinched. It was the fog-horn booming out on the Forth. Jessie screwed up her eyes tight as she had a flashback to many years before, in the kitchen of the lodge house. She tugged her arm out from behind the pillow. 'Rona, take this!' She thrust her hand towards Rona.

'What the hell is that, bitch?' Martha jumped back.

Rona swiped the gutting knife from Jessie's hand, clutching the baby tight to her chest with her other arm. An icy primitive fear overwhelmed her. In her hand she held a knife with which she could kill. And if Martha threatened her baby again, she would.

Jessie slumped back against the pillow. 'Who are you really, Martha? How did you find out about me?'

Martha moved her feet apart as if getting better balance then glanced from the tip of the knife to Jessie. 'Bertha's son, Peter, was a bad man, a double murderer, much older than me, but I loved him. He taught me loads.'

'Were you in prison?'

'The fire I'd made was perfect, but the kids got out, then they recognised me.'

'You tried to kill people? Arson?' Rona kept trying to hold the knife steady while Hannah jiggled about.

'Yeah, an arsonist, that's me. I was in a fire myself when I was ten. We all got out okay but it has fascinated me ever since. Then I found out about you, Jessie, and the diamond and, well, the rest is history.' She began to move towards Rona. 'No way will you use that knife, Rona. You're too nice, too sweet, too kind and—'

Rona thrust the knife forward at Martha who swerved away just as the blade nicked her arm. There was a crash behind them as the door swung open. Two policemen ran in, one grabbing Martha and yanking her arms behind her back, the other taking the knife from Rona. Craig and Ian rushed in and Rona ran to her husband, bursting into tears as she flung herself and the baby into his arms.

Chapter 57

1982

Rona gazed down at her tiny daughter as she suckled. She wanted to inhale her wonderful scent forever. After last night, she seemed even more precious, if that were possible.

There was a knock at the door.

'Come in, Mum.'

Morna entered carrying two mugs of tea.

'What time is it?' Craig rubbed his eyes and looked at the clock. 'God, it's half past eight, I've got to get to work.' He jumped out of bed.

'Craig, that nice nurse Fay came to the door just now. She asked if you could go and see her as soon as possible. She said to tell you you've to call Purves and that they have procedures in place, whatever that means.'

Rona sighed. 'Oh no, another death. Go and see who it is, Craig. Hope it's not dear old Mr Burnside, he wasn't great yesterday.'

Craig pulled on his jeans and a t-shirt and went to the door. 'I'll just nip out and see what they need doing.' He took a gulp from the mug. 'Did that actually happen last night? It was like a nightmare.'

'Certainly was for Jessie and me.' Rona turned to the window where her mum was opening the curtains. 'Oh, the fog's gone, looks like a nice day.'

'There was a shower earlier but it's sunny now. There was a beautiful rainbow a wee while ago.' Morna sat down on the bed beside Rona and stroked her granddaughter's plump cheek. She sighed. 'Did you have any idea that woman was so ... so evil?'

Rona shrugged. 'Mrs Bell used to call her Lady Macbeth and warned us to watch her, but I would never have imagined what she was capable of. Or what she was prepared to do last night.' Rona shivered. She lifted Hannah's chubby hand and kissed the tiny fingers.

'Did you actually do her any damage with that knife?'

'I would have killed her, Mum. I mean, I'd have stabbed her through the heart if she'd come any nearer Hannah.'

'It's amazing what a mother would do for her young.'

'I think I just grazed her arm. There wasn't much blood. I remember looking at the floor when the policemen were dragging her away and thinking we wouldn't need to get a new carpet, it'd just need a good scrub. Funny how your mind works.' Rona looked at the clock. 'Can't believe we slept in.'

'It was well after three when you eventually got to bed. The police will be coming back this morning, I presume?'

Rona nodded. 'Thanks again for calling 999, Mum. If you'd left it to Craig and Ian, they might've tried their heroics again and it could all have ended so badly.'

Rona removed Hannah from her breast and handed her to Morna, who snuggled Hannah into her shoulder, rubbing her back with the palm of her hand.

'What I've been wondering, Mum, is how on earth Jessie had a knife under her pillow? It looked ancient.'

'It was a herring gutter's knife. It was just like my granny's, remember Granny C who was a fisherlassie in Stornoway?'

Rona nodded. 'That poor woman, she must've been tormented for the past three years since Martha moved in. Well, we'll be able to make her nice and comfy in here now.'

The door opened and Craig stood there, shaking his head.

'What?'

'It wasn't Mr Burnside, Rona.' He walked towards the bed and sat down. 'It's Jessie. Fay reckons she must've died about an hour ago. Peacefully, in her sleep.'

Rona sighed. 'Oh, I'm so sorry. Bless her, the shock must have done it. I wish I'd killed Martha, she deserved it.'

'Forget about her, Rona. Fay said Jessie was lying flat on the bed, her arms crossed over her chest as if she'd been somehow ready to die.' Craig fished in his back pocket. 'There's a note.' He handed it to Rona who began to read.

> Dear Rona and Craig,
>
> It is 6 a.m. I have not been able to get back to sleep since you left with the police, so I thought I would write you this note.
>
> I placed the diamond in your pram for Hannah. I am so sorry I caused your beautiful little daughter to be in such danger.
>
> Something good must come out of what has happened and I feel now, by giving this to you, I might lift the curse that has hung over me all my life. They used to call me Winzie when I was younger. I shall not go to my death cursed, of that I am sure.
>
> I now feel safe in the knowledge that Martha has gone forever out of my life. I'll shut my eyes and sleep, a long peaceful sleep, perhaps one without any dreams at all.
>
> The diamond is now in your care. Use it as you wish.
>
> Yours,
> Jessie Mack

Tears trickled down Rona's cheeks.

'Mum, can you go over to Hannah's second drawer down, please? Bring over the brand new pink bootees?'

Morna hoisted Hannah onto her other shoulder then opened the drawer and lifted out a tiny pair of knitted bootees. She handed them to Rona who loosened the ribbons. Rona slipped her fingers inside one but there was nothing. Then she felt something bulge inside the other. She pulled it out. It sparkled and shone. It was a huge, glittering diamond.

Acknowledgements

Thanks to Anne Dow, Elisabeth Hadden and Isabelle Plews for reading and commenting wisely.

Thanks also to Fiona Campbell, Mary Duckworth, Anna Hadden, Gordon Hay, Margaret Hickey, Sheila Jardine, Michael Laing, Ann McCluskey, Val Rankine, Flora Sharp and Stephen Turner for their help and professional advice.

Thank you, as always, to my brilliant agent, Jenny Brown, for her encouragement, support – and patience.

Thanks also to my excellent editor, Anita Joseph, to Katharine Allerton for her editorial assistance, and to all the wonderful team at Saraband for their commitment to this book.